Praise for Gr.

Beach Rental

FINALIST IN THE 2012 GDRWA BOOKSELLERS BEST AWARD

DOUBLE WINNER IN THE 2012 GAYLE WILSON AWARD OF EXCELLENCE

FINALIST IN THE 2012 PUBLISHED MAGGIE AWARD FOR EXCELLENCE

"No author can come close to capturing the awe-inspiring essence of the North Carolina coast like Greene. Her debut novel seamlessly combines hope, love and faith, like the female equivalent of Nicholas Sparks. Her writing is meticulous and so finely detailed you'll hear the gulls overhead and the waves crashing onto shore. Grab a hanky, bury your toes in the sand and get ready to be swept away with this unforgettable beach read."
—*RT Book Reviews* 4.5 stars TOP PICK

Beach Winds

FINALIST IN THE 2014 OKRWA INTERNATIONAL DIGITAL AWARDS

FINALIST IN THE 2014 WISRA WRITE TOUCH READERS' AWARD

"Greene's follow up to *Beach Rental* is exquisitely written with lots of emotion and tugging on the heartstrings. Returning to Emerald Isle is like a warm reunion with an old friend and readers will be inspired by the captivating story where we excitedly get to meet new characters and reconnect with a few familiar faces, too. The author's perfect prose highlights family relationships which we may find similar to our own, and will have you dreaming of strolling along the shore to rediscover yourself in no time at all. This novel will have one wondering about faith, hope and courage and you may be lucky enough to gain all three by the time *Beach Winds* last page is read."
—*RT Book Reviews* 4.5 stars TOP PICK

Kincaid's Hope

"A quiet, backwater town is the setting for intrigue, deception, and betrayal in this exceptional sophomore offering. Greene's ability to pull the reader into the story and emotionally invest them in the characters makes this book a great read."

—*RT Book Reviews*, 4 STARS

"This is a unique modern-day romantic suspense novel, with eerie gothic tones—a well-played combination, expertly woven into the storyline . . . She rode the wave of excellent writing in her first novel with the same complex writing style which easily draws the reader in."

—*Jane Austen Book Maven*, 5 STARS

The Happiness In Between

"*The Happiness In Between* overflows with the warmth, healing, and hope Greene fans know to expect in her uplifting stories."

—Christine Nolfi, author of *Sweet Lake*

the
memory of
butterflies

FICTION BY GRACE GREENE

Emerald Isle, North Carolina Novels

Beach Rental
Beach Winds
"Beach Towel" (A Short Story)
Beach Christmas (Christmas Novella)
Beach Walk (Christmas Novella)

Virginia Country Roads Novels

Kincaid's Hope
A Stranger in Wynnedower
Cub Creek
Leaving Cub Creek

Stand-Alone Novels

The Happiness In Between
The Memory of Butterflies

the
memory of
butterflies

A Novel

Grace Greene

LAKE UNION
PUBLISHING

Published by Lake Union Publishing, Seattle

www.apub.com

Amazon, the Amazon logo, and Lake Union are trademarks of Amazon.com, Inc., or its affiliates.

ISBN-13: 9781542045674
ISBN-10: 1542045673

Cover design by Laura Klynstra

Printed in the United States of America

The Memory of Butterflies is dedicated to parents and children, and to love—selfless love that promotes the best in us, and, without ego, sacrifices itself for the betterment of others. May that love, freely given without expectation, succeed and be passed on to each generation, and may it be returned, stronger and more glorious in form, back to the ones who gave it.

PROLOGUE

My daughter, Ellen, will graduate from high school this year.

The closer we get to graduation, the harder the past is coming at me, kicking like a living creature and forcing its way back into my life. With it, it brings happy memories but also those that were gladly forgotten—including the memory of how I lost my Ellen seventeen years ago, then found her again.

I grew up in Virginia, in the woods of Cooper's Hollow amid the leafy green shadows of Elk Ridge. The rough banks of Cub Creek cut through our land from north to south such that one was never far from the music of its dark water.

Our small house had sheltered many generations of Coopers, including those resting in the family cemetery on the hill opposite the house. I never wanted to be anywhere else except for a brief time, eighteen years ago, when I, myself, was about to graduate from high school. Six years after that, our home in Cooper's Hollow burned down, and we were forced to move into town—*we* being Ellen and me.

The nearby town of Mineral wasn't big by most people's standards, but from my perspective, it certainly was. Moving into town was scary, in part because Ellen was kindergarten age. I'd never wanted to draw attention, and it would be noticeable if she didn't start school. It was time for it anyway, and it turned out that when it came to school and being around teachers and other children, Ellen was like a lively duck landing in a sparkling lake—it was made for her. I'd taught her some at home, and the school administrators, recognizing her quick mind, moved her into first grade early. Our new life was a perfect fit for Ellen. So, while I talked for the next dozen years about rebuilding our house and going back to live in the Hollow, I never actually got around to doing anything about it. Instead, I settled into the daily life of being a mom, working at my pottery business, and even volunteering at church and with the ladies' auxiliary. How my grandmother would've laughed at the idea of my toting a homemade pound cake or a pasta casserole to a function! But you fit in as you can where you find yourself, and residing in town was social. Very different from living in the Hollow.

For these last several years, I've been biding my time, waiting until the timing was right for both of us—for Ellen to graduate and begin her college career and for me to return home to Cooper's Hollow permanently—to finally face the past.

CHAPTER ONE

I always knew Ellen and I would be separated one day. Not forever, of course, but time moves on, and children grow up. We'd visited her first-pick colleges early in her junior year, and once she made her choice, there was no changing her mind. The University of Virginia was closer, but Ellen wanted to attend Virginia Tech along with most of her friends. Those college visits had happened last year when her graduation had seemed distant. Now the reality of it was smack in my face.

I'd been fighting a growing melancholy over the last few months, and one morning I woke up and knew it was time for me to move forward, too, as my Ellen was doing. The plans I'd been making since leaving Cooper's Hollow, plans I'd put off for the benefit of my daughter, would now come to life. My dreams were now in the sure hands of Roger Westray. With his expertise and his unfailing friendship, I never doubted he'd get this done for me.

Roger, sandy-haired and blue-eyed, was waiting for me at Dell's Diner near his office. I parked my car in the paved lot between his office and the diner and went inside. Roger already had the blueprints and was working on the construction plans for the house. This was no ordinary house he was preparing to build for me. We were blending rustic with modern while keeping the flavor of the original homeplace by salvaging and incorporating the old logs and stone at the site. I wanted more space, too, and definitely more luxuries than the original house. Living in town had given me a taste for conveniences I wasn't willing to do without.

Roger waved his pencil at me as I entered. His preferred table was the corner booth next to the windows on the shady side. He was friendly and sociable, but he always preferred to face the room. He'd never said much about it, but I understood from remarks here and there that it was due to his years in the army. He liked to see what was coming at him. This morning it was me, and he waved.

"I hope I didn't keep you waiting," I said, smiling as I took my seat opposite him.

He grinned and raised his coffee cup in salute. "You're late."

I looked past the counter with its stools and at the digital wall clock over the order window. "I'm on time. That clock's fast. It always is."

The diner was less than half-full. The morning was moving on. The chatter was low and seldom, and the clatter of dishes and activity back in the kitchen sounded relaxed.

Roger reached into his leather case to pull out the plans.

"What do you have for me?" I leaned forward, eager to see.

We were interrupted as Shelby approached the table, and I sat back.

"Morning, Hannah. Coffee?" She placed a white mug in front of me and set a napkin and spoon near my hand.

Shelby had waitressed for Dell's longer than I'd been coming here for coffee and the occasional meal. Before that, we'd attended the same high school. The schools were regional here in the country and served a large area, so we'd known each other but hadn't been close friends. I didn't know the details of her personal story any more than she knew mine. What we did know was that high school was a generation ago now, and neither of us was quite where we thought we'd be all these years later. But waitressing was honest work, and a smart waitress was a treasure. The café wasn't known for its cuisine, but the food was tasty and inexpensive, and the atmosphere was congenial.

"Yes, thanks," I said. "And a sweet roll, too."

"You got it." Shelby whisked away.

"Is that your breakfast?" Roger asked as he moved his cup and saucer to the side and ran a napkin over the already clean table before laying out the papers.

"You're one to talk."

He shrugged. "On second thought, it hasn't done you any harm that I can see."

"Flatterer." He was right, though. I must've been some kind of throwback genetics-wise, not at all like my grandparents. I had a natural tendency to be slim and was delighted that despite being in my late thirties, I could eat pretty much whatever I wanted without repercussions. It was a silly thing to be proud of, and definitely of no particular credit to me, but my "atta girl" list was pretty short, so I didn't scruple about including it.

"I like your hair," he said.

That had come out of nowhere. "Thank you," I said. "But it's the same as always." It was long and straight and dark blonde except for where the sun had bleached it lighter. Today I'd pulled it back with a headband, and flyaway ends kept tickling my cheek. Suddenly self-conscious, I smoothed them back and away from my face.

"Maybe." He smiled.

"You're in a strange mood this morning."

"Am I?"

His tone and expression were unreadable. I was relieved when he turned his attention to the papers on the tabletop. These weren't the actual blueprints but copies of specific areas. He waited as I gave them a close look.

I touched one of the papers. "The front of the house is one level with the back half being two stories." After a pause, I added, "It's so large."

"Building is expensive. It's not much more expensive to build larger. Besides, it's not that large."

"Tell me the truth. What do you think? Is this a silly expense? Ellen is leaving for college in a few months. It'll be me. Me alone. Would it make sense to scale the plans back?"

"She's not leaving forever. Besides, you may marry yet, have other children. There are only three bedrooms and an office area. Rooms fill up before you know it."

Marry? I wanted to scoff at the idea. Instead I swallowed the quips. Roger's eyes were too revealing. I knew what he wanted, but I couldn't offer him my heart. There was too much he didn't know about me and could never know. The invisible barrier between us wasn't there by my choice but of necessity.

"Here at the entrance," Roger continued, "we're incorporating part of the original foundation. Though, as we discussed, the logs are mostly for show. They'll come from the springhouse and weigh a lot more than two-by-fours. We'll run them across this front section with plenty of support below and behind them. The ground is good, but we can't forget the 2011 earthquake, and small tremors still occur from time to time. What happens once can happen again."

"True," I said. "The damage was hit or miss. The high school was wrecked and had to be condemned while houses a few blocks away had no structural damage. Every time I drove past Cuckoo . . ." I shivered remembering the damaged home with its tall, stately chimneys half-crumbled, and the brick walls leaning away precariously from the historical mansion. But the owners had fixed it. It was beautiful again.

Likewise, the new school building had finally been completed. It seemed odd that although my daughter and I would both be graduates of Louisa County High School, we hadn't attended the same facility. Ellen was about to graduate from a new, very grand building. It reminded me of her fascination with butterflies. She saw mystery in their beauty and in how metamorphosis wrought that change. But she was still young. I knew that sometimes the most significant changes were natural, but often they were painful or forced. There was no irony or mercy in nature but rather unsentimental, practical reality. Nature had destroyed the old building, but out of the destruction of the old, the new had been built, much like what we were planning with my home in the Hollow. It said something about the cycle of nature, the inherent logic of . . .

Roger's fingers tip-tapped on the tabletop, interrupting my thoughts.

I looked at him and he said, "You were far away."

"I was thinking about Ellen and her graduation."

"It's not an ending. It's a beginning."

"Exactly what I was thinking." New beginnings were coming around again for both my daughter and me.

He motioned at the house plans. "About the logs—they're only for the small front part here at the entry. I wish you'd let us dismantle the old cabin. We could do amazing work with those logs. They're in great shape."

I shook my head. "I have plans for that cabin. It stays as is."

"It's your decision. No argument." He motioned across the diagram. "The rest of the house will have the usual framing and structure. Windows will span the back. You'll have a sweeping view of the hills, the creek, and the forest."

Anxiety and eagerness fought for prominence within me. I accepted the coffee gratefully from Shelby and wrapped my hands around the steaming cup, enjoying the aroma. "I wish we could just imagine it and make it happen."

"Wave a wand? I'd be out of business pretty quickly if that were possible." He laughed.

When Roger laughed, his blue eyes lit up, and the squint lines beside them rearranged themselves into happiness. He had two vertical lines between his eyebrows—Gran had called those worry lines—and when Roger smiled, those smoothed out. I couldn't help responding, as if I'd been part of the reason for that smile, or maybe it was the sense of a shared moment. I tried hard to mute my reaction, but even his hands, moving over the diagrams and layouts as if he were crafting my house with the motions, spoke to me. I knew the language that hands spoke because it was the same for me when I was shaping clay at the wheel or sculpting using my fingers as tools.

"What?" he asked. "Don't you like the plans?" He shook his head. "What are you thinking about?"

I smiled. "Nothing too deep. I was remembering when we met. Duncan Browne had sent you to our house on Rose Lane right after Ellen and I moved in, after the fire in Cooper's Hollow. You and I talked about the changes I wanted at the house. You made me believe we could turn the house on Rose Lane into a home. You communicated what would be done so clearly I felt like I could see it, and that hasn't changed."

"That was a long time ago."

"Time flies," I said. "But you did what you said you'd do, and I have total confidence in you for this project."

Was he blushing? I didn't want to embarrass him, so I changed the subject. "What about the well?"

He nodded. "The well is looking good. We'll have to bleach it and drain it, but the casing looks sound. You'll need a new pump, of course. We'll revamp the sewage system, too, and bring it up to code. Permits are almost done."

"The bank said the construction loan is ready." I was funding a lot of the project. I was comfortably well-off, but I wasn't wealthy and didn't want to drain my accounts. On the other hand, this would be my forever home, the one that took me back to my roots, to my family, and hopefully honored them. It would be the place for Ellen to come home to, even someday bringing a husband and grandchildren with her. If Ellen had her way, I'd bring a husband home myself—a whole different subject altogether.

Roger had a funny look on his face again. I was glad he couldn't read my mind.

He said, "This means a lot to you. I can see it in your face and in your eyes."

I stared down at the plans. "It does. More than I can say," I said softly, surprised at the rough edges in my voice. I looked up and added, "Remember, I want to be there in person for site prep or any other work on the property."

He frowned. "I'll tell the crews to be careful, but we're deconstructing and clearing the whole site. What should they be careful of? What are you worried about?"

"Back when the fire happened, after the ashes had cooled, I picked through and found personal items. They were charred but not destroyed. Other things, family things, might be buried deeper under the debris. I know it's unlikely, especially after so long, but I want to be there to make sure nothing is disposed of that shouldn't be." I shrugged. "The kind of stuff that looks like junk to most might mean something to me."

"The workmen aren't going to handpick through a pile of charcoal and debris, soaked and settled for twelve years. It's not reasonable, Hannah."

"I understand, and I promise to be sensible. But if I stay away and dismiss it all as trash, I'll always wonder. Plus, there's the family cemetery. It doesn't look like much. The stone wall is tumbledown, and not all the graves have markers. Workmen might not respect it or protect it."

"The cemetery is on the far side of the creek and up the slope. It shouldn't be impacted at all. You can be sure it will be protected."

"Excellent, but I want to be there. I insist."

Roger groaned softly, then nodded. "Fine. We'll go out there together. I'll show you there's nothing to worry over."

I touched his hand. "Thanks, Roger. I appreciate your efforts and all you've done. Once things are underway, I'll relax a little, but for now—"

His eyes had shifted. He was no longer looking at me. I turned toward the entrance to see what had caught his attention.

A tall man. Broad-shouldered. Dark, longish curly hair with lighter streaks. Wearing jeans and boots. He was standing at the counter beside a stool talking to Shelby and was mostly turned away from me.

I picked up my purse and eased out of the booth. "Sorry, Roger, I have to run. I just remembered an appointment."

Roger frowned and half rose as I stood, but I slipped discreetly through the diner, keeping my eyes fastened on the front door, and I didn't stop until I was outside. Then, despite myself, I paused and turned back toward the window.

There was no way that man could be who I thought. After all these years, I wouldn't know Liam anyway unless he was wearing a name tag. This was a coincidence. A stranger with a familiar look. Nothing more.

Roger was watching me through the glass. I'd made myself look foolish for no reason. At least it was with Roger. Roger might be curious, but he wouldn't press the issue or hold it against me.

Feeling slightly ridiculous, I forced a smile. I gave Roger a breezy wave and went straight to my car. As I unlocked the door, I stopped. The idea that I shouldn't take Roger for granted intruded, and I almost turned back.

I didn't take him for granted, but I could see how it might look that way. Still, there were things I couldn't explain to him or to anyone else.

Other worries aside, I could count on Roger. He'd cover my tab for my coffee and sweet roll, and he'd build my house, and I'd make sure to let him know how much I appreciated his friendship and help.

I should've gone to my pottery shop. I drove right past it on my way home from the diner. At the shop, I could've been productive and worked off my lingering anxiety. Instead, I went straight home to Rose Lane, kicked off my shoes in the foyer, dropped my purse on a chair, and threw myself down on the living room sofa. I hugged a pillow and stared at the sunlight playing around the open blinds in the front windows.

Quiet. Peaceful. Clean. No dust coated the slats of these blinds. Not a single fingerprint marred the window glass. The frames on the wall—paintings, drawings, family photos featuring Ellen and me—were the same. Clean surfaces. Shiny glass. Everything was in its place, and all was well with my world. The glazed pots from Cooper's Hollow, the ones formed by my grandmother's and her mother's hands, were displayed on special shelving Roger had made for me after the earthquake. I'd been lucky during that shake. One couldn't expect such luck every time. With this shelving, the pots wouldn't go anywhere unless the house itself fell down.

The man who'd walked into Dell's . . . could he have been Liam? How unlikely would that be? Would it matter if it *was*?

I put aside the sofa pillow and sat up. Collapsing had never worked to relax me. I took a clean dust rag from the pantry box and began polishing the knickknacks and keepsakes.

Back when the house in Cooper's Hollow burned, some of the old hand- and wheel-thrown bowls and pots had been stored in the nearby log cabin. The house itself was small. It didn't have much display space. Besides, my grandparents were people who viewed a house as practical and utilitarian—much as the women had viewed the pots when they'd crafted them. Attractive was good, but an item must first and foremost be useful. As it turned out, it was fortunate these pots had been stored in the cabin, or I would've lost them all in the fire.

I ran my fingers over the pots. These were my history, and I'd continued the family tradition in a quiet storefront on Main Street in

Mineral. The sign in the window read **CUB CREEK POTTERY**. It didn't get many shoppers with ready cash, but it was mostly for me anyway. It was a place to work on the clay without messing up the house and a business address for my few clients to send requests or payments. Sometimes I gave lessons. But I never opened the store on Monday, even when I was there working the wheel. That was my time—time when I was guaranteed peace and quiet in which to work.

Ellen would be home from school in a couple of hours. She'd need a ride to her job at the grocery store. She filled in at the customer service desk and checkout during supper breaks. I found it rather a pain in the butt for the few hours she worked each week, but Ellen was that kind of kid. She needed to be out and doing, and I figured "doing" might as well be productive. She'd be home for a late supper after and to take care of her schoolwork. Finals and graduation were less than two months away. She was already set for college, and some might think the GPA didn't matter much now, but it did for her.

She was the best part of my life. My beautiful, intelligent, charming daughter. My Ellen.

I tossed the dust rag into the bin, fluffed the sofa pillows, and straightened the cushions, then went to the back door. I paused to grab a bottle of water from the fridge and to slip my feet into my yard shoes. The backyard garden was relatively shady this time of day, and nothing relaxed me like working with my hands. I donned my gloves, knelt on the rubber kneepad, and spent a couple of quiet hours searching out the tiny weeds from the dirt. As I turned the soil with the spade, I amended it with fertilizer. I wouldn't plant anything outside until May due to frost worries. My grandmother had always insisted I wait. I laughed softly at the memory. She would've told me yet again about that Easter snow when she was young, of how deep it had been. And then she would go on to recite stories of late frosts that had tricked many an unwary gardener. Small wonder I learned early to start the seedlings in the safety of the house. In a few short weeks, I'd move them out here.

If the house building went as planned, I'd end up transplanting the herbs, the tomato and cucumber plants, and whatever else I decided to grow, to the Hollow come June. Knowing I'd be putting the plants through a second move, a good start was especially important.

Using the back of my gloved hand, I brushed my hair away from my face. The sun was warm on my back. The breeze touched my cheeks. It made me smile. I couldn't collapse properly, but at least I knew how to laugh at myself. Nerves got me going. No wonder I stayed slim.

I was feeling better now. It was time to put away my tools and wash up. Ellen would be home soon, and she'd be hungry.

Her friend Bonnie dropped her off at the house. I heard the car drive up and then drive away, and Ellen came through the front door, calling out, "Mom? Mom?"

She was always upbeat. I glanced at the clock. Right on time. Her snack was waiting on the island in the kitchen.

"Here you are," Ellen said as she dropped her notebook on the granite counter and hopped up onto the island stool. "Guess what?" She took a sip of lemonade. "Remember I told you Bonnie was waitlisted for Tech?"

I would've nodded, but Ellen barely paused, saying, "Bonnie got the letter." Her face glowed, and her dark eyes flashed with amber sparks.

"For Tech?"

"Of course. We'll be there together! We'll room together. Or get an apartment together. Oh, Mom, it's going to be great."

"Wow. I don't even know what to say." I tried to match her excitement, but many emotions swirled inside me and it was hard to sound genuine.

Luckily, Ellen didn't seem to notice my hesitation. "I know, right? How amazing is it?"

"Amazing. For now, though, you'd better eat. What time do you have to be at work?"

"At five. I get off at seven."

I walked over to stand beside her. "What about your homework?"

She sighed, tossing her long, dark hair. It fell across her shoulder and cascaded down her back again in perfect lines, like a fan spreading wide. I couldn't help myself. I pulled the locks back and away from her face while she bit into the sandwich. She allowed me a few minutes of play-braiding her hair while she chewed.

"Soon, homework—at least for high school—will be a thing of the past," I said, her hair entwined with my fingers. "What am I going to do when you take off for college?"

Ellen was suddenly still. She leaned the side of her head against my palm. "I'll only be three hours away."

"More like four," I responded.

"Are you going to be OK, Mom?"

I was appalled at myself. I didn't want to lose her, but more than that, I didn't want to hold her back. I released her hair and put my hands on her shoulders.

"Don't you worry. I have plans, remember? Be patient with your old mom? I have to do a certain amount of moaning and groaning. How else will you know you'll be missed?"

"Old? You're the youngest mom I know of in the whole senior class. People think you're my older sister."

"Nonsense."

"You were my age when I was born."

"No, ma'am. I was nineteen. You are seventeen." I watched the braid fall apart, slowly unwinding. "Besides, I have plans. Plans I've put off for many years. It's time now."

Ellen smiled, her eyes sparkling with mischief. "So those plans of yours . . . do they include Roger?"

"Of course. He was showing me the house plans earlier today."

"You know what I mean."

"Roger and I are friends. Good friends. That's it."

"Fine." She shook her head. "You're wrong, but have it your way. Tell me, then, if not Roger, then someone else? You should have someone special, someone all your own. A boyfriend. I worry about you, Mom."

"Well, don't. If I meet anyone I'm interested in romantically, I'll be sure to lasso and hog-tie him until you have a chance to pass judgment." I patted her shoulder. "Now finish your sandwich and I'll drive you over." Then I saw it. I touched her wrist. "What's this?"

"My butterfly?" She saw my expression and giggled. "It's temporary, Mom. Not a real tattoo."

Earlier in the school year, Ellen had drawn a big, colorful butterfly on the front of her notebook. Now she'd inked one in black on her forearm above her wrist.

"It's a felt-tipped pen, Mom. It'll wear off." She sounded sad. Then the end of her mouth quirked up, and she put her wrist next to her cheek and asked, "What do you think? How would this look? A butterfly on my cheek?"

I pulled her arm away from her face. "No tattoos."

She was teasing. I was horrified anyway.

"No tattoos. I mean it."

She touched the flesh where she'd drawn the butterfly. "Bonnie and I want to get matching tattoos. Just a small butterfly, Mom, that's all. On our arms, I think. Monarchs. Those are the orange ones."

"Don't even consider it."

She groaned. "Mom, no fair. Everyone has tattoos now. And this one is appropriate. Symbolic. We are starting whole new lives. Leaving Mineral and high school behind. Becoming adults and being on our own at college—"

"No tattoos." I frowned and pointed at her. "Promise me."

"For now, I promise."

"I don't like surprises. Not that kind, anyway."

"I promise I won't do it without telling you first."

15

"Not without my agreement."

"But, Mom, you'll never agree."

"Don't say never. Nothing is forever or never, and stuff happens all the time whether we want it to or not. But tattoos? When you're thirty, if you still want one, then I won't interfere." I paused. "Probably."

Ellen stopped in the doorway between the kitchen and the living room. She turned back toward me. "I love you, Mom, but I'm not a child anymore. I'm about to graduate."

"And?"

"And," she said, "that means you have to trust me to make my own decisions. That means it's *time* to trust me. Now. You've taught me everything I need to know about handling life." As she spun away, her words trailed off and I couldn't mistake the blithe note in her voice as she said, "We may not always agree . . ."

"No tattoos," I repeated as I grabbed my purse. "And no piercings, either!"

The next morning, I dropped Ellen off at school and drove out to the old homeplace.

In those first years after the fire, Ellen and I had visited Cooper's Hollow often. We'd worked together in the shade, cleaning up the graves and sharing our memories. As she moved from elementary to middle and then high school, she became less enthusiastic about going. It seemed to me her attitude was normal and healthy for a teenager. Life seeks life, and young people are like magnets for each other. Ellen went less often, but nothing changed for me. It was important to me to keep the memories fresh, along with keeping the graves weeded and neat.

Going out there with Roger for the preconstruction visit would be different. There would be workmen and strangers with big clumsy equipment and their own agendas. It would be nice when the construction was finished, I didn't doubt it, but Cooper's Hollow would be changed forever.

Nothing stays the same, I reminded myself.

This might be my last peaceful visit. The house had burned down twelve years earlier, yet each time I saw the blackened pile of debris, the acrid smell rose again—at least in my memory—and reminded me of our fear that night and of our loss. Beyond the dark, charred heap of what had been our home stood the outbuildings. Those rickety old buildings of weathered gray wood had been untouched by the fire. They still stood, but in varying degrees of collapse. The chicken coop was in shambles. Same with the dog pens. When my grandfather died during my senior year of high school, Gran gave the dogs away to his hunting friends. With the dogs gone, the coyotes grew bolder, and we gave up keeping the chickens.

Grand's toolshed still stood. I hadn't opened the door in years. I suspected the junk filling the shed kept it upright as much as its construction did. Beyond the shed was a ramshackle barn. Its stalls had sheltered a few cows and goats through the years. Even a barn cat or two had called it home. We'd had a horse for a short time when I was a child. Upstream, the springhouse was almost lost amid the trees. It straddled a natural spring and caught the water as it bubbled up from the ground and flowed down the hill to Cub Creek. Closest to hand, very near the burned house, was the original log cabin.

No one knew how old the cabin was, though Grand had mused about it a time or two. His great-grands had built the "new" house where I'd lived growing up. It was roomier than the cabin with a living room, two bedrooms, a kitchen, and, eventually, indoor plumbing. The log cabin was used for storage, but when I was teenager, it was where I worked my potter's wheel and where Grand had set up the kiln. He'd ordered the parts by mail, assembled it, and rigged the kiln to work with propane. The wheel was secondhand but a beauty, and Grand was as tickled to give it to me as I was to receive it.

He ran an electrical line out to the cabin to make it work and for me to be able to plug in a lamp for light. An old treadle wheel my grandmother's mother had used was stored in a dark, musty corner of the cabin. Grand said the old treadle wheel was too heavy to move because it might fall apart and break Gran's heart. I was happy with the electric wheel, plus I had a table for wedging and handwork. When I was young, Gran would sit out there in a chair by the hearth to keep me company. She'd share advice while I worked the clay. I had plenty of room, and over time I moved more of Grand's stuff out of the way. By then we'd stopped calling it the old cabin and referred to it as my pottery cabin.

Grand died while I was in high school, and his death, more than anything else, marked the biggest change in our lives and in our plans, though we didn't necessarily understand it at the time. In our grief, we simply mourned. He was laid to rest in our cemetery, the Cooper family cemetery. Its stone walls occupied a spot across the creek and up the hill—the natural stone aged and blending in with the trees and leaves and shade, such that, sometimes one could hardly pick the cemetery out from its surroundings. Grand's remains rested there with his parents, my parents, and others whose graves weren't marked.

In the years since the fire, when I came out here to the homeplace to reminisce and tend the cemetery, I always paused in the driveway in the spot where Ellen and I had huddled together in shock as the flames rose, and the old wood snapped and crackled, and smoke filled the air, and had watched as our home and our worldly goods were consumed by a mindless force.

As the curtains had flamed in the windows and fire bloomed up from the roof, men did arrive. They brought a tanker truck, but it was far too late for the house. They prevented the fire from spreading into the forest and gave us a ride into town where a local pastor and his wife took us in for a few nights. Ellen and I didn't sleep that first night. We bathed to rid ourselves of dirt and ash, but the smell of smoke was stuck in our noses, and the night-terror images were too stark in our brains. Our daily lives and our possessions had been so freshly in our hands. I found myself repeatedly staring at my palms as if the lost items might suddenly be there, perhaps a favorite book or Gran's doilies. Even her pearls, safely stored away for many years, and one of the few nice pieces of jewelry she'd had, were gone. I'd let them burn. Not by choice but by action, along with my drawings, our keepsakes, and everything in the house not on our backs. More than once, I'd relived the memory and wondered if I should have left Ellen outside and dashed back in to grab things, anything, that meant something to us. These many years later, as I stood here in the driveway, and though our losses had been sad, I was also grateful.

At the time of the fire, as young as I was, it had felt too late for me but not for Ellen. She was reaching school age. Would I have left our secluded Hollow on my own? Would I have recognized her need to be among other children and attend school and allowed it to conquer my fears? I liked to think I would've put her first, but honestly, I wasn't sure I would've had the courage to risk it.

The fire had been tragic. It had also been liberating in a way I couldn't have foreseen at the time.

This morning, I took my work bucket from the trunk where I kept my tools for cleaning the cemetery. I slipped on my rubber garden clogs and gathered my gloves, my spade, and the rest of my gear. It wouldn't do for the cemetery to look shabby. The workmen would be coming in a few days. I wanted them to understand that precious people, gone from this earth but not from my life, had lived in Cooper's Hollow, and their remains and their memorials dwelt within those stone walls.

The workmen, and anyone else who came here, should tread carefully and respectfully among my memories and my past.

And not judge me.

CHAPTER TWO

We'd planned for me to go to college, but I couldn't leave home right after high school. My grandparents had raised me, and when Grand died during my senior year, my grandmother needed me. I loved her and didn't want to lose her, but the honest truth was, I didn't think she'd last as long as she did. Grand's death had been hard on her, and I'd already grieved for her, too, almost in tandem with the loss of my grandfather. She'd either get better or she wouldn't, and, at this point, I wasn't seeing a recovery on the horizon. *One year,* I thought.

Gran herself didn't think she had more than a few months left in her. She made me promise that when she passed, I'd go on to college. The high school guidance counselor warned me I was making a mistake. She said the grants and scholarships wouldn't wait forever. But a person has to do what they can live with. Meanwhile, Mildred Harkin, Gran's longtime friend and nurse, had dropped by, as usual, to check on Gran and deliver her medications, and she'd realized my dilemma.

I sat on the sofa while Mildred checked Gran's heart rate and blood pressure. Gran's bed was in the living room. We'd moved it there after Grand died. The tiny bedroom in the back of the house had been mine for most of my life, but without Grand, my grandmother said she'd rather have my small bed moved into the living room. She'd be near the direct warmth of the woodstove and handier to the kitchen. She insisted

I take the larger front bedroom with the big bed. Gran tended to be cold, and now a widow, she preferred to trade privacy for more warmth than a couple of quilts could provide.

Mildred arranged the blanket across Gran's legs and gathered her doctor's bag and sweater. She came over to the sofa.

"Can I speak with you, Hannah?"

"Yes, ma'am." I stood out of courtesy.

She touched my arm, signaling me to follow her. As we went out the front door, she called back into the house, "Clara, I'll drop the ointment by tomorrow. Be sure to use it. It will help with the soreness in your shoulder and knees. And make sure you take your water pills like you're supposed to."

Mildred had gray eyes and gray hair. She didn't wear nurse's garb, though. She dressed like a neighbor come to call, except for the old-style doctor bag she carried. The casual clothing and their longtime acquaintance were probably why Gran tolerated the intrusion of personal questions, stethoscopes, thermometers, and such.

I walked with Mildred from the porch and into the yard, suddenly anxious. No matter how set you thought you were about losing a loved one, you were never really ready.

"How's Gran?"

"About the same, dear, but I want to talk about you, if you don't mind." She nodded toward the driveway where she was parked, and I followed her. When we were well away from the house, she stopped again.

"So you're staying home? Not going off to college after all?"

"Yes."

Mildred sighed. "You have a right to your own life. You should consider what's best for your future."

I tilted my head. I could hear her words, but I didn't get where she was going with this. "Sure, but what would happen to Gran? She can't manage on her own. She took Grand's death hard."

Mildred put her bag on the front seat of her car, gave me a long look, then patted my shoulder. "I understand. She may recover somewhat. She may not. Time will tell. The fact is her heart isn't getting better, and the edema will continue. If we could convince her to go to the doctor, the hospital, and get treatment that could make a difference."

I shook my head, knowing Gran would never go, but asked anyway, "Would that cure her?"

"No, honey, it wouldn't. It might improve her situation, though. It's worth a try."

I looked back toward the house. "She'd never go. You know she hasn't left the Hollow in many years."

"Please encourage her to consider it." She touched my forearm and held my gaze. "In the meantime, you need to move on with your own plans. College. We could find someone to stop in and help her on a regular basis, or maybe it's time for her to go live elsewhere."

Elsewhere? Put Gran in a nursing home? I was shocked.

"You shouldn't have to bear this alone. You're so young."

"We do fine." I stood taller. "We have everything we need here. What we don't have is brought in. Grand arranged the deliveries long before he died. Plus, I have his car and can get about as I need."

"Unfortunately, Hannah, you have to face reality. Your grandmother is going to need more care than you can give her no matter how willing you are or how much you want to help her."

I tried to find the right words. I knew the truth of what she was saying, but I also knew the truth of what could be, and what couldn't ever be, not in a million years.

Mildred patted my arm again. "Close your mouth, dear. No need to look horrified. Think about what I've said. Accepting and dealing with reality can be hard, but moving a person to where they'll get the care they need can be a good thing. Sometimes it's the only choice we have. You need to figure out how long you can live this way and how much you're capable of handling." She shook her head. "I'll leave it for now. If you get in too deep here, you let me know. I'll help you figure something out."

She gave me a quick hug. "I admire your love and loyalty. I see it often when loved ones are sick or dying. But people take on too much and don't understand they can't fix everything for a loved one, that sometimes their paths must part."

She waved her hands. "We'll talk about it again. Meanwhile, I'd like you to get out. You need a break from time to time, and it won't hurt Clara to be on her own for part of the day. You don't need to hover."

"I've been thinking about finding a part-time job, maybe earn some money because I'm definitely going to college next year. By then, Gran will be better or . . . not, but I have to give her this year. She gave the last eighteen to me."

Mildred shook her head. "Hannah, you are one of the most reasonable, practical people I know, but you're very young. I worry you won't recognize when things get beyond your ability to manage or mend."

She opened the driver's side door. "It's good to have plans and goals. I have a friend who cleans houses—mostly light housework—and from time to time she needs help. Would you be interested? It would get you out a bit and give you a little money to set aside for school, yet still give you time to be here and do the things you enjoy, like your gardening and pottery."

I had to admit the idea of leaving the Hollow on occasion appealed to me, and cleaning houses would be easy work.

"I'd be willing to talk to your friend. See what we can work out."

Still looking worried but somewhat reassured, Mildred left.

Gran expressed misgivings when I explained the house-cleaning plan.

"If the money's tight, Hannah, we'll talk to the man in town."

The Man in Town. My grandparents had mentioned him over the years. My grandfather had been careful about money and distrustful of society. I'd overheard them talk about an annuity, and I knew cash came from somewhere, presumably from that mysterious man, on a regular basis. Certainly I never went without. When I needed clothing or anything else, Grand had driven me to the store to get it, whether the store was in Charlottesville or Richmond, and, of course, there was always mail order. For food, we gardened and hunted, and we bought the rest at the grocery store in Mineral. The only thing we lacked was online shopping, but we had no computer and no connectivity for Internet or cell phone.

Honestly, the lacks didn't bother me. I'd rather be at my potter's wheel or walking through the woods if spare time offered itself.

Bottom line: Grand gave careful consideration before every expense. He said we had to keep our money safely in the bank in case of hard times. We lived lean here in Cooper's Hollow, and aside from the losses money couldn't solve, like Grand's death, I couldn't recall any problem hard enough to disregard his admonition about saving.

I told Gran, "Mildred thought it might be good for me to get out and about some. Plus, I can put the money aside for college."

Gran nodded as if in conversation with herself, but all she said was, "If that's what you want to do."

Mildred's friend, a scrawny woman named Babs, had a regular route of houses she cleaned. Many big houses dotted the county both from folks who'd lived here a long time, plus the newcomers. I let Babs know I wouldn't take customers from too far away because it wouldn't be worth it if the gas and travel time outweighed the pay.

The people in the big, fancy houses lived very differently from us. I enjoyed seeing how they lived, but I wasn't envious. Curious, yes. Babs gave me a turquoise T-shirt with her company name printed on it, but otherwise I wore jeans and sandals. I cleaned several houses a week. It wasn't hard work, and my personal savings, tucked in a small box in a corner of my dresser drawer, benefited. In the evenings, over supper, I'd tell Gran about the houses and the people who couldn't or wouldn't clean their homes themselves, who had to hire others for such basic stuff like dusting and sweeping, and we'd have a good laugh.

Late one afternoon, I returned from my cleaning job. My brain was busy, but I didn't feel talkative. Gran was seated by the woodstove, reading. I went about tidying up and remaking her bed until she rapped her cane against the floor. I looked up.

"Hannah, honey, you've been in another world since you walked in the door. What's got you so preoccupied? Are you regretting the job? Because if you are, that's fine by me. Like I said, we can work out the money issue ourselves."

I looked at her and saw her lower legs and ankles were seriously swollen. Her slippers couldn't fit on her feet properly. I moved the footstool closer to the chair.

"You need to keep these up when you're sitting." I lifted her legs one by one and gently placed them on the footstool. "Now keep them there."

"How was the job today?"

"It was fine. Nothing special. You stay put, and I'll get supper going."

The cleaning job that day had been a little different. Maybe special, too, despite what I'd told Gran. As nice as some of those houses were, they didn't feel harmonious inside. The air felt wrong—not congenial— as if the folks living there were often at odds.

That was the case with the house off Cove Road farther along Elk Creek. By all appearances, it was a beauty, and it was a pleasure to mop and dust while I considered what I might like in my own home one day, a long way down the road of time. The beauty of it was almost enough to disguise the disquiet. I saw the framed photos on the wall and recognized a boy I knew from high school. Spencer Bell. We hadn't traveled in the same circles, but he was a looker and one of those kids with good teeth who smiled all the time. He had plenty to smile about. We weren't friends, but he wasn't a jerk, either, and I had nothing against him. He surprised me while I was working in the kitchen. Gave me a double look.

"That you, Hannah?" He looked around. "Mom said the cleaning lady was here."

I laughed a little to dispel the oddness of it. "That's me." I waved the dust cloth. "I'm earning extra for college."

He pulled a stool up to the kitchen island and drank from the milk carton. I gave him a glass, and this time, he laughed. His dark hair fell in locks across his brow. He had a good haircut, the kind that fell carelessly and still looked right. He was wearing shorts and a knit shirt. Nice stuff. Probably cost more than what I'd earn for a week's work. Maybe more.

He asked, "Where are you going?"

"Me?" I fidgeted with the dust cloth. "To college? I was planning to go to Tech, but I have to wait a year. My grandfather died, and I can't leave my grandmother yet. She needs a little time to get back on her feet, so to speak."

He frowned. "I'm sorry. They raised you, right? You lived with them?"

I nodded. "Yes, my parents died when I was a baby."

"Yeah? I think I heard that somewhere along the way. Sorry." He fixed his eyes on my face. "I never thought much about it. You never talked about being an orphan or acted like it."

"An orphan?" I almost laughed. How did orphans act? "Honestly, I never felt like an orphan. Things happen. Everybody has troubles of some kind or another. I was lucky to have my grandparents." I didn't add, though I could've, that family business is private business, not to be discussed with the outside.

"I like that," he said. "You don't go around feeling sorry for yourself. You know what you want. My dad says that's being self-directed. A self-starter."

"That's how he raised you? That's good."

"Well, he tried. Not sure it really took." He glanced at the digital clock on the microwave.

Holding up the cloth again, I said, "I'd better get back to work."

26

"Sure, I have to be somewhere, too." He left the stool but paused on his way out of the kitchen. "You interested in hanging out . . . I mean, going out sometime?"

I think I blushed. I tried not to show his invitation meant anything, even if my face did turn a little pink.

"I know what you're thinking," he said.

My tongue was stuck to the roof of my mouth. I couldn't answer.

He continued. "Melissa and I have been together forever. But here's the thing—we split up. She's going to one side of the country for college, and I'm going the other way. We agreed it's time to see other people, so if you're interested in having some fun . . ."

"Sure." I tried to sound cool. "Call me sometime."

He grabbed a marker from beside the kitchen phone. "What's your number?"

I told him and watched, amazed, as he wrote the digits on his forearm, like a tattoo. Like something important he wasn't willing to risk losing.

He tossed the marker back onto the counter, grinned as he said "Bye," and took off.

I put the milk carton back in the fridge and rinsed his glass and set it in the sink. I'd wash it up later with the rest of the dishes. But the whole time, I was seeing his grin and the scrawled numbers on his arm, and I knew he'd call.

A few days later, the phone rang. I'd just come into the house from working my pottery wheel. I didn't have running water out there in the old cabin where my wheel and working area were, so I paused to wash my hands at the kitchen sink, and Gran answered the phone. She pressed it to her bosom and called to me softly. The house was small, and I had young ears, so it didn't take much volume. Despite Gran's ears being older, the principle of proximity still applied, and it wasn't possible for me to have a truly private telephone conversation in this house.

"Hi. Sure, I can talk."

"Great. A group of us are having a cookout down by the river. Stan, Bruce, and some others. Gina and Angie. It'll be fun. I thought you might like to go."

These were his friends, not mine. On the other hand, I didn't have anything against them.

"I'd love to. Thanks."

After we hung up, I turned to find Gran staring at me.

I shook my head and shrugged all at once. "I'm going out Friday evening. A cookout. A group of friends."

"Friends? That sounded like a young man on the phone."

"He's a friend from school."

Gran turned and muttered for a while. She was talking to Grand. I came up behind her and rubbed her shoulders. She sighed, then said, "I wish your grandfather were here."

"Me too. All the time. But why do you wish it this time in particular?"

"Because when a boy shows up to take a gal on a date, he ought to see a male family member. It doesn't hurt to see a man on the porch, maybe with a gun or at least a big stick, lest the boy forget any good sense he might own."

"You sit on the porch, Gran. You can hold Grand's old rifle," I joked. I knew she would never do any such thing. The very image of Gran with a gun or bat across her knees was hilarious. Almost.

"Oh, you can laugh, missy, but I'll be sitting on the porch, make no mistake about it." She walked off, muttering, "It won't be the same, though . . . an old, worn-out grandmother."

I hadn't dated in high school. My life had never been centered in town but in the Hollow. I'd engaged in a few school activities and made some friends, but most of those kids were like me, awkward and solitary. None were the partying kind, and I wasn't around them enough to feel like I was part of a close group of friends. As the week wore on to Friday, I got nervous. I almost called off our date, but then decided that since it was a party, it would be appropriate to drive myself. I could leave whenever I wanted, which reassured me.

At supper, after I set Gran's plate on the table, I told her what I was intending.

"I've decided to drive myself to the party. Instead of anyone coming to pick me up, I'd rather drive. That way if I'm not having a good time, I can leave without asking someone to take me home."

"That so?" She sipped her coffee before she began cutting up the pork chop. "If you're not sure about it, maybe you shouldn't go." She shook her head. "It's not as if I don't think you should socialize. You should do more with friends your age. But I'm picking up vibes from you, Hannah, and it's making me nervous."

I set my plate opposite hers and took my seat.

"You're picking up on my nervousness, Gran. I've been too content to stay here at home. Mind you, I love being here, but maybe I've . . . Maybe I should do more about getting out and living life."

"Don't mistake me, Hannah. I know you love me and love home, and heaven knows you've been bound here far more than you should've been. It wasn't your fault you had to be raised by your grandparents, and old grandparents to boot. You're a young person and should be having fun. But are you driving yourself to this date because you don't want your friend to see where you live?"

I was stunned. I hadn't thought of it like that. Perhaps there was truth in it. Our home was small and shabby, but we owned many acres of forest. When the laurel and azaleas were in bloom, and then the honeysuckle vines and trumpet flowers, there was no sweeter, more beautiful place on earth.

"No, Gran." I shook my head. "I know who I am. I'm Hannah Cooper, and I'm proud of my home and my people."

"You had to grow up too fast, honey, and without the fun," Gran said. "If your mama had—" She broke off, and her eyes turned red, as they always did when she mentioned my long-deceased mother.

29

My parents had died in a car accident when I was a baby. When I grew older and started asking questions, my grandparents told me about it. It was real and it was tragic, but it didn't feel like a fact of my life because I was so young when it happened. I had no recollection of them and would never know what I'd missed. The loss had been different for my grandparents. It had punched a huge, unfixable hole in their lives.

I thought of what Spencer had said about my being an orphan. Maybe my Grands had viewed my childhood through a similar lens— that of loss. But for me, when I considered my life, I thought of my freedom in the woods, my love of home, my pottery, and my grandfather who drove me into town for school day in, day out whether I wanted to go or not, because he cared about the person I would be.

"I had plenty of fun. No regrets, Gran. I promise."

One of Spencer's friends had an uncle who farmed acreage out past Route 33 near the South Anna River. There was a turnoff that went through the trees and ended at a picnic table and a fire pit. It wasn't dark yet, and it certainly wasn't cold, but the guys already had a fire going. There were about eight coolers lined up in the bed of a truck, and a couple of guys were unloading them. Spencer saw me watching, and he laughed.

"These parties have a way of growing and getting very thirsty," he said.

He'd moved closer, and I stepped a few inches away. I was glad I'd driven myself. Whatever I'd expected, this wasn't it.

As the crowd grew, along with the noise and music, I recognized a few faces. A girl from my senior English class came over, and some others joined us, and soon I found myself laughing with a group of people I hardly knew. Some were total strangers. The last I'd seen of Spencer, he was with some of the guys cooking on a huge grill someone had towed in and was going hard at the beer.

As darkness fell, the clear skies reflected in the river. I maneuvered away from the crowd. My ears were ringing, and my head ached a little.

As I stood at the riverbank under the arching branches of a large oak, I was buffered from the worst of the noise, the blasting music, and the smells of alcohol and smoke.

I watched the river flow by in the night. The river water, even in daylight, was dark like Cub Creek, but otherwise, it was very different. The South Anna River wasn't as wide or graceful as the James River but much wider and more forceful than Cub Creek. Yet the difference was more than that. I tried to imagine this river flowing through the Hollow and decided I wouldn't want it. It was powerful and beautiful, but it was too accessible. It wasn't private. It would be too hard to shut out the world.

"Join us," Spencer said. He handed me a bottle.

"Where'd you go? I haven't seen you in a while."

"I had to help get things set up. It's my fault, though. I should have smarter friends." He laughed. "That's a joke, you know."

I held the bottle but did no more than that. Spencer touched my arm and got bolder and put his arm around my back.

"I'm sorry, Hannah. I should've told them to fix things themselves." He touched my hair. "Listen, if this isn't what you want . . . If you want to leave, just say the word. I'm with you either way, stay or go."

I believed him. "No, this is OK. It's . . . loud."

He laughed again. "Yes, it is. Look, if you're willing to stay, then I'm glad because I'm kind of one of the hosts, and it would be rude to leave, but I will, I mean it." He tapped the bottle. "Take a drink and come over by the fire. Relax and have fun."

I took a sip and grimaced. Spencer laughed again and pulled me closer. I leaned against him, and we turned away from the river and joined the group.

In the end, the party was a blast. Gran was awake in bed when I came in. She did some pronounced sniffing when I came near, and she might have picked up on the beer because displeasure showed in her face, but she only said, "Did you have a good time?"

"I did." As I told her good night and bent to kiss her cheek, I was grateful that the heavier smoke from the fire pit probably disguised the worst of the alcohol smell, or else I would likely have gotten a lecture.

"They treated you right, Hannah? The boy and his friends?"

"Yes, ma'am, they did." In fact, I hadn't felt the class division I'd experienced in high school, and here we were, barely out of school. Had we grown beyond the artificial social boundaries of that brick building so quickly, or had I imagined they existed? More likely, my welcome was no more than a temporary acceptance because the guy I was there with was one of them.

As I drifted off to sleep that night, I wondered if Spencer would call again. I thought of his laughter and his breath on my cheek when he lowered his voice and spoke only to me. I remembered his arm around me as the evening had worn on. And I thought he probably would.

Spencer and I went out a few times after. I thought I was in love—a sudden love that was all the more amazing because I'd never imagined it was lurking anywhere around us when we passed in the school hallway. Because I was in love, I made some poor decisions. We'd graduated. We were adults now. The kissing and hugging combined with the alcohol, and I said yes. But in the end, it was a crush. Just a crush. I knew it for sure when he didn't call me afterward, and then I was *truly* crushed. When I called him, he didn't answer or return my call. Finally, one day, he did. I happened to answer the phone. When I heard his voice, my heart nearly flew out of my chest and heat rushed up my body to burn my face.

I blurted out, "Why haven't you called?"

"I'm sorry, Hannah. Really. Things have changed, you know?"

"What things?"

"Well, college is coming up, and I've got stuff to take care of and all that."

I didn't answer.

He added, "I don't have time for you right now."

The words felt like a knife twisting in my gut. "Time for me?"

"Not right now." He sounded awkward. "I don't mean not for you, but for hanging out with anyone. Not even with my friends."

I shook my head. He couldn't see my head shake, but honestly I was speechless. Gran was nearby. The house was small. She might try not to listen, but how could she not hear?

"Hannah." His tone changed, softened. "I'm heading off for college in a couple of months. My dad and mom want me to do some things with them, a trip, and my dad wants me to spend time at work with him."

Which didn't preclude spending time with the person you loved, right? Unless you'd realized you didn't love the person after all, at least not as much as the fun stuff you might miss out on by choosing the tougher path of integrity and loyalty.

"I see. I have plans, too. You should've been more considerate, had some guts, and not made me chase you down. Have a good life."

I hung up. I'd tried to keep my voice low, but what were the odds Gran hadn't heard? I couldn't face her. I walked out the kitchen door and crossed the yard to the pottery cabin. I sat on the seat at the wheel. All around me, in the corners and above my head in the loft, were things Grand, or others, had stored here over the decades. Sometimes it was like being buried amid someone else's junk. Other times it was like hugs and memories wrapping around me, a certainty that life had gone on for centuries in our Hollow, not only for the Cooper family but for the Native Americans here before us and for whoever might have preceded them. *Life goes on*—I'd heard it said many times.

I wanted to be devastated over what amounted to the boy's abandonment of me. His perfidy. My Grand had been a lover of impressive words, and he'd taught me a bunch of his favorites. *Perfidy* was a fine one that sounded exactly like its meaning. Treachery. Disloyalty. And I *was* hurt and angered by the boy's cowardly actions, but the truth was, I wasn't really all *that* hurt. My pride, yes. My feelings, certainly. I'd made some bad choices and tried to fit myself into this person's life, a life in which I didn't belong. I lived in Cooper's Hollow. This was where I belonged. One day, I'd go off to college and be smart and successful, and when I came back to Louisa County and our cozy Hollow, everyone would see how brilliant, beautiful, and fabulous I was.

"Hannah?"

Distantly, I heard Gran's voice. I'd left the cabin door cracked open for light and air. I got up to look out. She'd pulled a kitchen chair over to the back door and had wedged her cane into the door hinge to prop it open. She was wearing the knee-length housecoat she called a duster. Her legs were encased in the tight white stockings Mildred made her wear for swelling. On her feet were the same worn-out house slippers she'd scuffed around in for years, and she rested the soles on the threshold. She saw me at the cabin door and yelled, "Are you all right, honey?"

Despite a tear or two trickling down my cheek, I laughed. It was a short, embarrassed laugh but already a strong sign of recovery.

"I'm fine." I wiped at my cheeks and joined her on the porch.

"Never you mind that boy. You should go on to college. Don't worry about me."

"I already deferred the grants and the scholarships for this year, so I can't. Besides, money wasn't the reason I decided not to go."

"Hush, child. I'll do well enough on my own. Our groceries are delivered, as is the propane. Anything I want"—she snapped her fingers—"I can have it delivered out here anytime. In fact, having to do more for myself will be good for me. I'll get more exercise and grow stronger. Never mind those scholarships. Go talk to Mr. Browne in town. He can work it out."

"Mr. Browne? The mysterious man in town who sends us money and pays the bills?" Regretting my snarky tone, I added, "Sorry, Gran."

"He isn't mysterious at all. He worked for Grand and me, and now he works for me and you. He can advise you. He'll tell you how much we can afford."

"Are you talking about going into Grand's savings? College is very expensive."

"We can sell off land or the timber. Though," she muttered, "I don't hold with selling off the timber." She added, "But land. We have a lot of that, and we can part with a few acres for your future. I should've insisted before. In fact, I'm going to give Mr. Browne a call. Let him know what we're thinking, and then you go talk to him."

"No."

"I mean it, Hannah. I know your grandfather handled all this sort of stuff, and I've never stepped up and taken on the responsibility, but I'm serious this time."

"So am I. It's too late. I'd have to reapply by certain dates and get accepted and all that. Plus, I don't want to leave you here alone."

"Never mind me. Selfishly, I wanted you here with me, so I let it be when you said you were putting off school for a year. But you need this. I see it now. If it's too late for this coming school year, then we need to get cracking for next year. Or what about midyear? Can't you start between semesters? You've got time to work it out, and we'll talk to Mr. Browne and find out how best to proceed."

We were connected to the world by our landline. Here, in our beautiful, homey Hollow, we had no cell reception. That yellow phone on the wall was our link to the outside world, and it brought in both good and bad news. A few days after Spencer's phone call, Gran said she spoke to Mr. Browne, but she must've done it while I was out in the pottery cabin or working outside otherwise. With Gran tied to the house, as she was by her physical limitations, there was never an opportunity for me to communicate privately via phone, unless I left home and drove somewhere.

In the end, I didn't go to see Mr. Browne. Very soon, other things came up to interfere with the plans we thought we needed to make. I was reminded of something Grand had often said. He'd quoted Proverbs with all the fancy wording of the King James Version, but he'd said the message came down to one certainty: "Man plans; God disposes."

When I suspected I was pregnant, I didn't tell Gran. I could be wrong, and there was no sense in getting us worked up over something that might not be true. And there was no point in taking those tests from the drugstore. Either I was or I wasn't. It wasn't as if I needed to know by a certain day. I preferred not to think about it. Instead, I spent longer hours out at the potter's wheel. It was the only place I could hide from Gran without raising questions. She might be old, and her body was worn out, but her senses were sharp.

One morning in September she made me face the truth. I was fixing breakfast, and she was sitting at the kitchen table waiting for her coffee to cool. The bile was rising, and I tried hard to think the nausea away, but my stomach was determined to betray me. As I scraped scrambled eggs onto her plate next to the toast but not touching it—just the way she liked it—Gran confronted me.

"You're paper white. You think I'm old and don't know, but I do. Tell me the truth. Is it the boy you were dating? What's his name? You only ever called him by his first name. Who are his people?"

I wanted to pretend I didn't know what she was talking about, but any moment now I was going to lose what little I'd eaten that morning. I pressed my hand to my midsection and tried to breathe evenly.

"You don't need to know his name. He's gone. Out of the picture. This is on me." My stomach lurched.

"Gone? What does *gone* mean?" Her voice rose on each word.

My coffee and toast were abandoned as I flew to the sink and hovered there. So far, so good. Nothing had come up, but it was a near thing. I clutched the counter and answered her.

"He's not in the picture, that's all."

"What about college, Hannah? And a baby . . . a baby is a gift from God, but babies should have daddies in their lives."

"I didn't. Not a mother or a father. I had you and Grand. You were more than enough."

Gran shook her head, her face full of worry and misery. She rubbed her cheeks, then said, "It wasn't a choice. Nobody wanted it that way."

A tear wet her cheek. Tears always happened when I mentioned my dead parents. She couldn't bear to speak of them. Next, her body would start shaking, and she'd cry in earnest. I went to her and wrapped my arms around her.

I whispered, "He's a boy, Gran. Not a man. The last thing we need is a grown child to take care of. We're better off without a boy who doesn't want to be here and doesn't want to be an adult."

Her body shuddered in my arms, and she gripped them with more strength than I could've imagined was left in her scrawny hands. "We don't have Grand anymore. Just you and me. Two women. One too old and one too young. How on earth . . . what in heaven's name are we supposed to do?"

"Hush, Gran. You're right. A baby's a gift. This baby is a gift from heaven, sent to comfort us for all we've lost."

She patted my back. "You have to do the right thing, the honest thing. Hard as it may be, Hannah, that boy, whoever he is, has a right to know. It's right for his family to know. A baby should be celebrated and loved, not hidden." She paused and pulled back, her eyes open wide. "Unless he's a criminal or sick in his head or . . ." She covered her face with her hands, and her shoulders quaked.

A criminal? For heaven's sake. Where had that come from? I kissed her forehead. "No, Gran, he's a foolish boy fresh out of high school with no good sense and no proper home training."

Gran quieted. I fixed us both fresh toast with butter and jelly. I left hers on a plate beside her bed and put her coffee there, too. I helped her move from the kitchen to her bed and settled her in, propped up well so she could eat and drink. My nausea had passed, maybe in part due to relief now that Gran knew the truth. I carried my coffee and toast out to the cabin, ready to be alone for a while.

I sat at the wheel and gave my dilemma some thought while I nibbled at my toast. When the toast was eaten, I brushed the crumbs from my fingers and centered the wedged clay on the wheel. I wet my fingers in the water bucket, and the spinning started. The hum of the motor below the wheel pan established a rhythm. My wet fingers, slipping along the clay body, strummed the one-note tune, but within that single note were variations unimagined and songs uncounted. Sometimes those songs had words, and I heard them in my head. Soon I was humming along in harmony.

When the shaping was done, I stopped the wheel, took my wire, and worked it carefully under the edge of the soft clay pot, pressing it close to the base, and then pulled it toward me with a smooth, deft movement. When the pot was freed, I carried it over to the shelves and found a prime spot for it to dry. Drying had to happen slowly. I dampened cloths in a water bucket and wrapped them loosely around it.

Clay required timing and patience. Whether to work it or leave it be to dry properly—the process was driven by the needs of the clay. The potter was a tool whose wants and needs were extraneous. It was a humbling occupation. Plus, a potter had to have a true disregard for messy hands.

I took another lump of clay, one I'd already wedged. Wedging clay was powerful and violent. It eliminated the air bubbles that made the clay body weak and prone to exploding when fired. I liked to wedge clay when I was feeling upset or angry, so I usually had clay, already wedged and wrapped, ready to hand.

Wetting the wheel, I pressed the clay onto it, hard, then beat at it with my fist to make the suction right. As the wheel began to spin, I worked on centering the clay with my hands. I dipped my fingers in the water again and went to work shaping. The focus, by necessity, blocked my extraneous, darker fears and worries. As I pressed into the lump of clay and worked my thumb and forefingers down and then up, over and over, to create the walls, I realized Gran was right about telling the boy. He—no one else but him and me—had the absolute right to know.

The next morning, I bathed and washed my hair. It was long, half-way down my back, and would dry straight and shiny without help, but standing in front of the medicine cabinet mirror over the sink, I saw the ends were uneven. I took Gran's sewing sheers and pulled the tresses forward over each shoulder and trimmed up the edges. I wanted to look respectable, someone worthy of inclusion in another family. After fixing breakfast, I dressed in slacks and a dressy top. It was early days yet, and the slacks fit fine.

I drove over to the boy's house. Some other woman was cleaning it now, I assumed. I hadn't been here since that woman was me. The grass was green and freshly cut, and not a leaf marred it. When the leaves began turning, they would fall, but they would fall as colorful, crisp ornaments to be whisked away as soon as possible. My experience with these people, and those like them, was that they weren't mean, but they were self-directed and self-focused. They weren't the sort of human beings tenderhearted people should get in the way of.

There was no sign of life. No car was in the driveway. But there was a four-car garage, so the empty driveway meant little. I knocked on the front door and waited, then rang the doorbell. My gut was thumping. I felt it throughout my body and tasted the bile in my mouth.

No one answered. Light-headed, I stepped back and leaned against a post. Relieved more than disappointed, the gut-thumping diminished, but I felt teary now. Had I cherished hopes after all? Maybe that these people would be kind and welcoming?

Maybe I had hoped Spencer would be glad to see me despite what he'd said. I didn't love him, no pretense there. My good sense and morals had been crushed by a crush, enhanced by alcohol and proximity, and a new life was not an uncommon result. But we could make this right. We could make a life together. This wouldn't be the first baby that resulted in a happy marriage.

No one was home, and I was in no rush. If I returned home too quickly, Gran wouldn't believe I'd tried. I sat on the concrete porch steps to rest and gather myself.

Hinges squeaked behind me. The storm door, its etched glass perfect and shiny, opened a few inches.

"Hello?" his mother said.

I stood. "Hi. I don't know if you remember me?"

She tilted her head. Her hair looked freshly colored, and her hand resting on the doorframe displayed her manicure.

"Oh, sorry. You're Anna, right? You cleaned our house?"

"Hannah, ma'am. My name is Hannah." I cleared my throat, suddenly suffering from a burning stomach again. "I wondered if your son might be home?"

"My son?"

Apparently more explanation was called for.

"Well, yes, ma'am. We went to school together, and we . . . he and I talked the day I was cleaning your house. Might I speak with him?"

Her eyes had grown cold. I didn't know if she was suspicious, or protective, or if I was boring her.

"I need to speak with him."

"Hannah, you said? Well, Hannah, my son is at college. If you're friends, then I'm surprised you don't know."

Dismay hit me. My eyes wanted to close, and my body tried to turn away in shame, but I refused. I forced my distress from my face, mentally smoothing away the hurt, and straightened my posture.

I cleared my throat. "Yes, ma'am. I knew he was already in Charlottesville for school, but this being the weekend, I thought he might be home . . . with the university so close."

"He isn't. I'll be happy to pass on a message to him, if you like."

My thoughts and fears all stuttered and stammered around in my brain. I tried to sort out the best response. Meanwhile, my nausea increased. Black specks danced before my eyes. I held on to my stomach, trying to keep it all at bay.

I managed to say, "Could you ask him to call me, please?"

Between the floating specks obscuring my vision, I saw in her eyes how badly she wanted to say no. I saw her suspicion. Her lips shaped to say no, but instead she said, "What's your number?"

"He already has it. I guess you didn't know *that*, did you?" Then I turned and barfed. I missed the door and the porch, but the neatly trimmed bushes suffered. I would've been embarrassed, but the immediate relief the vomiting brought made it worthwhile. If not worthwhile, then surely inevitable, and the sense of well-being flooding through me in its wake gave me strength.

"Sorry, ma'am." I nodded as I wiped my lips and chin with my sleeve and turned for the car.

The woman's mouth hung open, then she slapped her own hand over it and bent a little at the middle. Vomiting can be catching, I knew. I also knew Spencer would never call because he'd never get the message, and part of me was happy. Gran had the honesty she wanted—at least I'd tried—and I wouldn't have to wonder if his family would have welcomed a new little one and me.

I stopped cleaning houses before I was far enough along to draw questions. I had a little money saved up, and it didn't take much to keep us fed. Mr. Bridger, who lived over the ridge, shared his venison with us, and sometimes a squirrel or rabbit. Gran and I grew veggies and canned them, and I'd kept that up after she got too sick. We had electric for the lights and propane for cooking, and the man in town mostly handled the bills. If I were laid up for a few days after having the baby, we'd manage well enough.

❧

On a visit to Gran, Mildred saw my condition and had another, sterner word with me.

"You need to see an ob-gyn."

I set my lips to closed and scowled at her.

"It's not only about you. You're pregnant. You owe it to this baby to give it the best start possible."

My stern expression may have wavered because Mildred pressed harder.

"I'll make the appointment." Mildred moved close to me and put her hand on my arm. She lowered her voice. I was forced to lean toward her to hear better.

"This doctor is near Charlottesville. You won't run into anyone from around here. I know you want to keep your business private." She glanced at Gran, and Gran nodded.

I didn't respond, but Mildred saw my doubt. After she left, Gran pressed the subject further.

"She's right, Hannah. The babe deserves the best. And you, too. It's no easy thing to have a baby. You need to be at your best."

When Mildred called the next day with an appointment time and an address, I agreed to go. She gave me directions. She offered to drive me. I told her I could handle it.

I found the doctor's office with no problem. I was early, and the parking lot was all but empty. I sat in the car trying to get up my nerve. I'd rarely been to a doctor for any reason, and this felt far too personal and intimate. On the other hand, intimacy had led to this whole thing, so that felt like justice of some sort.

That morning the sun shone brightly in a pure-blue sky. A flock of birds flew overhead, low enough that I could hear them squawking through the rolled-down window. Other cars drove into the lot and parked. Several women emerged from the cars and gathered near the office door. They wore pink and blue scrubs. They must work for the doctor. One of the women laughed loudly and turned toward my car.

She couldn't see me, not with the glare of the sun on my windshield, but I saw her and recognized her as the mother of a girl I'd gone to school with. The girl and I weren't close friends, but we'd known each other for years, and her mother would know me in a heartbeat.

I tried to tell myself that she wouldn't know why I was here. It could be for one of those wellness visits, right? At this point, I was thicker in the middle, but it wasn't obvious. All the same, Mildred had figured it out pretty quickly, hadn't she? And this woman might come in the room with the doctor for the examination. Even if she didn't, my records would be right there in their files. I imagined how natural it would be for her to mention to her daughter over supper, "Guess who I saw today?" And the next reasonable question would be, "Why?"

My fingers gripped the steering wheel so tightly that my joints ached.

I'd learned it well from my grandparents—the value of privacy and self-reliance—and I wouldn't let my Grand down now. Likely, some of my own pride was at stake as well, though I didn't want to admit to it. I didn't have much in life, neither possessions nor social position, but I had my reputation as a decent, practical, respectable young woman who minded her own business, and I didn't want to be the subject of anyone's gossip. I was a Cooper from Cooper's Hollow, and that's who we were.

I drove home. Gran welcomed me as I came through the door and started to ask about the visit. I shushed her. Her smile dimmed, and she rubbed her hands over her face, but she didn't persist.

Mildred called later that day and asked why I'd missed the appointment. I was honest with her. I owed her that.

"I saw people I knew. Someone who worked there. I'd like to keep my business as my business."

"We'll try another doctor."

"No. Thank you for your concern, but definitely no. Babies have been born for centuries without doctors. I'm young and healthy, and I'll take my chances."

There was a long pause, a moment of silence wherein I let Mildred gather her thoughts, hoping we could resolve this now and put it aside.

"What about your baby?" she finally said. "You have a responsibility to your child."

Out of respect, I'd given her the opportunity to speak her mind, but this was enough.

"We'll be fine. Thank you for your concern." I said it firmly, leaving no doubt there was a period at the end of the sentence and an end to the conversation.

Mildred showed up a few days later with prenatal vitamins and books about pregnancy, childbirth, and bringing up babies. She began checking my blood pressure along with Gran's. I allowed her to do that, and it seemed to ease her mind.

The book she'd given me about childbirth was almost enough to send me running back to the doctor's office. I was curled up on the sofa, reading, and Gran was in her bed doing the same. I must've made a noise because she asked if something was wrong.

I looked down at the picture of the crowning baby and slapped the book closed. "No, ma'am. It's all good." I stood up and walked toward the kitchen. "Thirsty? Can I get you something, Gran?"

"Hot tea would be nice."

"Yes, ma'am." In the kitchen, I stood at the back door. We'd left it cracked open for fresh air. I clutched the book to me and stared out across the yard and the creek. Beyond the creek and amid the trees on the far side was the cemetery. Its stone walls had been there long before Grand and Gran, and maybe before Grand's grandparents, too.

For untold years, women had been having babies. There was no disputing the value of doctors and hospitals and all the conveniences, but in the end, babies were conceived and born with or without them.

My reasoning wasn't without flaw. I knew that.

I closed the door and put the book on the counter while I filled the teakettle. I felt assured. All would be well for both my baby and me. We'd do just fine.

⚬⚬

Before my baby was due, I drove up the interstate to the next town. My house-cleaning savings were tucked in my purse. I wandered through the infant section in Walmart and picked out what I deemed most likely to be needed early on. I did everything I could to make sure we were ready for the big day.

My baby was born in late February. It was a cold, bitter, rain-spitting morning. Per our calculations, we'd been planning on an early March delivery, but when the contractions started and didn't let up, Gran called Mildred. Mildred lived a few miles up Cross County Road, nearer Mineral, so we were lucky there was only rain.

Mildred arrived ready to do business. No more suggestions and second-guessing—she set to work helping me deliver my baby.

The contractions weren't pleasant but not as bad as I had feared, though the last one made me yell. That was it. A push or two and Mildred was holding the baby and looking almost surprised. Her all-business demeanor vanished as a smile transformed her face.

"A daughter," she declared as she wiped the baby's face, then wrapped her in a soft cotton baby blanket. "Sometimes fast births have their own challenges, but you're one lucky mom, Hannah Cooper. This little girl is pinking up nicely and already eyeing me. She's small but perfect. I've seldom seen an easier birth, especially for a first baby, but some women are built for it. It's all in the hips. I'm glad for you, but make no mistake,

45

you are truly fortunate." She smoothed the baby's blanket and placed her in my arms.

"Thank you, Miss Mildred, for your help."

I touched my baby's hand and her cheek. I untucked the blanket from around her feet and inspected them, too. She was perfect, as Mildred had said. I was glad my baby was a girl. She'd fit right in with this household of women.

"I'll register the birth for you when I go into town. What will you call her? Have you decided?"

"Her name is Ellen," I said, caressing her cheek and fluffing her soft cap of very light-brown hair tipped with gold. "Ellen Clara Cooper."

Gran beamed when she heard it. Her first name was Clara and her maiden name was Ellen.

Mildred wrote down the name, then fixed her gray eyes on me. "And the daddy? What's his name?"

"No need to list him. We're good as we are."

"I have to list someone. If I don't, they'll put unknown."

"Then so be it. Let people think what they will." I tucked the soft baby blanket up under her chin, and she turned toward my fingers. "Ellen, daughter of Hannah Cooper, great-granddaughter of Clara and Edmund Cooper. That's good enough for anyone."

Mildred shook her head but bent forward to place a light kiss on my forehead.

"You're hardly more than a baby yourself. I'll have social services come out and visit. They'll be able to offer assistance."

As with Mildred's suggestion of going to the doctor, Gran didn't object outright. I was shocked at her. I fixed my stare on Mildred and said, "Don't. We are fine as we are. I won't let them in. We don't need them, and if we ever do, I'll summon them myself."

"Hannah," Gran admonished.

"No, Gran. You know about babies, and I've read the books Mildred brought. Between us, we'll do fine. When I'm fit to drive, I'll take her to see a pediatrician. I'll be a good, responsible mother." I leveled my gaze at Mildred. "I appreciate all you've done for us, truly, and I mean this sincerely—you are welcome to drop by anytime you wish to check on us in case you think we aren't up to the challenge, but otherwise, we have everything we need." I looked down at the newborn in my arms and whispered, "Aren't I right, my sweet Ellen?"

Ellen slept and ate and cried and laughed and thrived. Her eyes were blue, and her hair stayed wispy and curly. When I rubbed her forehead and scalp lightly with my palm, she'd close her eyes and her lips would part, and her expression was pure and angelic. That, and rubbing the soles of her feet, were her favorite things, and would always soothe her when she was gassy or fretting.

Gran hovered nearby. She tutored me in diapering, burping, and all such things. What she couldn't do was to spell me at night, so if Ellen didn't sleep between feedings, I didn't, either, and I was tired. During that first week, Mildred had brought a baby car seat and secured it in Grand's car. She drove Ellen and me to visit the pediatrician. The result was gold stars for all of us.

For the first two weeks, Mildred dropped by daily, but as time wore on, she was reassured by Ellen's progress and my ability to manage despite the sleep issue, and she eased off on the frequency. I was pleased and proud. It felt like a seal of approval.

One day when Ellen was three weeks old, I was sitting on the porch with my feet up. It was early March, but the air was mild and the breeze was fresh and gentle. The cradle was next to me. Ellen was sleeping on a soft cushion with the blanket snugged up around her cheeks and looking cozy. I was half-asleep myself, listening to the woods and the creaks of the house and the soft sound of her breathing. The noise of a truck approaching woke me. I sat forward, wondering if I should rush Ellen inside. She'd been up half the night, and I was loath to wake her before time to feed her. By that point, the pickup truck was rounding the curve and in view. It was the grocery delivery. Eva Pullen did deliveries as a business. Gran had been placing orders for years, and Eva would do the shopping and deliver the groceries. I was surprised to see Eva driving and not her son, Anthony, who'd been taking over her delivery routes in recent months. I figured the reason for that was obvious—and sleeping in the cradle.

I waved, then put my finger to my lips to signal the baby was sleeping and went to meet her at the truck.

She handed me a grocery bag and carried the box herself. She whispered, "I saw diapers and wipes and formula on the order and decided I'd deliver it myself. I heard you had a little one. I hardly believed it. Can I see her?"

"You can peek, but don't wake her. Sorry, I was up with her last night."

"Colicky? Or got her days and nights mixed up?"

"Lonely, I think." I smiled. "Wanted some hugging."

Eva started toward the porch. I stopped her, saying, "Let's carry it around back. Gran's resting, too."

"Oh, of course, honey." She followed me down the side path to the back stoop. "How's Mrs. Cooper doing?"

"Gran is pretty good."

"Well, she always was stubborn, but a lady, certainly."

Once in the kitchen, she couldn't help but see through the kitchen door into the living room and see Gran on her bed. But she didn't approach her or disturb her. As we walked back outside and around again, she said, "Give her my best when she wakes, if you will." She went straight up onto the porch this time and paused by the cradle. She asked, but softly, "Who does she favor? You or her daddy?"

She was casting about for personal information.

"Ellen got lucky. She looks like her great-grandmother." I let Eva know by a hard look that no further questions would be welcome.

"I got ya," she said. "That Melissa Meese just had a little one, too. A boy, I heard."

Melissa and Spencer? It seemed like their breakup hadn't been that serious after all. And he'd run off on both of us. I almost laughed at the foolishness, the recklessness, of young hearts. We'd thought we were grown up.

I didn't have to hide resentment or hurt feelings from Eva. There were none. If I had a touch of regret, it was about my poor choices, like dating Spencer. Certainly it wasn't over losing him. Good riddance. Taking care of Ellen was exhausting but rewarding. Not so with Spencer. I was thankful I didn't need to deal with him.

She continued. "I reckon the father's family will be paying her bills, since I hear he's run off to college like he had nothing to do with it." She gave a short laugh. "Or more likely his parents packed him off lickety-split. Easier to pay the bills and not let the relationship go further. Mama and Daddy have bigger expectations for their only son than a local girl."

If Eva thought she might pry a secret loose from me, she got nothing but my tired smile.

Eva nodded good-bye. As she went to the car, she added, "If you need anything out here, you let me know. I know you're a strong, smart girl and devoted to your grandma, and I can see you're a fine mommy to the babe, too, but no one can handle it all. You let me know and I, or my Anthony, can be here in twenty minutes. And happy to do it."

She meant it and had a good heart, but she was also an information broker, as I called such folks. Grand had explained such things to me when I was a child. People like salesmen, and people who did deliveries and paid lots of visits around the county were the purveyors of personal and interesting information long before the local newspaper was being printed and sold. The worst of all such invasions of privacy were local diners and doctors' waiting rooms. Frequent those places, per Grand, and you could never expect to have a modicum of privacy. Needless to say, we didn't eat in town a lot. My grandparents considered Mildred to be the exception, and they were never proven wrong.

It occurred to me, almost belatedly, that my Ellen had a half brother out there. Beyond a moment of speculation, the information held no meaning to me whatsoever. I had plenty of other things to concern myself with, and I put it out of my mind.

Eva had stuck the latest issue of the local newspaper in the top of the food box. She'd also tucked a baby book in the side of the box. The book was pretty and mostly pink. I thumbed through it. There were pages for all sorts of dates and events and pictures. I left the baby book on the kitchen table and took the newspaper out to the porch to read while I kept my eye on my sleeping Ellen.

There it was, in the section with engagements, weddings, births, and obituaries. I hadn't submitted an official notice in the paper, but it didn't surprise me. No doubt they pulled the information from legal records, and Mildred had said she'd file notice of the birth for us, so I guessed she had.

"Baby Girl Cooper, born to Hannah Cooper," and the date. That was it.

I decided this wouldn't be my baby's birth notice. It wasn't good enough and didn't deserve a place in Ellen's baby book. I went into my bedroom and found a school notebook, my spiral notebook from history class with plenty of empty sheets left in it, and took it back out to the porch.

I wrote:

Ellen Clara Cooper, daughter of Hannah Cooper and great-granddaughter of Clara and Edmund Cooper of Cooper's Hollow, was born on a cold, overcast day in February—a day that was immediately made bright by virtue of her shining countenance, her charming blue eyes, and her sweet smile and voice. She was born with light-brown hair, almost golden, and curly and feathery, and she grabbed her mama's hand with a strong grip. She knew she was exactly where she belonged—in her mama's arms.

Feeling life's rhythm strong in me now, I flipped to the back inside cover. It was a lightweight cardboard with more substance than the thin sheet of lined paper, and while my Ellen slept, I sketched her sweet baby profile and the tiny, slightly curled fist resting near her cheek as if she'd fallen asleep before the thumb could complete its journey to her mouth. Her lips, soft and full, were posed as the traditional cherub's bud mouth, and the nose was perfect. Simply perfect.

This would start the baby book off as it should. Only the best that love could give was what my Ellen deserved.

I wasn't a great artist, but I had some skill, and I did one more sketch later that day. Gran was holding Ellen, and when I put the pencil to work, I kept glancing up at her.

"What's this?" she finally asked. "Why are you looking at me?"

Ellen reached toward Gran's moving lips. Her hand, with its chubby fingers, waved, and she smiled. The pediatrician had said she was too young to smile, but Gran and I knew better.

"Hold still and don't get her stirred up," I said. "I'm drawing a picture for her baby book."

"What? Of who? Me?"

"Hold still, Gran. This is for Ellen. For her baby book. A picture of her being held by her Great-Gran."

Gran chuckled, and the sound and movement delighted Ellen. Her arms swung and her feet pumped.

"Hold still, girls. Show a little respect for the pencil, please."

Gran smiled and didn't protest again. Instead, she touched the pert nose, the rosy cheek, and Ellen waved her tiny hands again and gurgled happily.

George Bridger was a lean, angular man with a beard that had gotten whiter and longer over the years. It had grown straggly and wasn't always clean. Every few months, Mr. Bridger bestirred himself to cross over Elk Ridge and hike down to our Hollow. Only once did I ever remember his driving over. Instead, he walked. Gran and Grand had known him since before water ran in the creeks, as they liked to say, and they were some kind of distant kin. Mr. Bridger had been fast friends with Grand in particular. He lived alone. I think the old man walked down to visit and to check on us, feeling a family sort of responsibility, and to let us have the honor of checking up on him, too. Sometimes I think he hoped he'd find his old friend, at home and miraculously restored, no questions asked. I understood, but I couldn't help him with that. Other than Mr. Bridger, Eva Pullen's one visit, and Mildred, we saw no one, which was fine with all three of us gals.

He visited one day while I was working with my clay at the kitchen table. He didn't approve, being as it was a kitchen table, and he'd wanted to pull up to it and have a cup of coffee and share a little conversation with Gran. Gran insisted they could settle at one end while I worked. After a bit, I realized the conversation had ceased. I looked up to see him watching.

"What're you making?" he asked. "A bowl?"

"A bowl or a pot. I suppose it would work for a cup, too."

"It's got wings?"

"Butterfly wings." I motioned with my hands. "Or rather hands and fingers shaped to mimic butterfly wings. I made the bottom, the bowl part, on the wheel, and then came in here to make the wings and attach them." I finished smoothing a missed edge into the main body. "This is Ellen's long naptime during the day, and my only time to get things like this done."

"That so?" he asked.

"I'm going to carve her name in it. I'll save it for her till she's older."

He laughed.

Gran spoke up. "What's so funny, old man?"

Mr. Bridger finished his last swig of coffee with a slurping noise and said, "Well, you'd best make two of 'em. I never knew a child who didn't break a breakable." He chuckled, appreciating his own wit. "That pot with its wings looks like an invitation, an outright temptation, to little hands to touch."

I considered what he said. It made sense. After all, if one was good, two was better, right? Smart to have a spare.

Despite her ailments, Gran lived beyond either of our expectations. I liked to think it was because I gave her such loving care. On good days she'd get up and move around. On other days she sat in her rocker or lay abed, but for those few months we shared baby Ellen, I had glimpses of a time I, myself, couldn't remember—of my own babyhood, of when Gran had made funny faces and spoken to me in baby talk. I didn't doubt her face had shone as brightly back when I was a baby as it did when she made faces over Ellen. In those long-ago days, Gran's hair had been the color of corn silk, though already mixed with gray, and while her wrinkles were fewer, they would still have been in evidence, as she was just over sixty when I was born. Back then, she said, she'd still had shapely legs and nice ankles. She and Grand had used to go dancing, at least until my parents died. Now those swollen legs burdened her. Sometimes they seemed to weigh a ton, she said. On the days she spent abed, Gran would ask for Ellen to lie beside her at naptime or when I was fixing meals.

I'd place my daughter in the crook of Gran's arm. Gran would offer a finger, which Ellen would grasp and hold on to with every ounce of her baby strength even while they slept. We both knew the time was coming when Ellen would become mobile. She'd start crawling, and our current arrangement wouldn't work so well. Gran wouldn't be able to chase after Ellen, and I'd have extra burdens on me. I worried about it. Gran said not to borrow trouble, that things would work out. As it turned out, there was nothing to worry over. Not in this case. Before crawling ever had the chance to be a problem, we lost our sweet Ellen.

CHAPTER THREE

Ellen was in my bedroom in a small wooden fold-up crib. My grandparents had used it for me when I was little bitty, and for my mother when she was a newborn. It was a simple bed with a two-inch mattress and wooden slats to let the air through. I kept fresh linens on it all the time. I'd fed my sweet baby Ellen, and she was dozy. The heat and humidity made her extra drowsy on top of her meal. A summer storm was trying to roll in. It had bunched the bad air up ahead of it, and we all felt the heaviness. I put Ellen into her small crib for her nap that day instead of with Gran, because Gran was hurting especially hard. Storm fronts always tortured her joints and bones.

I'd given Gran some herbal tea to help. She was finally dozing. Ellen was quiet in her crib, her eyes still peeking, but with the half-conscious, unfocused look they'd get before she slipped off into sleep. I was eighteen and bone-tired myself. A five-month-old daughter, an eighty-year-old grandmother—they depended on me. My body ached with the oppressive front, too, but never as hard as Gran's did. I supposed my time would come one day, but not for decades yet, I hoped.

While Ellen and Gran slept, I went into the backyard to watch the trees. Up high, the boughs bent in the fitful winds, not yet breaking through to the thick air closer down on the ground. I felt the storm approaching and yearned for the freshening breeze to blow through and push out the dirty air. The clouds were dark and massing. Thunder rumbled in the distance. The rain was likely to be heavy. On impulse, I arranged some old bricks around my herb patch to divert the runoff that was bound to happen. The slope could be a problem, but thankfully the creek was far enough downslope I didn't need to worry about flooding. Cub Creek was likely to get itself a nice replenishment today. I stood there in my bare feet, sniffing the air and feeling the change. The leaves in the trees near the edge of the forest seemed to be growing larger and turning over, so I knew I was right—there'd be real rain. I checked the window and door to the toolshed, and the pottery cabin, too. Everything was shut up tight.

The atmosphere was uneasy. My bones and my brain were uneasy, too, and felt brittle. I checked on Ellen. She was sound asleep. I saw the slight rise and fall of her back as she slept. I didn't touch her lest I disturb her. Even through the closed windows, I felt the electric pull of the coming storm. I needed, wanted, to focus on it. Grand had been the same when an electrical storm approached, and Gran had said it was in my genes. Gran, herself, had fallen off into real sleep, and I was grateful. The heavy, anxious air pressing around me made me restless. I was always one to meet it head-on instead of running or hiding.

The storm came as promised. I sat on the porch rocker, not rocking but leaning forward as I watched the clouds turn nearly black. Then I stood at the steps, eager, as the freshening wind blew its way through and bent the trees by force.

I wanted my share of it and lifted my arms. The skin on my arms prickled, and then my whole body shivered with the electricity. When the clouds opened and the rain fell in sheets, I stayed out of reach of the drops but enjoyed the clean feel of it washing away the thick, dirty air the storm had bunched up in our Hollow. A sharp boom of thunder sounded and reverberated from hill to ridge. I poked my head back inside the house to listen, but neither of my charges showed any sign of having been disturbed.

When the wind shifted and the rain began to pelt the porch floor, I went into the house. I left the front door open, taking a risk that the rain would wet the floor because inside felt like a stale, dusty sauna badly in need of an influx of new air.

Despite the noon hour, the day was dark as the storm continued around and over us. Too dark and very quiet. I stood in the living room. Gran was in her bed, and I listened to her breathing. She'd slept through the thunder and lightning and the downpour. Her chest rose and fell evenly. She was resting easier. The weather front was passing, and the air pressure was rising. My own bones felt better, too.

Careful not to disturb her, I walked softly through the dim room and went to check on Ellen.

My baby was sleeping. She was due to be waking up soon, but she wasn't moving. Maybe she was feeling the break in the weather the same as Gran did. I touched her back through the lightweight cotton gown she wore. It was pink with burgundy roses, handworked by Gran's own mother.

The house rattled in a strong gust. There was a sucking sound, then a loud crack outside. Part of my brain recognized a tree was going down, its root ball being plucked from the wet ground. I didn't care as long as it didn't land on the house.

I touched my baby's back again, this time more firmly.

My instinct, more than my intellect, knew something was wrong. No stirring at my touch? I pressed the flat of my hand against her back. Her back wasn't hardly wider than my stretched-out hand. There was no rise and fall.

Roughly, I rolled her over, hoping the infant-size assault would offend her, scare her, or startle her into wakefulness. I called out her name. The house shook. Or I did. Maybe both.

I grabbed her up and held her small body close to my chest and neck. Her hair still had that precious baby smell, but her eyelids were tinged with purple. Her body was too cool. I wrapped her in her pink blanket. I swaddled her tighter and tighter as if to prevent her escape and to warm her up again.

Gran called out from the next room, "What's going on, Hannah? Was that a scream? Did I hear someone call out? Are you hurt?"

Gran's voice was thick and slurry sounding, and it made less of an impression on me than the rain and wind and the thudding of my heart. I rushed past Gran as I ran through the living room to the kitchen with Ellen in my arms. I grabbed the wall phone and dialed. Nothing. No dial tone. I flipped the wall switch. No light. The lines were down.

The car keys were in the dish by the door. I didn't pause for shoes or an umbrella but dashed straight out, the screen door swinging wide behind me and slamming into the outside wall. Beyond the steps, it was mostly mud. The rain, lighter now, continued to fall, hitting the thick leaves. Greedy leaves. The greenery seemed to have multiplied, and it brushed my face wetly. I pushed the leaves and branches aside, got in the car, and laid my bundle on the passenger seat.

"We'll get help, baby. Sweet baby, sweet Ellen, don't leave your mama." The words came from my mouth and were formed by my lips, but that desperate voice didn't sound like mine.

Grand's car was old, but the engine turned over and came alive. The driveway was red clay and mostly graveled. Up around the curve where the road sloped down, the low spot in the S curve might be flooded a bit but shouldn't be a problem if I had enough speed and didn't stop. I'd take the last hill fast and be up to the level spot where it joined the paved road before the tires could give a thought to getting mired. I hit the accelerator hard. And instantly slammed to a jolting stop.

My neck. My head. Pain, bright and blinding, hit me. I raised my arm to shield my face, and in the same instant, with my other hand, I grabbed at the precious bundle on the seat.

The downed tree. I'd heard it fall, hadn't I? Back in the house when nothing had mattered but my Ellen not waking? Yes, and in my haste to get help, I'd been fooled by the mass of thickly leaved branches. I should've realized why so many leaves were draped around my car and blocking the view.

Time was precious—each second—and it continued to tick. In that same moment, I understood time didn't matter. Its continued passing would only carve grief more deeply into my heart and brain.

My hand rested on the still form beside me. The leaves from the fallen tree covered my windshield like a green grave, and told me there was nothing more to be done here.

But hope dies hard. Taking my Ellen in my arms and holding tight to her, I opened the car door. I stepped out into the mud and sticks and other storm debris and stumbled my way under the now-slanted tree trunk and through the hanging boughs. On the other side of it, clear of the tree, I slipped and fought through the mud until I reached the driveway. The drive was muddy, too, but the surface still had enough gravel in it that it provided better footing. I tried to quicken my pace, not feeling the sharp rocks underfoot and ignoring the pain that shot up my back to the base of my skull with every movement. Clutching my bundle, I ran along the driveway.

If I could make it to the main road and flag down a passing car . . . Stranger or not, they'd help.

Where the drive curved away into the woods to begin its long slope down and nearly out of view of the house, I missed my step and went down. I never lost hold, though. I held tight. But when I tried to rise, I made it only as far as my knees.

There was nothing to be done. I rocked back and forth, holding to my heart my dearest little girl, who, through all this turmoil, had never cried, never stirred. She was gone, her spirit flown away.

I looked skyward at the dark clouds clearing overhead, almost as if I might see her . . . what? Ascending? No, all I got was a searing pain wrenching the back of my neck and down my spine.

Distantly, I heard Gran's voice. She must've come out onto the front porch.

Some rational spark in my brain cried out, *Get up and go back, Hannah. Heaven help us if Gran tries to walk down here. How will we ever get her back to the house?* And then the spark died, and I was fully back, enveloped in misery and pain.

I struggled to my feet and limped home, my face buried in the folds of Ellen's blanket.

Gran was standing in the doorway braced against the lintel. I ignored her and sat for a while in the porch rocker in my own hazy bubble. I was dizzy. My head and neck hurt, but the only thing that mattered was my loss. Gran was talking. I didn't answer her, and finally she stopped. My baby and I kept rocking.

It was summer. July. The afternoon was passing. No matter how tightly I'd wrapped her, no matter how hard I held her, I couldn't warm her small body back to life, nor keep out the damaging heat.

I knew she wasn't coming back.

I wished I could lay her back in the crib. As if I'd never disturbed her nap. All would be as it had been.

But it was too late.

Gone, as they say. Passed. Lost.

Our nearest neighbor was Mr. Bridger. I could hike up and over the hill. It was quite a walk, but once I was over the ridge, if he was home . . . He had an old truck, and it wasn't likely blocked in. His phone might be working, too. But to what purpose?

If he took me into town, would I be able to say to whomever one reported such events . . . say my baby was . . . I bit my lip, tasted blood, and bit down harder.

There was no way I could utter those words.

I held her more tightly and rocked harder back and forth. The jerking motions made the pains in my head worse.

No point in seeking help, anyway. No one could help. Not in any way that mattered. Time had passed, taking hope with it. One hour? Two? More than that. It was done. Over.

If no one could help bring her back, then I wouldn't give her up to the hands of strangers. People who'd never seen her laugh, had never experienced her temper when she was hungry.

She was my baby. My Ellen. Whether there was breath in her lungs or not. I had a duty to her.

I left the chair and the porch and entered the house. Gran had sat herself in a chair in the living room. Her face was red and pale all at once. She was panting through parted lips, her chest rising and falling in a quick, jumpy way. Her hair was wet and stringy. It clung to her forehead and cheeks. I noticed her state only peripherally as I carried Ellen past. Gran's eyes were big, her expression stricken, but I couldn't feel her pain. I was too full up with my own.

In my room, I laid my baby on the bed and opened the blanket. Her face and body were perfect. Not a mark. I tried one last time to wake her, not able to see how this could have come about, but the effort was too cruel to both of us to try more than once. I washed her body and pinned a fresh diaper on her, and then re-dressed her in the same gown. It was my favorite, and it had meaning. Gran's mother and other family, perhaps my own mother and father, might recognize the dress and know who she was when she arrived in heaven. It was a light thought—a thought without weight because I had to keep certain things at a distance.

Nobody was coming to clear the downed tree. I would have to do it myself with the chain saw or wait until the power company came to check on the outage, and they'd help me. But such help could be hours or days in coming, depending on how widespread the storm damage was.

No help was coming. This was on me.

I'd heard of crib death. I didn't know if that's what had happened, but there was nothing to indicate otherwise. She was as beautifully perfect as she'd been when I put her down for her nap, except now she was limp and cold. Her lips were tinted the soft lavender of a summer sunset, but there was no pink in her cheeks, no life in her flesh.

I brushed her brown-gold curls, kissed her perfect cheeks and smooth forehead, and then wrapped her again in a dry, fresh blanket. I took a clean sheet from the linen press and spread it on the bed. I laid her in the middle of the sheet and, kissing her soft cheeks one last time, I folded the fabric around her with all the love in my heart.

Tucked in is how I thought of it. Her mama was tucking her in.

Inside, I was breaking. Only great care could hold me together. And I had to hold it together. If not me, then who? Who else would take care of this?

Not Gran.

Not the hands of strangers when, and if, they ever showed up.

Human noises—breathing hitches and exhales, wet-sounding, almost painful in their gasping, were coming from the next room.

No help there. Not to be received or given. This was on me.

How would I explain it to people? My poor, sweet babe was gone, lost to me—an unworthy mother who must've done something wrong. That's what their eyes would say, and their mouths might say it, too.

I should've kept moving, but I let in these thoughts, and my heart failed me. My legs got weak. I sat in the chair in my bedroom and held the bundle. Gran was grieving and calling out questions and saying something about fetching Mildred.

But we had no phone service, and it was too late. The fact was it had been too late even before I'd known there was a problem.

Gran's breathing was ragged, and her voice was hoarse. "Hannah."

I nodded, yet stayed in my chair. I wouldn't go to Gran, but I owed her some words. "She's gone. She didn't wake from her nap."

It seemed indecent that a few words, such simple words, could represent something so unthinkable and horrendous.

"Child, call Mildred." Gran had made it to the doorway. She was standing there, held up by the doorframe and her cane.

"Phone's out and the drive's blocked." I tightened my arms and shrank back. There was a high edge to my voice that hurt my head. It rang in my ears, but with a nails-on-chalkboard edge that seemed to be growing in my head. An answering wail echoed in my body, like a vibration from within the earth, shaking below me and inside me. I tried to speak. I opened my eyes, but everything around me was awash in red.

A sharp, hard pain stabbed my leg. My vision cleared enough for me to see Gran, closer now, the tip of her cane hovering near me.

"Hannah, child, stop that screaming." She stumbled forward and ended up sitting on the bed, shaking her head and repeating, "I can't lose you, too, Hannah."

I dragged in a breath and tried again. My voice was no more than a hoarse whisper.

"She's gone, Gran. Gone too long. There's nothing anyone can do to help her. If they can't help her, then they can't have her."

There was a long pause before Gran spoke. Her tone was stronger, and there was steel in her words as she demanded, "Help me to my bed, Hannah."

I looked up. Her face was wet. Tears flowed from her eyes and followed the wrinkles in her cheeks, then dropped onto the bodice and skirt of her dress. I looked beyond her to see that, somehow, the afternoon had slipped away, and evening was pressing in on us.

"Yes, ma'am." I put my bundle carefully onto my bed and took Gran's arm.

I helped my grandmother back onto the living room bed. The mattress sagged and sighed as she returned to her place. I pulled the light coverlet up over her legs and hips. Despite it being high summer, she tended to feel the cold in her extremities.

"Bring her to me."

My mind blank, I stopped. I glanced toward the bedroom. Had Gran not understood?

"Bring her," she repeated. "Now, Hannah. Bring her here. Ellen and I will nap together again for a while." She fixed her teary eyes on mine and spoke a truth we both understood. "Grand's shovel is in the shed."

I brought Ellen to her. It was a good thing. Horrendous to settle Ellen in Gran's arms as if to nap, but it was also right, because I had decisions to make and work to do. That work was unspeakable and horrific, but it was also a duty of love, and the task had fallen to me.

⁂

I carried Grand's shovel across the creek bridge and up the slope to the cemetery. There, I dug a hole beside his grave—between his and my mother's grave where Gran had intended to be buried. She would now rest on the other side of Grand when her turn came.

Generations of Coopers are buried here, I thought. *Our baby will rest between her grandmother and her great-grandfather.* Grand would be there to welcome her to heaven, and I presumed my mother would, too, but I hadn't known her. She'd never felt real to me. Gran would join them there sooner or later and make sure all was right. Sooner rather than later, if she didn't take better care of herself.

It all made sense in my head while I was digging up the earth and creating a nice, neat pile of dark soil.

There were a few cedar boards in the barn. I fetched them and laid them side by side in the bottom. The scent was faint but reminded me of the cedar chest Gran had her wedding gown stored in. I went back to the house and took some loose chips from inside Gran's wedding chest. I sprinkled them on top of the boards.

The blue butterfly pots I'd made—they had wings shaped almost like fingers tightly pressed together, wings that wrapped themselves up around the sides of the pot. George Bridger had suggested making two, and I'd taken his advice. I'd pressed Ellen's name into each before glazing and firing. Now I took one of the pots and set it gently in the grave.

When I paused in passing beside Gran's bed, she looked at me with wide, dark eyes—the rest of her had faded into nothingness—and we didn't speak. When I picked up the bundle from beside her and carried it out, she didn't stop me.

After that . . . I remember it all, but like I was someone else, watching from afar, bemused, as a young woman laid her precious bundle into the midst of those cedar chips. Somehow the woman reached into the pile of dirt and took it, handful by handful, and returned the earth from whence it came. I held my breath, watching her. I didn't think she could do it, but she did.

Gasping and breathless, I watched her, and when it was done, she mounded the dirt with her bare hands, shaping it and patting it into place. I could read her mind. She kept telling herself, "Just this—this and no more—and then you'll be done. Do this, and then you'll be finished and able to rest."

But still the woman wasn't satisfied. She looked around, this cold creature, and decided to pry up a cement slab her grandfather had made as a step at the shed door. She dug it out with her bare fingers and rolled it end over end to the creek, across the bridge, and up the slope.

When she reached the cemetery wall, despite the weight of the slab, somehow she managed to lift it over and lay it on top of the mounded dirt. She climbed back over the wall and searched the woods and creek bed by moonlight. She gathered up rocks, large and small, and carried them back. She arranged them like a necklace around the perimeter of the block. The mica flecks and milky quartz crystals glittered like earthbound stars in the light of the moon.

Was it deep enough? Secure enough with the concrete block on top? Rocks all around to mark it as special? I heard the woman's voice in my head asking, *Is she safe now?* Not asking about herself but about the bundle. Baby Ellen. *Is Ellen safe?*

There were noises in the dark night. The woman stared, her eyes fixed on the stone wall. I, myself, saw a small figure move, not much more than a shadow on top of the wall, but it remained indistinguishable. Meanwhile, small animals—rabbits, possums, and a raccoon or two—crept from their burrows. They prowled for food and were driven by the other needs of life. They, and the insects, came alive with the dark, and filled the air with their noises.

The woman's knees grew wet and cold as the earth soaked through her clothing and the night settled damp around her. A gentle breath of wind swirled the air. The branches overhead moved, shaking up the moon-cast shadows. The wispy almost-form on the stone wall vanished. The woman lifted her arms, her hands grasping at the empty air as wails and cries filled the darkness. Wild, crazed sounds. Creatures emerging into the night stopped, then slunk away. There were better places to hunt and mate. Tonight, this landscape had become a hostile, nightmarish hell.

Finally, only the woman remained. The continued cries hurt our ears, but I was helpless to stop her. They issued from her, hurting her chest, tearing at her throat, and over some period of time I knew the truth—the coarse sounds emanated from us. They came from inside us—her on the ground and me at what should've been a safe distance—the wails screamed from a consciousness whose reality had been torn fiber by fiber, beyond acceptance.

I was pulled back roughly from my distant perch, but I couldn't come in all the way home, not back to where I'd begun. Instead, I found a place to dwell within Hannah but that was not Hannah. Hannah, the girl who'd lost her child, went to sleep, and then I was finally able to rest.

A few times I heard Gran's voice from a distance.

At false dawn, I awoke. I was curled up in the loam, sheltered only by the moss and lichen-covered low stone wall of the cemetery. The predawn sky lit up this patch of land and the flat concrete block, and I knew my baby was gone from me. Really gone.

I pushed up to my knees. My fingers screamed. The early light wasn't enough to give me the details, but they felt torn and bloody. My joints ached. I made it to my feet but couldn't stand all the way up. I was hunched over like an old woman, older than my Gran even, and I crept, drained and hurting, back to the house.

Gran was on the floor in the open doorway between the kitchen and the living room. She was half-propped against the doorframe, and her legs were sprawled out. Her eyes were closed. I was so near the floor already that it wasn't a long trip down. I touched her face.

"Gran? You there?"

She murmured something. Her eyes opened slowly. "Hannah?"

I sagged. "You're OK, then?"

She nodded. Even in the near dark, I could see her eyes were red and wet. The lids were swollen; she could only peek out. Her cheeks had sagged long ago, and her jawline had grown soft as her wrinkles had deepened, but tonight she looked like she'd grown old twenty times over. She put her arm around me, heavy but firm, and pulled my face into her midsection. I let her hold me close for a few minutes but then struggled free.

"I'll help you back into bed," I said.

"All right. Help me get to the bathroom first, and then a drink of water would be welcome."

"Yes, ma'am."

Everything hurt me, inside and out, but the necessity of getting my grandmother onto her feet and sorted out stirred the life back up inside me. I found I could put one foot in front of another, as long as she didn't ask. When we passed the bedroom door where Ellen's crib was clearly in sight, she didn't comment. She coughed. She sniffled. She groaned. She muttered. But she didn't ask. And that was a good thing.

I'd tossed the rain-wet blanket into the crib when I was changing her that last time. In the dim light and from a certain angle, I could almost believe she was still there, and the past almost twenty-four hours had never happened.

After Gran was settled, I fell into bed and curled up, filth and all, into a ball. I closed my eyes and left this world again for a while. I hoped I would never have to return.

Gran never brought up our loss, and I never mentioned it. I put fresh flowers or greenery on the grave every day. I sang softly while I worked and spoke quietly to the grave. I prayed, too, but I never exchanged a word about it with any living soul.

The next grocery delivery came about two weeks after the storm. By then, the power company and phone company had cleared enough of the downed trees to restore services. After the utility workers left, I took the chain saw and removed the rest of the tree blocking the drive, leaving the larger parts of the trunk. I'd have to hire someone else to split it for firewood, but at least I could get in and out of the Hollow now if I wanted. I didn't want to, though, and I didn't go anywhere. We did wonder why Mildred hadn't been by to check on us.

"Maybe she's still clearing debris herself," Gran said. "Did you try calling her again?"

"Yes, Gran. Her phone's still out."

"Well, she hasn't missed a visit in more than a decade. She'll be showing up anytime now, I'm sure."

I knew better. Something bad must've happened. As a dedicated nurse and a family friend, she would've found some way to get here when she realized she couldn't call us. I'd been worried about how to explain our own grief to her, fearful the fault for our loss would fall on me due to something I'd done or not done. And yet, I'd also wanted her counsel. Gran had gone back to dozing. I'd never felt so alone.

When the groceries were delivered for the first time post-storm, we didn't answer the door. I'd hung a note on the door telling Eva to leave the goods on the porch. When I went to the window and peeked around the curtain, I saw it was her son, Anthony. I rushed out to the porch and caught him before he reached the truck.

"Oh, hey there, Hannah. Need any help?"

"No, we're good."

"Lost a tree, I see." He pointed at the branches and leaves still littering the ground, and at the most obvious part, the trunk.

I nodded. "We did."

"It was a mess all around."

For a moment, I had a brief flare of hope that maybe the extent of the storm damage across the area explained Mildred's absence, but then Anthony spoke again.

"Did you hear about Mildred Harkin?"

"No," I whispered.

"I'm sorry to be the one to tell you. She had a heart attack during the storm."

My lips parted as I intended to say something, even to just echo his words, but nothing came out.

"Apparently she was attempting to pull some branches off her car and keeled over. Must've had somewhere to go that couldn't wait. Her neighbor found her shortly after the rain ended, but it was too late." He gave the yard another look. "If you need any help, let us know."

I'd forgotten about the wood, but Anthony noticed.

"You want someone to take that wood? I know a fella who'll split it, take some, and leave you some. Want me to have him call?"

"Sure. That would be great."

He left. I carried the grocery box inside and set it on the kitchen table. *What would I say to Gran?* Too many losses. How could we bear them? Would the county send a new nurse? Mildred's loss was a sign—a sign to keep my own counsel because with Mildred gone, there was no one with whom I could discuss what had happened to us. Selfishly, I found a small, warm comfort imagining Mildred had likely accompanied Ellen, had seen her safely arrived to where I would someday greet her again.

Thereafter, we always left the note on the door for grocery deliveries. Eva came a couple of times and put the box on the porch. The first time, she stared at the door and the note for long minutes before leaving. Eventually, she stopped coming, and Anthony took over full time, and he had more interesting things on his mind than our personal business.

The only person who ever asked after my baby was George Bridger, and that was no doubt because he was being polite, not really being a baby sort of person and not knowing of our loss. I walked away. He joined Gran for a cup of coffee, and she must've told him about our grief because he never asked again. He always looked at me a bit askance after that, as if he thought he'd angered me and didn't want to risk ticking me off again. Or maybe he was afraid my grief might be catching or would demand some sort of response from him. He was a lonely man and didn't interact much, but I let him go on thinking it. So long as he didn't ask me questions.

The propane deliveryman was the only other person who came out during that time, and he'd never known about Ellen or the pregnancy. Aside from George Bridger, no one knew about our loss, and I wanted to keep it that way. As long as it wasn't official, there was still some part of her alive in my heart. The world, if it knew, would ask questions and make judgments and force me to speak of it. As far as I could tell, Gran hadn't told the man in Mineral who paid our tax bills and whatnot. In my head, he was a kind of clerk with a long beard and angel wings who wore a brown suit. Brown, I guess, because she'd called him Mr. Browne, and wearing angel wings because he sent us money from time to time. And the long beard? Maybe because he seemed like Santa sending us gifts of money.

We saw few people. After Mr. Bridger's last encounter with me, he didn't wander in as often, and I began to feel badly about it.

In February, on the day when Ellen would've turned one, I stayed in bed until Gran started poking at me with her cane. I expected her to cater to my right to be miserable and grieve. I saw by her face that she, too, was grieving, but today I couldn't help her. I obeyed her cane but went outside and spent the warmest part of the day in the pottery cabin. I hadn't been in here since I'd lost my baby girl. It was too cold to work the clay, but I did anyway. Not on the wheel but on the table. I sculpted a small child. The figure was rough. Before I was done, my heart failed me, and I left it unfinished, knowing that meant it could never be fired or glazed. It would be a simple dried clay form, subject to breakage with the least jostle. Fragile.

I washed my hands at the outside pump. The cold water set me to shivering and drenched my shoes. I went back inside, still not speaking to Gran, and started a hot bath to thaw myself out. My hands had cracked from the cold air and wet clay, and they were bleeding. Later, I noticed I must've been crying because raw, chapped tracks marked my flesh from my eyes to my neck.

After the first anniversary, and especially once spring began to peek in on us, life began to feel normal again. Not as it had been before our loss, but survivable.

Over the years, when Gran had been in a baking mood, I'd take a walk up the hill and deliver a pie to Mr. Bridger. I decided it was overdue. Gran wasn't up to baking, but she supervised while I put together a cobbler with the peaches Eva's son had delivered in the grocery box. When the cobbler was done baking and cool enough to carry, I took a walk up and over Elk Ridge. It was already September. I'd survived the anniversary of Ellen's birth in February and also the anniversary of us losing her, and I could see promise ahead, distantly, barely present on the horizon but there. That had to be enough for right now. I crossed the high point of the ridge and came out of the woods and emerged in Bridger's old fields. I followed the overgrown farm road through the fields. He rarely farmed anymore, but stuff grew anyway—stuff the butterflies liked. As I walked, a bunch of them rose in an orange cloud. I paused and watched them flutter around me. A couple came close to my face and hair. One landed on the top of the dish I was holding. I stood still, waiting, then blew on it softly. The butterfly fluttered its wings and floated away. But it had lifted my spirits.

I found Mr. Bridger sitting on his porch in a cane chair. He'd rocked it back onto its hind legs and balanced with his boots propped on a box. His firearm was set alongside the chair. He was sipping tea with perhaps a little extra in it and smoking a cigar. The left side of the porch was loaded with boxes and all manner of stuff, including some tools, and had a noticeable sag at that end. Above us, though, the Bridger house rose two stories and had once been known for its beauty. Not a huge house but a substantial one, and not kept up. It was slowly disintegrating.

"You look peaceful, Mr. Bridger."

"I am. You've brought me something, I see."

"Peach cobbler."

He dropped his feet to the porch, and the chair clunked forward. "That's real nice of you. Tell Clara I appreciate it."

"I did the cooking. Gran's recipe, of course."

"Double thanks to you, then." He stubbed out his cigar. "Maybe my boy, Liam, will be here in time to have some."

"You heard from Liam? That's good."

Mr. Bridger was an odd character, even with my limited knowledge of human beings. He wasn't natural with people. His son was older than me and had rarely been around when I was growing up. I'd seen him a few times, of course, being neighbors of sorts, and he was a good-looking guy, as I recalled. Rough but handsome with a bad-boy reputation. He'd left the area long ago, and no one had seen him around here in years. It was hard on old Mr. Bridger, but I didn't doubt it must've been hard on his son, too, growing up with him, and that likely accounted for his decision to make himself scarce as soon as he was old enough.

"Is he coming to stay or just for a visit?"

"Stay awhile, I reckon. It was his wife who called. She rang me on the phone and said they were coming."

I couldn't imagine what they'd think of this house. I'd heard it was a beauty years ago, one of the nicest in this area back when his great-grands had built it. When I was a child, I'd been fascinated with the gingerbread fretwork on the porch, the fancy woodworked door, but most of all by the stained glass windows on the second floor. Butterfly panels, Gran called them, because of the side panels. I learned in high school art history that the set of three panels was called a triptych. In the last several years, the house had continued to go down, and that was from the vantage point of the outside. I'd never been inside.

Did Mr. Bridger realize how this place would look to an outsider? One thing I'd learned when I started going to school in town, especially by the time I hit middle school, was that a person's brain grew used to seeing their surroundings in a certain way and didn't realize how it looked to others. That front window upstairs, stained glass panels with lilies and butterflies in pieces of glass in brown and blue and gold and red, was a marvel. I would've loved to see it from the inside, so it might be worth the price of offering my help. Gran always said he had lots of money but you'd never know it, and he wouldn't be likely to pay me for the work. Still, he was a neighbor.

"You need any help getting things ready?" I asked. "I could give you a hand."

His expression was scornful. He probably picked up on my lack of sincerity.

I looked down and shuffled my feet, then reminded myself I was an adult. "Shall I put the cobbler in the kitchen?"

"You can set it right there on that box. I'll enjoy smelling it. I'll take it in when I go."

"All right, then." I set the dish on the upturned crate he'd been using as a footrest.

"How's Clara doing?" he asked.

"Well enough, considering. She's got the sniffles, though. I hope it doesn't settle into a cold." It nagged at me, my own hard-heartedness toward this old man. "Are you sure you're good here getting ready for company and all? I can spare some time."

"I'm fine. I can manage on my own, no problem. Give Clara my regards."

Sometimes people dwelled on things, especially if they were alone too much. I suspected George Bridger couldn't get past that one rebuff when he'd asked about my Ellen, and he held it against me. Or maybe he tried to steer clear of emotional women, especially those who'd proven themselves to be predisposed to rude and emotional reactions.

"You take care, Mr. Bridger. Have a good visit with your family."

❧

I didn't give Mr. Bridger another thought. Gran was having a lot of troubles. Mildred had been wiser than I knew. Herbal teas, warm poultices on her legs—I tried everything I could think of to help her, but when I mentioned seeing a doctor, she'd get mulish and wouldn't discuss it. A new visiting nurse came by, and I let her in, but she was a stranger, and Gran was grumpy. We were both missing Mildred.

Suddenly, it was November and snow was falling. It didn't linger on the ground too long, but it heralded a snowy winter, and I rarely left our cozy Hollow. I kept the fire burning in the woodstove, and the propane kept the kitchen stove operating. Even if we lost the electricity, we'd be able to manage—not preferred but doable.

I brought my good clay inside lest it freeze and did some sculpting on the kitchen table. Gran liked to watch. I was sculpting another child. This one, I thought, would be better than the first that still sat, unfinished, on a shelf in the cabin. I pressed a sliver of clay onto the shoulder and smoothed the edges in carefully. When I was satisfied, I sat back and met Gran's eyes.

"Sure you don't want to take a turn at it?"

She laughed softly. "Me? Been much too long. Lost the knack of it many years ago. Besides, it was always the wheel for me anyway."

"You taught me."

"My mama taught me. One of these days I'm going to take a walk out back to the old cabin and see their pieces again. That pottery is the work of three generations of hands."

"But not my mother's hands."

She shook her head. The good nature spilled right off her face into sadness.

"Sorry, Gran."

"No harm. Just what it is. But she never had a feel for it. Your mama was never one to sit still."

It was rare that Gran volunteered any reminiscence about my mother. I looked up, hopeful, thinking she might say more, but she didn't. The subject veered away from dangerous emotional areas. Perhaps if I'd felt the lack of parents more keenly I would've pushed harder, but whatever caused hurt to my Gran hurt me nearly as much, and so, as always, I let it go.

"Hannah, honey. Are you running out of shelf space in the shed? Do you have what you need out there? Heaven knows I haven't been out there in years. The days do slip away."

Seeing an imperfect spot, I pushed another tiny wedge of clay into place on the back. Then I looked up and smiled at her. "The shelves are getting pretty full, but there's space left."

"One of these days I'm going to walk out there and see what you've made. You are wonderfully gifted, Hannah. What are you going to do with it all?"

I shrugged. "Give it away, I guess. Maybe try selling some of it."

Gran leaned forward, reaching for her cane. "That won't work hiding away out here in Cooper's Hollow."

"Then it's not time yet. That's all I know."

"Get a shop in town. You'd be good at that, Hannah."

"Gran, please."

"Or how about a roadside stand? Right out by the state road? Instead of tomatoes, sell your clay pots."

I looked up. She was grinning. I smiled back and said, "We'll set you up there with your rocker and your cane, shall we? You can be the one to talk to all those strangers."

That quieted her. After a while she spoke again.

"What about college?"

I focused on the clay and didn't respond. She didn't press me but got to her feet and, between touching the wall for stability and using the cane for support, she made her way back to the bathroom.

Gran was feeling better than she had in a while. I ordered turkey dinners to be delivered. Eva's son did the delivery, and I met him at the porch. Come Christmas, I thawed out a venison roast an old friend of Grand's had brought us. We celebrated in our quiet way. I'd never gone back to cleaning houses, nor did I try to find another job. I'd lost the desire to go to college or even to leave. Gran and I did very well on our own. Happy didn't really figure into it. We settled for contentment, and we were careful not to upset the emotional balance we'd worked hard to achieve.

February was difficult, and as if by prior discussion, Gran left me alone on what would've been my daughter's second birthday. I cooked for Gran, but otherwise we spent the day apart.

Spring arrived prematurely in early March. My thoughts turned to my garden. I felt like making plans for planting. I made a shopping list and tried to estimate how much it would cost. Gran called the man in town while I was out in the cabin. When I came back inside, she asked me to go to the bank in Mineral where money was waiting for us. From there I could go on into Louisa, a little farther than Mineral but larger, as it was the main town in Louisa County, and make my purchases. I did. It felt odd walking into the bank and speaking to the branch manager, but he checked my driver's license and handed me cash with a smile.

In April, I prepared the bed, but Gran allowed no outside planting before May because one hard frost would end the new growth before it had hardly began.

On a sunshiny morning in early May, the air changed. It felt genuine. Life was stirring. I felt it in myself, too, and after I'd cleared away the breakfast dishes, I made a batch of cookies. While I was baking, I heard a noise, like a brisk knock on the front door. I listened, but it didn't repeat, so I pulled out the last sheet of cookies to cool. Gran ate a couple while they were hot, and I didn't fuss at her. Instead, I kissed her on the forehead and left her to it. It was shortly before noon when I stepped out onto the porch expecting to see a broken branch laying on the porch planks, or perhaps an injured bird that had flown into the door.

There was no branch. No bird. Only a little girl, a toddler between two or three years old, sitting in my rocking chair. Her feet didn't reach the floor but hung there clad in some sort of plastic slip-on shoes, and they dangled above the wooden planks. Her dark-brown hair brushed her shoulders. A blue barrette held her bangs back. The barrette had slid halfway down, and her hair didn't look clean. She was wearing a blue quilted jacket, stained, and long pants, and a skirt, to boot. She looked bulky, so she was likely wearing extra shirts, too. She was silent and didn't move.

This child, this vision, stilled my heart. For a long minute, I held my breath. I thought I'd finally gone all the way over.

Is this how crazy happens? One moment you were good, or thought you were, and the next, you were living in a land to which no one else had general admittance. You lived each day thinking you were managing, handling your life, and then one bright morning, when you least expected it, a hallucination laid you out flat.

At first, I didn't breathe. I wondered what would happen to my poor grandmother now that I no longer had the mental or emotional wherewithal to care for her. Then the child moved. Her shoulders jerked, her feet crossed, and one hand, a small fist, moved up to rub her eye.

In a heartbeat, I crossed the few feet between us. I fell to my knees. Her eyes were brown liquid with amber flecks, and her rosy, chapped lips were pressed together tightly, quivering, as she struggled not to cry.

She must have a person, a parent, someone, nearby. Maybe up at the main road? Had there been an accident and she'd wandered down?

I gave her a closer look. Her face was dirty around the edges as if someone had taken a wet rag and given it a lick and a promise but no real washing. Her nostrils were a little crusty, but noses could run when it was cold. Black dirt lines were ingrained beneath her fingernails. The flesh of her fingers was cracked, almost like mine had been when I'd worked in the wet clay in winter. I thought this might be what was called chilblain in a Dickens book I'd read for school.

"It's OK, sweetie. Where's your mommy or daddy?" I reached toward her, and she drew back.

Her shoulders hunched, and she seemed to draw inward.

I wanted to run up to the road and see for myself, but I couldn't leave her here alone. She might wander off into the woods, and I'd never know what happened to her. I looked at the door. Should I take her inside? What about Gran?

"What's your name, sweetie?"

She pursed her lips, squeezed her eyes shut, and shook her head.

The door opened. Gran was there, up and using her cane and feeling well enough to be curious.

"Where'd you go, Hannah? I—" She broke off. "Why look here. Hey there, sweet girl." She paused, she frowned, and then Gran broke into the biggest smile I'd seen in two years. Her whole face lit up. "Well, there you are, my sweet Ellen. Where'd you get to, honey?"

Chills raced through my body. Feeling wrenched by her tone and words, I cautioned her. "Gran, I don't . . . this isn't . . . I don't know who this child is."

"Ellen. Our sweet baby Ellen. Gran's got cookies, little miss. Can you smell 'em? Come in here where it's warm." She let go of the doorjamb and held out her spotted, wrinkled hand.

The morning was a tad chilly, but it was nowhere near cold, and this child was dressed in bulky clothing. She gave Gran one long look, then scooted out of the chair. The child went straight to her, taking the offered hand.

What was I supposed to do? Snatch her back?

For now, it seemed well enough. Gran would come to her senses soon. She was indulging her own imagination and avoiding pain that seeing a toddler might cause. Gran took flights of fancy from time to time. Aggravating sometimes but always harmless. At least the child was safe for the meanwhile.

I slipped on my outside shoes and walked across the yard to the driveway. I thought of driving, but if something were going on in the woods between here and the main road, I'd likely miss it in the car. I walked fast downhill to the low point in our drive and then up the slope to the main road. It was a fair walk, and when I stepped onto the asphalt, I stood there looking both ways. No one was in sight. Not a soul. Not a single car passed. I walked along the narrow dirt shoulder far enough each way to see around the curves. Finally, a car did go by, and then a truck. They barely slowed.

I had plenty of time to consider, and the only thing I could think to do was call the sheriff's office when I got back to the house.

After that? What would happen?

My Ellen would've been about this age, this size. Except for the dark eyes and darker hair, this *could* be her. My heart gave a tug. No wonder Gran was confused.

What if the little girl was abandoned here on the state road? Had found her way down our driveway?

"Nonsense," I said. No one drops off a child the way they might do with a dog or cat that had become inconvenient. If no family claimed her, the sheriff and social services would take her and find her a reasonable home. I mean, for heaven's sakes, look at Gran and me—an old woman who'd passed her expiration date a long time ago and a youngish woman who'd been fatally broken before life had even given her a real try. Stuck out here in this Hollow. Cocooned out here. Not that Gran wasn't an amazing woman, but she took most of my time. No sane authority would allow me, twenty-one and with no means or prospects, to take charge of a child not my own.

This worry was pointless. This child's people would be searching for her. Or suppose she'd been kidnapped?

I looked up and down the road again, almost expecting to see kidnappers returning. Driving dark, dangerous cars and armed, no doubt. I stared up the road. Would I fight them? I would. I would welcome a fight that had a ghost of a chance of being won.

No kidnappers, then. Maybe hikers or tourists. They didn't deserve a child if they couldn't be bothered to keep track of her when in the woods.

I was being ridiculous. It was because I dreaded having to do what I must, and I feared for Gran, body and soul, if it came to taking the child away right at the moment.

Back down the driveway, and at the house, Gran and the child were seated at the kitchen table. Gran had pulled out the cookies. Only crumbs were left. A half-filled glass of milk was on the table in front of the little girl, and she wore some of it as a mustache.

From the kitchen doorway, I asked, "Did she tell you her name or why she was on the porch?"

"Her name's Ellen, silly." She turned to the child. "Still hungry?"

The child's blue jacket was hung on the back of the chair. I picked it up and checked the pockets. Something crumpled, a tiny noise deep in a pocket.

I felt it again. Something there. I reached in and pulled out a note.

I recognized George Bridger's hard, tight scrawl. It read:

Liam's girl needs a home. Her mama left her. I'm sick. Going to the hospital and likely not coming back. Take care of Trisha. Regards to Clara.

The last time I'd seen Mr. Bridger was in the autumn. September? He'd mentioned his son was coming to visit. Liam. Liam had left years ago. Mr. Bridger had mentioned his daughter-in-law, too. Had they ever arrived? They must have, judging by this note.

Likely, he'd said. Was there a possibility Mr. Bridger would return home? Was he asking me to take charge of the child until he knew for sure? Or was he asking me to do a favor for him as an old family friend? Whatever the reason, this was not an everyday kind of request.

I pressed my hands to my chest to calm my heart.

No, this was not merely a favor he was asking. I saw the child with such clarity it was like heaven itself had etched her features. He could've dropped this child in town on his way to the hospital. George Bridger had meant this twofold—as an answer to his problem and as a gift to us.

It wasn't a gift we could keep. This was someone's child. Liam and his wife's. But where were they?

Gran reached for her cane and pushed up from the table. "Ellen and I are going to read a story."

"What?"

"I promised."

The child scooted around me, still unsure, and when Gran's bulk hit the bed and it sagged, I helped her get her swollen legs up onto the mattress. The girl—*Trisha*, I reminded myself—stood at the foot of the bed like a statue.

"Prop the pillows, Hannah." Gran was intent. "Get the ones from the sofa, too. We need extra."

I did as she instructed. Gran patted the bed beside her and held out her hand. The child scrambled up and scooted into the crook of her arm.

"Fetch us a book, will you?" Gran waved her free hand in the direction of my room.

The storybooks. They'd been mine, and my mother's before me. They'd been in the bookcase in my bedroom for many years. The bookcase next to the crib. The crib I'd never taken down because taking it down meant . . .

Acceptance. Surrender.

Gran was talking to the child in a soft, comforting voice. I went to my room. I grabbed a few books and took them into the living room. The child looked up at me and held out her hands.

And grabbed my heart with her tiny fingers. It actually hurt.

My hands shook as I gave her one book and put the other two on top of her little legs.

While I was there, I eased off her shoes and put them at the foot of the bed where she could see them.

"Gran. Are you two comfy?"

She patted the child's hand and said, "My great-granddaughter and I are perfect right here together where we belong, aren't we, sweet Ellen?"

Trisha, aka sweet Ellen, nodded with a smile that about killed me. Blind and gasping, I found my way to the kitchen and fell against the counter. I needed air. I floundered through the back door and caught myself on the stoop railing. I slid down to sit heavily on the step. I put my face in my hands.

Beyond me, across Cub Creek and near the edge of the forest where the hill began to rise in earnest, were the resting places of my loved ones who'd already gone on. Gone. My Ellen . . .

This child wasn't my Ellen. Trisha was George Bridger's granddaughter. But Gran suddenly had a spark in her I hadn't seen in two years . . . not since . . . Maybe longer. In fact, not since Grand had passed.

One task at a time, I reminded myself. The first was to go see about Mr. Bridger.

I called back into the house. "Gran, I'm taking a walk. Keep an eye on . . . on the child?"

"We're fine. Take your time." I heard a child's high-pitched giggle follow Gran's words.

Laughter. There hadn't been any of that in this house in . . . how long?

The path was level in areas but steep in others. Louisa County was mineral-rich and mica schists ran through it. The tree growth was old, and Cub Creek cut through the small valleys. It didn't pay to tackle the walk up to Elk Ridge with tears in your eyes because the footing could be tricky in spots. So I dried up my distress along with my tears. I stopped at Ellen's grave and straightened the small clay bear I'd placed on top of it, then I began my trek, but empty-handed.

No cobbler for George Bridger this time.

CHAPTER FOUR

Without the old man sitting on the porch or working about the yard, the place seemed more desolate than ever. Or maybe it was more than that—a feeling that embodied emptiness.

The Bridger house had never been as fancy as the big brick mansion house at Cuckoo and of less historical significance, but it was memorable. Approaching it from my side, the Cooper side, and coming up Elk Ridge, was like coming through a wilderness where you might run into anything—coyotes, maybe even a bear, though rarely. The main approach to the Bridger place was from the other side, and it was a reasonable, if unpaved, road. His road didn't dip and curve like ours. His house had a nice porch, and I'd heard about the pretty parlor and lovely wood paneling in most of the downstairs rooms. It had a true upstairs where the bedrooms were. It was vastly different from the small house where Gran and I lived.

I peeked around back before trying the doors. No cars. No sign of anyone.

The outside had grown shabby in recent years, but that was to be expected. I didn't know how old Mr. Bridger actually was, but he had more than a few years on him and was living alone . . .

The front door was unlocked.

It was May. Despite the warmer days, the nights were cool. The air inside the house was musty, though he hadn't been gone very long. *To the hospital,* he'd said. What had happened to his son and daughter-in-law?

It was easy to see where Mr. Bridger spent his days. Small piles of clutter began at a sagging chair in the living room and grew as they defined the path through the dining room with its amazing fireplace with the inset mirror. I'd seen some fancy houses when I was working for Babs's cleaning service, but nothing quite touched the elegance of this deeply grained wall paneling and the mirrored fireplace.

The kitchen was usually where a person's truth lived, and that was true here. Mr. Bridger hadn't washed a dish in a long while. It was early in the warm season, but likely there were insects living amid the disorder. I could hear mice scurrying, unseen, around the room, happy with their home. I flipped the light switch. The power worked. The chill throughout was pervasive, with the walls and furnishings still holding on to the memory of winter. The heat was by woodstove and fireplace, and those ashes were long cold. That was a good thing, I thought, in terms of keeping the kitchen mess from stinking worse than it did.

I could only presume Liam and his wife had brought their child to his daddy's place and had left her here. Hard to imagine what need would drive such a decision.

Gran and I lived simply, but we lived clean and decent. This house had the feel of a time warp. Stepping in here was like stepping into a place where life had stopped years ago. Nicer than our place, bigger than our place, but it felt abandoned. Forgotten.

Judging by the condition of the main floor, Mr. Bridger had lived down here and slept on the sofa. He might not have gone upstairs much anymore, but his family must have while they were visiting. I faced the stairs. They were steep, narrow, and dark. I hesitated.

Hoarders had chronological piles. If the child had been living only downstairs, her clothing would've been atop the piles. I would've seen her belongings.

I held tight to the stair rail. The steps looked sound, but it was too dark to see for sure.

All the bedroom doors were closed. Closed off is what they felt like. I opened the door to the front bedroom. Mr. Bridger's room, yes, but I was right. He'd been sleeping on the sofa downstairs. The room was furnished and probably had a fortune in antiques, but there was nothing that felt "recent" about it. I walked in, mesmerized by the stained glass window. I'd never seen such a thing except in church, and Gran and I had left off going a while ago.

The light fell on the glass panes from outside and filtered into the room to paint my hands and arms with a myriad of colors. The colorful glass pieces, joined together by dark leading, depicted lilies and butterflies. The window was positioned to capture the morning sun. The sun-infused color streamed in, lighting the room. *What a way to start each day,* I thought, *with this glory greeting you.*

Reminding myself to be respectful, I backed away and pulled the door closed behind me. My business here was about the child and Mr. Bridger. Not to be nosy.

The next room must've been Liam's because it had the look of a boy's room. Mr. Bridger had married late in life, and Liam's mother passed when he was young. A boy, growing up in this house with only George Bridger as a parent, must've had a difficult time of it. I felt empathy for him. We'd both had grievous losses. Many did. Everyone handled them differently.

There were several posters on the wall, plus a faded football program from the high school we'd both attended but at different times. The bed was roughly made, as if in a hurry. How long ago, it was impossible to tell. That was about all the room told me. No indication of where he'd come from, what he did for a living, or why he'd left—back then and now.

The next room was where the child had slept. Only a small body had mussed this sheet and coverlet. The room and furnishings looked scary—or would look that way to a child. No kid stuff, no fluff. A bed in the corner and a dark wood dresser and a creaky cane chair. A grim place. Not right for a child.

I checked in the drawers and found a few clothing items that surely belonged to the little girl. Left-behind stuff. I took what there was because it was more than we had for her. It fit easily in one small bag. I searched in her daddy's room again for anything that might belong to her. I found a child's book, a woman's headband, and nothing else.

For no good reason, I stopped in the kitchen and rinsed and stacked the dishes. I collected the trash and bagged it. Despite the mess, it went quickly, and so I washed the dishes, leaving them to dry in the drainer. Finally, I swept the floor and added that litter to the trash bag. If Mr. Bridger did return home, then he'd have a nice surprise. Because he might come home, right? His note had been uncertain, really, hadn't it?

As I washed and cleaned, I considered. The only right and reasonable thing to do was to keep the little girl safe until he returned, or until we knew for sure he wouldn't.

Trisha. I tried speaking the name aloud, but it sounded wrong. Gran had already fixed on the name Ellen. Would it be so wrong to call her that? Would the child care? It wasn't likely to do her any harm for a short time. Forcing Gran back to reality would be cruel. She would find her way back to the truth on her own. Surely she would, given time.

"Wait and see" seemed to be the wisest course. Meanwhile, if I kept the child safe and happy, then we were doing our old friend's bidding and helping the child at the same time. Liam was bound to show up soon.

Many doubts traveled with me as I crossed the ridge and descended the path back to our house.

The child's mother, I dismissed. I didn't know anything about her. But Liam, I knew him, yet I had no idea how to reach him. Presumably the sheriff could figure it out, but only if I told him, and if I did, the law might not choose to respect Mr. Bridger's wishes, and that would likely kill Gran and let down Mr. Bridger.

By the time I reached home, I had decided what to do. I would call the hospitals and see what I could find out about Mr. Bridger. Until then, I'd keep my own counsel. We saw few people. Only Gran and I, and Mr. Bridger, knew baby Ellen had been born and then lost. Gran seemed to have misplaced the knowledge, for a while anyway. Mr. Bridger wouldn't talk out of turn about anyone else's business.

If Mr. Bridger recovered and returned home, or when Liam turned up—well, I could feel pleased, knowing I'd helped out a longtime family friend and neighbor. In the meantime, would it hurt to let my grandmother have her small fantasy?

When I reached home, I came in the back door quietly, not sure what I'd find. Gran was asleep, and the child was snuggled against her. They fit like two pieces, snug and tight. I hadn't realized the degree of tension in the child's face until I saw her now, unafraid and secure.

It was a sweet, loving scene. Maybe George Bridger hadn't meant this as a twofold solution, but rather threefold. For him, for us, but also for the child. The safety and love of this child.

Her clothing fit easily into a drawer in my dresser. I returned to the living room and considered waking them. A nap this time of day might make sleeping hard tonight, but I let them be. It was obvious we were going to have a guest, at least for this night.

In my room, I removed the blanket from the side rail of the small crib, the one that had blocked my view of the bed's interior. I stripped the small sheet. It had needed washing for close to two years. Then I removed the mattress and the hardboard beneath it. I unhooked the hinges and folded the crib. This crib was too small for a child of two years. I stored it in the back room.

Where should the child sleep tonight? With Gran? I didn't think so. Maybe on the sofa where she could see that Gran was nearby? Or with me? There was plenty of room in the double bed, and I didn't mind the idea, but thus far the child hadn't shown any signs of warming up to me. Maybe after supper, she'd be more open and approachable.

Simple was best. Eggs and toast and juice. Jelly, of course. Gran and I'd put up that jelly several years ago. The eggs came with the grocery delivery. Luckily, the last delivery had been recent and the milk was fresh.

I started singing as I cooked. It had been a while. I had a fair voice, and Gran used to sing with me before her breath got so short. Neither of us had done much singing in the last couple of years. This felt odd yet exhilarating. I was on the third verse into Gran's favorite, "Church in the Wildwood," and was planning to launch into "Barbara Allen" next as I stirred the eggs. The smell of toast filled the air, and I felt eyes on me.

Big eyes. Eyes so richly dark despite the amber flecks that they reminded me of the brown waters of Cub Creek when the sunlight flickered through the branches overhead and reflected on the moving surface.

Softly, I said, "Hello there. How are you, sweetie? Hungry?"

She looked down at her feet.

I poured the eggs into the pan and then stepped away long enough to pull out a chair. "You can sit here if you'd like." I turned back to the stove as if I couldn't care less.

Gran groaned as she moved from her bed, then her cane tapped the wood floor.

"What do I smell? Breakfast for supper?"

"Yes, ma'am," I called back.

"What do you think about that, my sweet Ellen?" Gran said.

A pang of guilt seized me. This child had her own name. Her own family. An identity. How much damage was this doing?

Gran said, "I'll pay a visit to the ladies' room and be right back."

The child had a momentary look of panic on her face as Gran left the room, but she stayed seated. I took a chance. I set the glass of juice in front of her and asked kindly, "What's your name, honey? What would you like me to call you?"

She took a sip of the juice.

I tried again. "Are you worried about your grandpa? Your mommy and daddy?"

The child, her little fingers hardly spanning the circumference of the glass, eyed me warily and set the drink carefully back on the table.

Gran was already returning from the bathroom. The floor planks squeaked as she progressed. Record time, it seemed to me.

Once more I asked, "Trisha? That's your name, right, honey?"

"Toast. Jelly. Please." She spoke in a toddler voice, turning her *l*'s into *w*'s and leaving off the last consonants.

As Gran shuffled into the kitchen and pulled out her chair, the child fixed those creek-brown eyes on me and said, "Sweet Ellen."

It sounded like "Swee Ewwen," and the words and voice reached into my chest with exquisite pain. I faced the stove. I held my breath, closed my eyes, and waited for it to pass.

That night, at bedtime, the child's lips developed a tiny tremor as she pressed them together. Her eyes were big and tinged with fear. I asked her where she'd like to sleep. I reminded her of where Gran slept, as if a soul anywhere in the house could miss that bed jutting out into the living room floor. I pointed at the sofa.

"I can make up a bed there for you." Then I held out my hand and said, "Come with me."

She took my hand, but in a skittish way, and I was careful not to clasp her little fingers too tightly.

I turned on the light in my room and said, "I sleep here. Used to be Gran's room, but she wanted to be closer to the stove because she gets cold easily. So I sleep here, but you can see it's a big bed, and there's plenty of room. If you like, you can share my bed."

She'd gone to the bathroom and used the toilet already on her own. Night was sometimes different for young ones, but I didn't have any Pull-ups and hadn't seen any evidence of them at Mr. Bridger's place, so hopefully, bed-wetting wouldn't be a problem.

We stood there while she took in the room. She was quiet and self-contained, such a little bit of a person. Not a big talker, for sure. I released her hand. Instead of leaving the room, she stopped in front of the bookcase. The books, I thought at first, but then saw her eyes had fastened on a rag doll. Mine. Gran had made it for me and, of course, I'd saved it for . . . Yes. For Ellen. Not this child. I'd saved it for when my Ellen would be old enough to play with it.

I picked up the doll. I cradled it in my arm and straightened her skirt and braid, then I offered it to this little girl. She took it and mumbled something. Thank you, I think she said. She walked to the living room and sat on the sofa, clutching the doll tightly to her.

Gran was already asleep. Not surprising. It had been quite a day for her. Wryly and devastatingly I thought, *It's not every day that one's lost great-granddaughter returned home.*

The child looked at me, not crying, but her dark eyes were swimming in unshed tears, and she said, "Mommy?"

Wrong. This was very wrong. This child was asking where her mother was. I knelt by the sofa and smiled kindly. "Tomorrow, sweetie. We'll find her tomorrow."

I covered a pillow with a pillowcase and pulled the afghan from the back of the sofa. There was no nightie in her stuff, and I wasn't about to strip her down to her undies and expect her to sleep like that in a strange house with people she didn't know. It wouldn't be civilized. I moved to take off the shirt she was wearing because I could see there were multiple layers on her little body, but she pulled back and nearly disappeared into the folds of the sofa. If she wanted to sleep in her day clothes, virtually her whole wardrobe, then she could. If she were still here tomorrow afternoon, I'd figure out something better.

The exterior doors were securely locked, and my bedroom door stayed open, as usual.

I changed into a nightgown, and after a last check on Gran and the child who appeared to be sleeping, I tucked myself in. I tossed a lot. Too much was on my mind. Too many emotions swirled in my head to think clearly about what was best to do. *Did I really have a choice?* It wasn't only about me. In fact, for me, this probably wasn't a good thing no matter how one justified it. To get attached, to have the responsibility . . . my plate was already full with Gran.

The clouds moved off. It was still night, but the moon was full, and suddenly its light parted the night and lit the pathway through the house to my bed. The mattress shifted as a small weight climbed on board. I opened my eyes a sliver and saw her looking at me. Those dark eyes, so deep, stared at me. I felt her loneliness. Not truly fear. If she was afraid, it was because she was alone. I pulled the covers up over her shoulders ever so gently.

She put her thumb in her mouth and closed her eyes. Her long lashes brushed her cheeks.

I whispered softly, "Good night, sweet girl. Sleep well."

She was a child in need of shelter and comfort. What harm could kindness do?

As I'd promised myself, and whatever fates might have been listening and might seek to hold me accountable, I drove into town to call the hospitals. It wasn't easy to find one old man who'd gone to a hospital in an area that stretched from Charlottesville to Richmond. I tried the most obvious ones, but no one was willing to confirm he was there . . . or they didn't know . . . or he hadn't been. That was the problem.

It was time to visit the man in town. He was "our" lawyer, after all, and speaking to him would surely be more discreet than straight-out walking into the sheriff's office.

His office was in a small stone building. Grand had pointed the building out to me on a shopping trip before he died. The name on the door read DUNCAN BROWNE, ESQ., ATTORNEY AT LAW.

A well-dressed lady was seated at the desk in the main room. I asked to see Mr. Browne.

"I'm Hannah Cooper, the granddaughter of Ed and Clara Cooper. He knows them."

"Nice to meet you, Miss Cooper. What would you like to see Mr. Browne about? Perhaps we could make an appointment?"

"Is he here?" I experienced a brief flashback of having stood at an etched-glass storm door while a certain boy's mother tried to keep me away from her son. I bit my lip to keep from speaking harshly. I didn't like gatekeepers any better than I liked information brokers. "I need help finding our neighbor Mr. Bridger. I think he went to the hospital, but I don't know which."

"You could check with the sheriff's department."

I didn't answer. She was right, of course, in one respect, but on the other hand, it would not serve my purpose—a purpose I certainly could not explain. In that silence, a man spoke.

"Miss Cooper?"

I turned. A man stood in the office doorway. Behind him was an impression of dark wood, leather, and books.

He moved forward, extending his hand. "I'm Duncan Browne. I imagine your grandparents have spoken of me?"

They had, but rarely. In my head, he was the Man in Town. He wasn't wearing the brown suit I'd imagined but a nice dark-blue one with a silky green tie. Gray was sprinkled through his hair, and his face was tanned and lined. His eyes were clear. I liked him instantly.

He cast a quick glance at the desk lady, then looked back at me. "Would you like to come into the office? Is there something I can help you with?" As I followed, he asked, "May I call you Hannah?" Then he motioned me toward a chair facing his desk.

"Of course." I sat in the offered chair, and he settled into his own.

"How's your grandmother?"

"She's well. Our neighbor George Bridger told us he was going to the hospital but didn't say which one. I tried calling around but no luck." I looked down. I didn't like lying. Even omissions were a form of lying. *Prevarication,* Grand had said to me, was a fancy word but still a lie.

"I don't know whether he went to Charlottesville or Richmond. I presume Charlottesville, but I couldn't locate him. I was in town, and I thought of you, that you might be able to find out where he is. He's not back home yet, and I'm worried."

"George Bridger. I know of him. As Aggie suggested, the sheriff can probably help."

I bristled. "He's old and sick, but as far as I know, he hasn't broken any laws. He's private. I don't believe he'd appreciate my bringing the authorities into his business."

Mr. Browne frowned, but then it slowly shifted, and a smile grew on his face. "Spoken like your grandfather." He leaned back in his chair and tapped the shiny desktop with his finger. "He and George Bridger—I always thought of them as the old guard. The county has grown, changed, over the last decade especially. Your grandfather was one of the originals—those folks who lived in the back of beyond and minded their own business. They didn't invite or appreciate interference. George Bridger was garrulous. He spoke a lot when he was in a chatty mood, but he actually said very little. Your grandfather spoke very little and meant every word." He leaned forward again. "It was my pleasure to have known him. Your grandmother, too. You say she's doing well?"

I wanted to get Mr. Browne back on track. "She is. I'm not here about her, but rather Mr. Bridger."

"I'll make some calls and find out about him. Shall I call the house number with what I find out?"

"That will be fine. If Gran answers, ask for me. I don't want to worry her."

"Your grandmother calls from time to time about business. She's not much given to chitchat. I hope you don't mind my asking, but are you doing well out there? Do you have what you need?"

His questions made me uneasy. I fidgeted. "We're good."

"Your daughter? Ellen? How is she?"

I must've moved suddenly because I heard a thud and realized my purse was on the floor. I was grateful for a reason to hide my face. Leaning over, grabbing for my purse, I said, "Fine. We're all fine."

Suddenly questions abounded in my head. As I'd suspected, Gran hadn't told him of our loss. I wanted to ask him why he paid our bills. Why was he involved in our lives? But asking would've been trespassing on my grandparents' business and would invite him to question me further about us and our lives. I was curious, but mostly I was respectful of my grandparents and grateful we had financial support such that Gran and I had our needs met. I wanted to get out of here before I had to say more lies.

"Thank you, Mr. Browne. I'll be waiting to hear from you."

A day later, Duncan Browne called, and I made sure to get there first.

"I got the phone, Gran!" I turned away from the living room, going as far as the cord would stretch, and kept my voice down. "What did you find out?"

"He went to the hospital in Charlottesville."

"How is he?"

"I'm very sorry to say that he passed. He walked into the emergency room and collapsed. They were unable to revive him."

I was stunned.

"Again, I'm sorry to tell you like this. I didn't want to keep you waiting on the information."

"No, I was just thinking that George Bridger always did have his own way of doing things. I'm sorry he had to go through this alone."

"I understand."

"What about a funeral?" A thought popped into my head. "Do you know whether his son is arranging a service?"

"I don't know his son, but I don't think so. Apparently Mr. Bridger had already arranged to be cremated. I was able to obtain the name of his executor, a local pastor, who said Mr. Bridger didn't want a service. He didn't mention the son. There's a cousin by marriage, I believe, but she lives out of state somewhere. As I recall, his son left home long ago. Is that your understanding?"

This was a chance for me to say, *His son visited him recently, and before Mr. Bridger died he gave me his granddaughter to look after.* But I squelched the words before they were uttered.

I said, "As far as I know, he's still gone. Thank you for your help. If you hear more, will you let me know?"

"I will. If you or your grandmother need anything, please call me. And you're welcome to come by anytime you need to."

We disconnected. I stood there clutching the receiver. I'd turned back toward the living room and saw Gran and Ellen flipping through the pages of a storybook and commenting on the illustrations.

Mr. Bridger certainly did have a knack for doing things his own way and in his own timing.

But so many losses. Our own, then Mildred, and now Mr. Bridger. Grand, too. A whole generation was passing.

I decided not to tell Gran about Mr. Bridger. She was happy these days because of Ellen.

Trisha, I reminded myself.

For the time being, Gran was happy, and I wasn't inclined to shake that up. Fate would or wouldn't send Liam or his wife back here. If they returned, I'd do the right thing. Whatever that was.

∽

For a year after George Bridger left his granddaughter on our porch in Cooper's Hollow, our lives were blessed. Gran stood straighter and moved better. She laughed a lot. So did I. The county sent visiting nurses by to check on Gran from time to time. They were professional, but they couldn't take the place of Mildred. Plus, it wasn't always the same nurse. Even so, the general consensus was a thumbs-up on Gran's improvement, and Ellen charmed them. Our sweet Ellen had found her voice, and she didn't stop talking except when she was working in the garden with me. She'd talk then, too, but in a whisper. I asked her why, and she said she didn't want to frighten the bunnies and squirrels and birdies.

I showed her how to tell the difference between the plants and the weeds, but she liked the weeds, too, so her help was more in the way of companionship than useful action. One day in late June, almost two months after she'd come to us, she was holding a spade for me while I resorted to digging out a stubborn weed with my fingers, when I heard her whisper, "Mommy."

She was staring at an orange butterfly that had fluttered nearby and landed on the tip of her spade. Ellen's eyes had opened so wide they were nearly round. Her lips were pursed as if she'd been caught in midwhisper or was about to offer a kiss.

The butterfly moved its wings and fluttered away.

For the rest of the day, she wanted to talk about the butterfly, butterflies in general, and everything butterflies. *Why are they orange? Why aren't they all orange? How do they fly? Why do they like flowers?* I didn't understand everything she said, but I answered every "why" as best I could.

When July arrived and, with it, the awful anniversary, I paid a special visit to the first Ellen's grave. I tidied the rocks arrayed around it and put a sprig of wildflowers on the earth above her. The small, unskilled wooden cross I'd placed there still stood, but it was unmarked by name or date. I'd never been able to bring myself to write her name on something so inadequate. Now, I thought, it was just as well.

Peace, I thought. Peace had eluded me for too long. I shed a few tears and said good-bye, then returned to the house to find Gran telling a story and Ellen giggling.

The year passed swiftly. It sped through the leaves changing colors, the leaves dropping, and Ellen asking question after question. The same was true of the snow that fell in December, and Christmas was merrier than I ever remembered it. Soon February rolled around, and since I didn't know her exact birthday, we used the one I did know, and so Ellen turned three.

CHAPTER FIVE

On a sunny day during the summer that Ellen was three, she cut her knee on a sharp rock. It was more of a scrape really, but she screamed so loudly that Gran and I nearly had heart failure as we searched her for bites or wounds, perhaps hidden under her clothing and probably scaring her more, before we figured out it was nothing and could be easily fixed with a little soap, ointment, a bandage, and a kiss "to make it all well."

Gran insisted I scour the yard for obvious things like nails or broken glass that could pose a risk to little feet and hands and knees. Ellen, already recovered, was out and helping. Her help consisted of walking around with a stick, stumbling over roots, and generally being a busy little three-year-old girl.

As I searched the hillside near the cemetery, I heard a stone dislodge and tumble down. I turned and ran immediately to the cemetery wall.

I grabbed Ellen as another loose stone slipped from under her foot. I caught her under her arms, let her stand for a moment on the top of the wall while I secured my arms around her, and hugged her. I wanted her to be careful but not fearful.

She pointed at the smallest grave with its ring of rocks. "Ellen can play?"

I tightened my arms around her. "Not here, sweet girl. This is our family cemetery." How to explain it? No way that I could think of. "Not for playing." The headstones went in a row straight across—my parents, Anne Marie and Sean, and their date of death on a homemade headstone with their names scratched in while it was still wet. I'd thought it was odd that their last name wasn't included but long ago realized that being homemade, probably by Grand, it was no wonder if it wasn't quite what you'd find in a city cemetery. Next to Anne Marie was the first Ellen, next was Grand, and then the spot where Gran would rest.

"Too tight, Mommy. Ellen get down now."

She squirmed, and I held her up, kissing her cheek with a blubbery noise to make it fun, then I set her down, letting her get her feet under her before releasing her.

How could I explain loss and burial to a child of this age? The word *Daddy* was a bit of a minefield anyway. She'd asked for him, simply saying, "Daddy?" a few times early on. But she hadn't persisted. She hadn't said it in a while. What could I tell her? Someday, perhaps not too far off, she might begin to ask with persistence.

Mommy hadn't been a problem. Not since I started answering to it.

Hand in hand, we crossed the bridge over the creek, but as soon as I let her go, she wandered over to the toolshed. The door wasn't latched, and her little fingers fit into the gap easily, and it swung open.

"Stay out of the shed, Ellen. There's sharp stuff in there."

But she leaned inside anyway and came out with a bright-blue pot. The butterfly pot. I had no idea how it had ended up in the shed. I understood why it attracted her. The pain that shot through me at the sudden memory was undeniable but manageable. I made a point of smiling so Ellen wouldn't misread my expression.

"Bring it over here." I held it in my hands and turned it over and moved my finger around the outer edges of the wings. Her name, my daughter's name, was scratched into the side. Ellen.

"Butterfly, Mommy?"

"Yes, sweetheart. A butterfly pot. I made it long ago." I smiled, saying, "Come with me."

I held her hand as we stepped over the tree roots and other natural tripping hazards I couldn't move out of the way. Ellen was at an age where she needed constant watching, and Gran wasn't up to it, thus I hadn't been inside the pottery cabin in a long time. It could wait. This Ellen, our sweet Ellen, had been with us for more than a year now and had already grown so much that at this rate, it wouldn't be long before she would be a full-fledged child and ready for school. I didn't know what I'd do about it when the time came.

"What is it, Mommy?"

Had she read my expression? No, she was pointing at the pottery cabin.

"That's where Mama used to make her pretties."

I opened the door, surprised it moved easily, as if the many yesterdays meant little. Inside it was dusty, and webs hung in the corners and rafters, but it was dry and smelled clean despite the disuse.

The potter's wheel sat where I'd last used it. I ran a finger in the layer of dirt and dust that had settled over it. Nearby was the table for working the clay, and against the wall was a cabinet where I'd stored supplies. Time hadn't stood still here. The clay was hard, and the glazes were dried up and cracked.

Other than halfhearted attempts at clay sculpture after our loss, I'd let this all go.

"What's this, Mama?" Ellen was trying to spin the wheel.

"It's where I make clay pots."

"The butterfly pot?"

"Partly there, and then I finished it by hand."

She set the pot carefully on the wheel, then tried to climb onto the seat via her belly. For a moment, I thought she'd overbalance and fall headfirst. I was ready to grab her, but she made it, pulling her legs around and ending up on her butt.

"It's dusty." I lifted her legs and checked around underneath the seat and wheel to make sure no spiders were lurking. "All clear."

"Show me how?" She looked up, her eyes adding weight to her question.

"I don't have any good clay. Besides, your hands are small . . ." I let that trail off. "I don't have any good clay."

"Show me. Please?"

I came up behind her and sat on the back edge of the seat with her sitting between my legs. She'd grown so much that I was more off than on the seat.

I took her hands in mine. "We can pretend. Will that work?"

She nodded.

How much should I show a curious three-year-old? Likely she'd lose interest quickly, but a turning wheel would have far too much potential for temptation. I said, "Pretend the wheel is spinning."

"Spinning?"

"Yes." I cupped her hands in mine and held them over the butterfly pot. "And that this is a lump of clay, gray and like mud."

"It's a bowl, Mommy. A pretty blue bowl. A butterfly bowl."

"True. But before it was a pretty blue bowl, it was a lump of gray mud. Clay. Can you pretend that's what it looks like now?"

She shook her head no, but she said, "Yes." Her dark, glossy hair smelled fresh and clean. I kissed the part on the top of her head, and she giggled.

"Listen carefully," I said. "We hold our hands like this. We don't touch the wheel because it's spinning, right? Pretend spinning, I mean."

She nodded. The tension was building in her hands, and her small fingers were tight.

"Now this is important. You have to relax because if you don't, the clay will get confused because your brain won't be able to communicate its happy thoughts through your hands and fingers, right?"

"'K."

"Pretend the wheel is spinning and the blue bowl is, too, and you put two fingers from this hand inside and a knuckle on the outside from the other hand, and you pull up ever so gently, and the clay shapes itself bit by bit between your fingers as you move. Can you feel that?"

"I can. I can do it myself. Like rubbing Gran's fingers."

I chuckled softly. "Gran's fingers?"

"When they hurt, Mommy. Gentle, she says, when I put the medicine on them." She crinkled her nose and shuddered dramatically. "Stinky."

"The medicine is stinky? Yes, I suppose it is, but it makes her hands feel better. And yes, gentle like when you put the medicine on Gran's fingers. Exactly like that, my very smart girl." My arms moved to embrace her.

She wiggled against my hug. "Mommy, I can't make the bowl with you hugging tight."

I kissed her ear. "Or without proper clay, either. How about if I get us some fresh clay to work with?"

"K."

How could one letter, one syllable, represent a little one's laughter, the shining eyes, and the excitement, almost like a vibration in her being? I didn't want to let her down.

"It'll take a little while before we can do it, but I promise we'll make bowls together."

"Thank you, Mommy." She wiggled off the seat. "Can I take my blue bowl to show Gran?"

"Yes, ma'am, you may."

I watched her strong, young legs carry her out of the cabin. Her movements were graceful, almost like dancing, and she held the bowl between her hands like something precious. But once in the yard, she broke into a run. I wasn't so old that I didn't remember when there had been joy in kicking up my heels and running.

The funny thing was, I'd never missed my mother as much as I did now. I missed the memories we'd never made. I missed having the memory of her arms around me, and kissing my hair, and of her teaching me how to do the things she enjoyed. I didn't know what she had been good at or what she'd enjoyed. There was a big, huge blank of a missing generation in my mind. Whenever I'd given it any thought, I'd envisioned my mother and father as slimmer, younger versions of my grandparents.

I'd felt complete. Until recently.

I should ask Gran. Surely now, so many years later, she wouldn't mind. If I ever wanted to know, this was the time to ask.

Grand had ordered clay for me through the hardware store in Louisa, and the Man in Town had paid the bill. Now I knew the Man in Town, Duncan Browne, and I decided to have another chat with him. What would happen when we lost Gran? I was the adult now, the one in charge, and I truly did need to know.

I left the cabin and went into the house by way of the back door, and I heard a voice. A man was standing a few feet inside the front door. In horror, all within the time it took my heart to beat twice, I saw him accusing me, claiming his child, killing Gran and me by taking our child away. Then I heard Gran's tone, courteous and unafraid, and saw Ellen's legs swinging from the side of Gran's bed.

"Hello? Can I help you?"

"Hello, ma'am. Sorry to disturb you."

"It's OK, Hannah," Gran said. "New pastor. Paying visits. I haven't attended regularly in a long time, and I'm housebound now, Pastor, as you can see. I appreciate your stopping by."

"Yes, ma'am." He handed me a card. "I hope to see you soon, in church if you can join us, but regardless, I hope you'll let us know of anything we can do to help."

He nodded and left. But my heart was still galloping. I watched him drive away and went back inside. I shut the door slowly. Gran hadn't let him in, though she might have called to him to enter. But he wasn't someone she knew. He was the new pastor, a stranger.

"How'd he come to be inside the house?" I asked her.

She nodded at Ellen. Ellen's face had lost its glow, presumably from the tone of my voice.

Gran added, "I woke up, and there he was."

I went to Ellen, determined to moderate the fear inside me and instead make the message clear and firm. "You can't talk to strangers, Ellen. Don't open the door unless Gran or I tell you to."

How ironic. The unspoken truth of it nearly knocked me over. I leaned forward and hugged her hard. We'd been the strangers, hadn't we? And we'd kept her.

No, my heart screamed. She was brought to us. Given to us. Not at all the same.

"Promise, Ellen? You'll try to remember?"

"Promise, Mommy." She rubbed her eyes. "Mommy?"

"What, sweetheart?"

"My daddy. That man wasn't my daddy?"

I was stunned. Gran said, "No, sweet child. He isn't your daddy."

She didn't ask more, but I knew she would later.

Ellen went to play with her doll in our bedroom. Gran motioned me over to her side.

"Should I tell her?" I whispered.

"Tell her what? That her daddy didn't want her?"

I had a moment of confusion. I was thinking of Mr. Bridger and his son, Liam. Gran was thinking of the first Ellen's father.

"No, Gran, not . . ." I stopped. I'd lied to this child and had allowed Gran to live her own fiction, too. There was only one thing to do. "When she asks about him, I'll tell her he died."

Gran screwed up her face, thinking hard. "And say his family moved away, and you don't know where, else she'll want to know them, too."

My first instinct was no. *No and no.* This wasn't right.

But then reality set in.

"I'll be back, Gran. I'm going to take a walk." I needed to clear my head. Even my stomach was unsettled.

"You go ahead, Hannah, honey. If Ellen tires of her doll babies, maybe we'll color."

I started down the slope toward the small bridge over Cub Creek, but I stopped. I didn't want to walk to the cemetery. I veered left, and where the creek narrowed, I jumped it and started along the path to Elk Ridge.

Not thinking but only walking and looking and feeling the forest around me as the ground rose toward the ridge. I hadn't been up this way since the day Ellen was left on our porch.

Back then, she'd been someone else's child. Now she was Ellen, and she was ours.

And if Liam returned today? If he or his wife came knocking on our door?

It would be incredibly difficult for Gran, and for me, too, but there was no question in my mind that I'd do the right thing.

Would I seek Liam on my own? A father who'd never come seeking his child and, as far as I could tell, hadn't returned here despite his father's death? George Bridger himself hadn't suggested finding Liam. The executor hadn't mentioned him. George Bridger's message, in writing to Gran and me, had been that Liam's child needed a home, not that I should find her father.

No, I wouldn't look for Liam. I had his daughter, George Bridger's grandchild, in trust, and based on the present circumstances as I knew them, we'd go on just as we'd come thus far.

I crossed the ridge and walked onto Bridger land. There was an area of thick, shrubby growth near the forest's edge, but I could pick my way along the narrow path, and then the area opened up into a dirt track with fields on either side. The corn was long gone and had been for some time. Blackberry thickets and sticker bushes were moving in.

The house was at the end of the dirt track and beyond the old fields. I kept moving forward, each step telling me that the house was still empty.

The porch had sagged a little more. Some of the boxes and other junk were gone from the porch, but otherwise, it looked as deserted as any house would look if it had been empty for so long and ill cared for before that.

She was too precious for this. And too precious for the vagaries of chance. She was safe and loved with us.

I turned away and began my trek back to the Hollow. So my original problem remained. What about when Ellen asked more pointedly about her father? Preparing now would ease us into that talk later.

When I returned to the house, Ellen was napping. I went back out to the shed and found Grand's shovel.

At the far end of the cemetery, away from Grand and the rest, I dug up a few inches of dirt about the size and shape of an adult's grave, then shoveled it back, trying to mound it a little. I made a cross and wrote *William Smith* on the crossbar, then hammered it down into the soil. With each shovel of dirt and each downswing of the mallet to set the marker, I put the final touch to our lies. By my acts, I bound the lies to us forever, to secure the blessing of the gift of this child for however long we could manage to keep her.

Those lies hung like chains. Chains of love or of deceit? Chains were chains. Eventually, they would grow heavy and difficult to keep hidden, regardless of why one first chose to wear them.

CHAPTER SIX

It was late August, and I'd just gotten lunch on the table. Gran had taken her seat, with a little help from me. Ellen, as always, sat next to her. The sandwich today was peanut butter and jelly because our sweet Ellen had decided on the menu, and Gran was delighted with her choice. As soon as I sat down, Gran said, "I need you to go to town, Hannah."

"Sure." I'd been working up the nerve to tell her I was going to have a frank conversation with Duncan Browne. There were things I needed to know. This might be an opportunity.

"In fact," I said, "I need to pick up some clothing for Ellen. She's growing like a weed." I reached across and tickled her as I said, "Like a weed, but one with the prettiest, sweetest flowers." She giggled. "We need some clothing and other things, too."

"That's fine. But for this trip, don't take Ellen. I need you to go alone. I need for you to go see the man in town. I have a letter for him. It's under my pillow on the bed."

"Is something wrong?"

"Nothing's wrong. Just reality."

"Why don't you come with me?"

She shook her head. "No, ma'am. I haven't gone to town in more than twenty years, and I don't miss it. I have everything I need right here, thank you." She pressed her lips closed.

What Gran had said all these years was true. She was never going back into town. I hadn't believed the decision was absolute. It was an unreasonable choice, in my opinion, but it was hers to make, and she was a strong-minded woman. But I tried anyway.

"Gran, surely it's time to put old memories and fears aside and get out into the world again."

She turned away, ignoring my protest. "It's time for my nap. Settle Ellen down with me. We'll do perfectly well until you get back. Don't forget the letter, and he'll arrange for you to get cash, too. As you said, we need some things."

I put on a clean pair of jeans and a button-down blouse. This was about as dressy as I ever got now. My long hair was clean and pulled back into a clip. My shoes weren't much, but I owned only a couple of pairs, so it was what it was. Gran had written Duncan Browne's phone number on the envelope, but of course I'd been to his office before when I went looking for help to find George Bridger.

I pulled into the parking lot but sat in my car. This was too strange. My curiosity warred with sudden anxiety.

With my shoulder bag held tight against my body, I got out of Grand's car and locked it, then paused to examine the dented front bumper. It was an old dent and looked like it was rusting. I was stalling. I was nervous. I wasn't accustomed to being nervous, thus it unnerved me further. I blamed Gran for it. Her behavior. Sometimes she could be ornery. Sometimes odd. She was the most loving, but also the most stubborn, person I could ever imagine.

I pushed the door open and went inside.

Aggie smiled and greeted me by name. "Miss Cooper. Welcome back."

"Yes, ma'am." I nodded and tried to return her smile, but my jaw felt tight.

"Mr. Browne is expecting you. If you'll have a seat, I'll let him know you're here."

The waiting area wasn't fancy but certainly respectable. Last time I hadn't had to wait. Still, I couldn't sit. I noted the carpet on the floor, the papered walls, a painting of tall snow-covered mountains and flowered fields hanging over a small loveseat-style sofa. Looked clean. Neat. Reasonable.

My anxiety began to abate a little, but when the office door opened, it ramped back up.

"Hello, Hannah. Nice to see you again." He extended his hand, and we shook.

I held out the letter. "My grandmother sent this for you."

"Certainly." But he didn't take it. "Would you like coffee? Or water?"

"Nothing for me."

He turned to Aggie. "Would you bring me some coffee and a bottle of water for Miss Cooper?" He stepped back and motioned me to enter his office ahead of him.

I remembered his manner as being less formal than this. He seemed on edge. I stopped halfway through the doorway.

"Mr. Browne, is there a problem?" I held up the envelope again. "What's going on?"

"You are very perceptive, Hannah, but don't worry. This is mostly about business—your grandparents' business and yours. Your grandmother and I have spoken on the phone. I imagine the letter relates to what she's already asked me to discuss with you." He accepted the envelope and put his hand on my arm. "Come into the office, and we'll talk."

Aggie was right behind us with his coffee and with water for me. She set them on the desk and left, closing the door behind her.

As before, I settled on the edge of the leather chair facing his desk, but I stayed, tense, with my purse on my lap and my arms wrapped around it. I could read body language and knew how my own posture looked, but I couldn't help it. Maybe it was good for him to see I wasn't a fool or someone to be fooled with, but rather someone who could think for herself and wasn't likely to be taken advantage of.

He used a letter opener to slit the envelope.

I watched as he read. My eyes flitted from his expression to his suit to his perfect, graying hair. I saw nothing to give me alarm. In fact, his eyes seemed kind. My tension eased again.

When he was done reading, he said, "So, it's been a little more than a year since you were last here. How are you doing? How's your grandmother?"

"She's well."

"I only met her once. Quite a lady."

"What exactly is your relationship with my grandparents? Why do you manage their financial affairs?"

He nodded. "When we met before we discussed your grandfather. You know I had a lot of respect for him. He didn't want to be troubled with financial management, but neither was he the kind of man to neglect his responsibilities. His biggest concern was that his family be provided for, now and in the long term."

I waited.

Mr. Browne leaned back. His tone softened. "After your mother died, I think your grandfather recognized that anything could happen to anyone—something we would all do well to keep in mind—and he knew your grandmother wouldn't be able to manage in a real-world kind of way.

"As for him, I think he'd lost the heart for it years before. He'd left most of his business affairs in the hands of my father. I joined my father's practice early in my career and then took it over when he retired. I know how strange this must seem to you, but I feel as if I've known your family for many, many years."

Still, I waited.

"Your grandparents lived simply. Very. They had assets that they've drawn on but in a very small way, thus money isn't an issue. You should know this in case it becomes . . . I'm thinking mostly of your grandmother and her health, but also of your daughter. Life happens whether we're ready or not." He reached into a drawer. "Your grandmother called a few days ago and asked me to explain to you the details of the property and the will."

I hugged my purse harder. I'd known there was a will. Regardless of their financial situation, there was land and the house and outbuildings. I was the only heir. What needed explaining?

He took two documents out of the drawer. One was trifolded. The other was in a fat white envelope. He laid the envelope on his desk and patted it. "You don't need to do anything about the will. This is a copy for you. It's very straightforward. You are the sole heir, of course."

No surprise there. So what was the big deal? Yet clearly something was, because his demeanor became increasingly serious, and as his frown grew, I fought the urge to jump up and run.

He unfolded the other document and laid it on his desk. "This document is a conveyance of property. Your grandmother is conveying the ownership of the land, house, and all outbuildings, et cetera, to you."

I shook my head. "I'm sorry. I don't understand. I always knew Cooper's Hollow would be mine when she passed, but she's giving it to me now?"

He paused a moment. I could see him thinking. Finally, he said, "Your grandparents added you to all their accounts before your grandfather died. Joint ownership. Your grandmother asked me to change that over to you, as the sole owner where appropriate. Some accounts are payable on death and can stay as is. She asked me to review this information with you."

I saw the acreage spelled out, and I saw the plat. He showed me the list of accounts—he called it an investment portfolio—and the income from their stocks and bonds. It all whirled around my head. Though I was seated, I gripped the edge of his desk to steady myself.

"You may remember signing documents before your grandfather died?"

"I"—I took a deep breath and tried again—"I remember. He said it was a just-in-case kind of thing. In case something happened to him and Gran. He didn't say . . ." I ran out of words and stopped.

Mr. Browne continued. "An accountant in Louisa has been doing the state and federal taxes each year, and I ensure those taxes, and other bills, are paid. Unless or until you choose to make a change in our arrangement, I'll continue seeing that it's handled. I'm happy to meet with you anytime and review it again, and in more depth. You look overwhelmed."

"I am, and I'm confused, Mr. Browne. I feel like I'm missing something." I shook my head again. "We're poor. We didn't mind doing without because we had what we needed and more. But this . . . There's money. I don't understand."

"The estate built over the years. As I said, my father managed it before me. In addition to other monies, there were life insurance policies that were paid out and invested."

"For my grandfather."

He nodded. "And your parents." He looked away and cleared his throat, then turned back. "Your grandparents couldn't bring themselves to spend the money, considering how it came to them. There is something else. Your grandmother asked me to speak with you about your mother and father."

My mouth was so dry I couldn't form any words. I picked up the bottle of water and twisted off the cap. I took a few slow sips. The water was cold. Not as good as our well water, but it eased my parched mouth and throat. I closed my eyes and drank a little more.

"She wanted me to tell you about their deaths."

I set the bottle back on his desk. "I know about all of that. They died in a car crash soon after I was born. They were on a trip. I know because I asked Grand when I was a child. I wanted to see where the accident happened, and they told me it was a narrow winding road somewhere along the Shenandoah River. They didn't know exactly where. My grandparents didn't like to talk about it."

He shook his head. "I advised them to tell you the truth years ago. My father did, too, before he passed. It's a wonder you never heard of it from other kids in school or from other sources. Your grandfather wouldn't tell you without your grandmother's approval.

"I'm sure she wanted it to come from her and your grandfather. But obviously she can't do it, and she has asked me to tell you the story."

He'd urged them to tell me the truth? What truth?

I wanted to leave. How ridiculous would I look if I simply got up and moved toward that closed door? I looked at Mr. Browne, assessing. Was that pity I saw in his eyes?

"Hannah, your father wasn't from around here. He was new in town, a laborer, picking up work where he could find it, when he met your mother. I never knew either of them, but my father said your mother was a sweet, kind, beautiful young woman. Perhaps she saw his wounded nature, and it drew her in. We'll never know. I understand he was handsome and courteous. If he hadn't been, your grandfather would've run him off one way or the other, but he had everyone fooled.

"Anne Marie, your mother, stayed at home after high school, and your grandparents assumed she'd fall in love with a local man and marry, but your father wasn't what they had in mind as good marriage material. They spoke against him and finally, the two eloped. Your grandparents weren't happy about it, but they accepted it. What else could they do?

"Your grandfather said he behaved well, and your parents were happy until trouble hit. He lost his job, your mother became pregnant, and they moved into the house at Cooper's Hollow with your grandparents. They said he changed. He accused your mother of seeing other men, looking for someone else because he wasn't good enough. He insisted people were lying about him, and he threatened to kill her before he'd lose her. They kicked him out. Flat out. Your grandfather leveled his shotgun at him and told him if he came back, he'd have him arrested and shoot him to hold him there until the police arrived.

"Sadly, he did return. It was shortly after you were born. Your grand-mother was out in the garden and had you with her. You were napping in a basket nearby. She never knew aught was amiss until she heard the gunshot. Your grandfather said she looked up and stared at the house as if she knew that every bad thing that could ever happen had occurred in that one moment. He was working on a lawn mower repair for someone, and he was up on his feet and running to the house at the sound of the shot. The second shot came as he reached the kitchen door.

"You can imagine the rest. Your father shot your mother and then himself. Mr. Cooper said he and your grandmother stood there realizing their daughter and her husband were dead and then they heard you crying outside in your basket. Your grandfather said your cry was the sweetest sound he ever heard because he knew you were all right, despite the rest.

"There's no way of knowing if he would've shot you, too. Likely not, but gratefully, he didn't have the chance." Mr. Browne stared at me, but kindly. "It's a lot to digest. His name and what little information we have about him is in this folder."

There was a folder in his hand, and he offered it to me, but I didn't reach for it.

Where had the folder come from? I hadn't noticed it. Maybe he'd pulled it out while I was drinking the water? I wanted to think about the cool, fresh water. Nothing else. Not folders or secrets or anything like that.

"Hannah, your grandparents petitioned the court to annul the mar-riage and change your last name back to Cooper. They didn't want you to bear your father's name. I presume you're in agreement with that, but if you're not, you can always get it changed back. I can help you with that or anything else.

"This folder has newspaper clippings, too. My father and I kept it all together thinking it might be wanted one day. Maybe *wanted* is the wrong word. But it's yours now, to do with as you wish."

I stared at the water bottle. I drank what was left, so thirsty I felt I'd never be sated again. Then I remembered. My heavy heart lifted. This couldn't be correct.

"There's been a mistake here," I said. "My father is buried in our backyard, in our family plot. The stone says Sean, husband of Anne Marie. It gives the year of their death." The words were tumbling out one on top of the other, and I tried to stem them but couldn't. Nearly frantic, I struggled to find the words to refute what he'd said. "There's some kind of misunderstanding. Gran said they died in a car crash, together."

Mr. Browne put the folder back onto the desk with the other documents. "Sean Davidson was his name. He isn't buried there. He was cremated. Your grandfather disposed of the ashes." He went silent for a few definitive seconds, and then said, "I'm sorry."

"Is he in the house? The ashes, I mean." I cringed. The idea horrified me.

"Your grandfather said he poured the ashes into Cub Creek. He said they washed straight down the creek into the South Anna River and then the James. He wanted them scattered and lost forever in the depths of the Atlantic Ocean."

How long did I sit there? My brain had stopped on *forever*, and I was having trouble moving forward.

"We should schedule another meeting to go over the financial arrangements and make sure they're meeting your needs."

Still struggling, I nodded. I wanted to talk about clothing and shoes for Ellen. Pottery clay. Not about the murder-suicide of my parents. Right there where I lived. This had to be a mistake, my brain insisted.

Then I remembered the boards under the living room rug. Those boards were newer and didn't match the rest of the flooring. I'd asked him about it once. Grand had muttered something about termites or vermin wrecking the original wood.

Was it strange I hadn't heard these details before? Perhaps not. New arrivals to town wouldn't know about it. The longtime residents who knew my family might have gossiped about lesser things, but when it came to such extreme tragedy, they tended to band together in a . . . I groped for the right words. Almost a communal protective stance. Like an unspoken agreement to pretend some things, some truly awful degrading things, had never happened. Some things were not to be spoken of.

Dark currents were morphing and swirling inside me. It was hard to concentrate. I closed my eyes and tried to focus. I'd think about all this other stuff later. I couldn't deal with it now. Later, it would hurt less. For now, I'd deal with today and this task, this moment.

I opened my eyes and said with forced calm, "I had planned to visit you anyway."

My voice had cracked. I took a deep breath and tried again.

"Ellen needs things. I do, too. Can you tell me what the arrangement is for the allowance? From the annuity or bank or wherever the money comes from?"

I straightened the strap on my purse. Somehow it had become twisted. I tried to smile but couldn't manage it.

"Call me or come by when you're ready to discuss this further. I know it must seem a blur now."

Mr. Browne opened a drawer and removed a checkbook. "I'll walk with you over to the bank. This is the account I use as the power of attorney. It's time we have them set up a checking account for you, with only your name, and transfer money over. You can draw on it as you need it."

At the bank, the teller smiled when we entered, and the branch manager greeted us and steered us to her office. She gave me starter checks to use while I was waiting for the actual checks.

They gave me cash, too. Several hundred dollars without blinking.

The ease of obtaining the cash, the knowledge I now possessed about my parents—and my own lies, including living as the mother of my beautiful Ellen—all contributed to a sense of unreality. I wanted to be angry. Cruel, even.

Did that mean I was my father's daughter? Hannah Davidson? What about the girl, Hannah Cooper, who'd grown up with her grandparents in Cooper's Hollow, who'd never had much, and had never wanted for anything other than what she had, at least not until high school when she'd wanted to see the outside world, had wanted to go off to college. But hadn't.

Where was that Hannah? Who was she?

That girl, that Hannah, had stayed home for her Gran, had cleaned houses to earn cash. If I'd known the truth, what would've been different? For one thing, I would never have been put in the position of running into Spencer in his kitchen that day and all that came from that.

Yet who could say what else, what good things, might never have happened if I'd lived my life differently?

On the drive home, I pulled off into the lumberyard parking lot. There were enough cars in the lot that mine didn't stand out, but everyone was in the building or the fenced yard working, so I had privacy. The manila folder lay on the seat beside me. I didn't remember picking it up and taking it with me. But here it was. I reached for it.

With great caution, I opened the folder. The headline was stark. It read SMALL-TOWN TRAGEDY. The black ink was fading. The newsprint was old. Twenty years old. It felt brittle. I read through each news clipping in turn and returned them to the folder. I learned nothing new. Mr. Browne had been correct in his telling of the story. I drove home, but I didn't remember the trip. Everything I had learned, both about the truth and the lies—a lifetime of lies—had dredged up resentments I never knew I harbored.

My grandparents, the mainstays of my world as I knew it, the people I trusted as I trusted no one else in the universe, had kept this from me. Even the bare, basic fact of my father's empty grave. Gran had known all these years, and she'd let me go on in ignorance. I had to confront her. This was unacceptable.

But.

A big *but*. It occurred to me that I hadn't been the first to deceive, but I had embraced my own deceptions. Sweet Ellen's father's grave was also empty. For the purpose of saving questions. Of solving potential ugliness and keeping it from intruding in our lives.

No, I wouldn't confront Gran.

Our dirt road dipped and then rose again, and I stopped in that curve. It was the last stretch before the house became visible. I sat in my car, the trees tall and dense on either side of me, and picked up the folder again.

I'd dug an empty grave and put a cross on it for the same reasons. Would I, could I, have done differently?

If not, then I'd better embrace the truth and not allow it to trouble my reality. Apparently, we Cooper women had a way of writing our own history, either to suit ourselves or to save ourselves and our loved ones from pain.

In the end, did knowing the truth make me feel better about things? No.

Gran was sitting with Ellen on the bed and reading her a story when I walked in. She looked up and stared at me hard. I stared right back, until I realized she was focused on the folder in my hand.

I walked over to the woodstove. I used my shirttail to shield my hand as I opened the little door and shoved the folder in. I shut the door and turned back to Gran, who was still staring at me. So was Ellen.

"What's that, Mommy?" she asked. "What did you put in the fire?"

I kissed her forehead. "Nothing, honey. Mommy's getting rid of some old papers we don't need. Trash." I turned to Gran. "You two did OK while I was gone?"

Gran nodded, and I saw a tear swell at the outside corner of her eye and wet her cheek.

"I was gone longer than expected. You two are probably hungry." I tickled Ellen's tummy, and she giggled. "I'll get supper started."

I went into the kitchen, still confused but home again, and that counted for a lot.

What was truth anyway?

My truth was there in the living room where my Gran was again reading to Ellen in our snug, warm home where an old woman's chuckle could mix with a child's laughter and make my heart beat warm and steady again.

I chose that truth and whatever came with it.

❧

A few weeks after my meeting with Duncan Browne, Ellen nearly scared the life out of me. I heard her scream. Gran, who'd fallen asleep, awoke with a start and yelled my name. I ran to the living room.

Ellen was waving her hand and crying out.

"She touched the stove," Gran said. "Ellen, honey, why'd you do that? Hannah, fetch the butter."

Ellen ran to Gran and buried her tearful face in Gran's blouse. Gran began soothing her.

It had all happened very fast. What I took in, first and foremost, as soon as I saw Ellen wasn't seriously injured, was the open woodstove door and a piece of paper she'd drawn on. The drawing was on the floor nearby.

I closed the stove's small door, picked up Ellen, and carried her to the kitchen sink. I ran the water cold and held her fingers in the stream until her cries softened and then eased. The finger pads were reddened but not blistered. I sat her on the kitchen table and smeared butter on the burns, but more for show than for need.

As I tended her fingers, I asked, "Why did you touch the stove? You know better. So why?"

She used her free hand to swipe at her messy nose. She gave a little gulp and said, "Ellen had something she didn't need no more."

"Ellen?"

"Me, Mommy. Ellen. I didn't need it, and I burned it." Her sentence ended on a very high note, and a new sob began as she said, "But it burned me! It hurt, Mommy. It hurt my fingers."

This was my fault. I was Mommy. She was mimicking my actions and the way I'd defiantly shoved those clippings into the fire. A fine example I'd set for an impressionable child.

I held her hand gently and spoke firmly. "You must never touch the woodstove under any circumstances. Ever. You must remember that. If I can't trust you, then I can't allow you to be in the living room without me. I need you to be a big girl and promise me you'll stay away from the woodstove."

"I promise, Mommy."

She went to Gran for additional consolation, and I retrieved the drawing from the floor. In circles and slightly crazy spikes and geometric shapes, Ellen had drawn what appeared to be Gran and me. Next to us was a male figure, judging by the height and the short hair.

My darling girl had tried to draw a father. Did she have some memory of the time before she'd come to us? Had she not wanted me to see it? Or had she been disappointed by her ability to draw him? Ellen tended to be a perfectionist. My heart broke for her but instead of asking, I folded the paper and slid it into the side of the kitchen trashcan, pressing it down until it was well hidden.

It had been a painful lesson for my sweet daughter, but I felt sure she'd remember and keep that promise. I learned a lesson, too. One I thought I already knew. No action is without consequence, especially unintended consequences. What I'd done to reassure Gran had backfired and served as a poor example to my daughter.

I resolved to do better, and I took extra care from that day on to be vigilant. I would do my best to ensure that no action of mine or anyone else would result in harm to Ellen.

❧

It was a mild day in October. The poplars had turned golden, and the sweet gums were blazing red. The leaves were beginning to fall, painting the ground in vibrant color. Ellen and I were in the pottery cabin. I was teaching her to make a pot by hand. She was four. Her hands were small and so was the pot. It was such a tiny pot it wouldn't hardly hold a dollop of cream. I'd tell Gran that Ellen had made her a thimble pot. It would give Gran a chuckle.

A golden leaf floated in through the open door. Ellen and I watched it flutter toward us on this nearly breezeless day and land on the table.

"Like a butterfly, Mommy," she said, and she laughed.

It was getting late and about time for me to start supper.

"Ellen, please wash your hands, then let Gran know I'm coming in to cook."

She jumped down from the stool and ran inside. I used my larger, more practiced fingers to smooth out the spots she'd missed, then wrapped the project loosely in damp paper and plastic to let it start drying. I made sure everything was switched off. I took special care with that since the incident with the burned fingers, and I routinely disconnected the power cord from the house line. Ellen was getting bolder about trying things without asking, and I wouldn't put it past her to come out here and try the wheel on her own if she took the notion.

As I left the cabin and walked to the house, I saw Ellen standing on the back stoop, her hands hanging by her side. The clay still covered her arms, all the way up to her elbows. It was a lot of mess for one tiny pot. I smiled, and then realized she wasn't. Her chin was quivering.

"Mommy?"

As I came closer, frowning, I saw the quiver in her chin working right down the rest of her body. She was shaking.

"What's wrong, sweetie?" I put my arms around her. "Ellen?"

I looked at the open door.

"Stay here, Ellen. Right here."

I went inside, my instincts alert and wide open. The lighting was dim, and Gran was sleeping. The front door was shut and locked from the inside. I turned back to face the bed.

My heart was breaking and my eyes were stinging before I knew why. My conscious brain was slower to accept reality, and I stared.

Gran's arm was half off the bed, and her hand was dangling.

Gently, I touched her wrist, intending to move her hand back onto the bed. Her flesh was cool. Her eyes were semiopen, like she was peeking out at the world. The lines in her face had eased, almost vanished.

She was gone. Gran was gone.

Every bit of starch in me evaporated. I sat on the bed. I couldn't do anything.

"Mommy?"

Ellen stood in the kitchen, her eyes big and round and dark. I held out my arms. She hesitated.

"It's OK, sweet Ellen. Gran loved us both very much. Let's love and hug each other and remember how important we were to her."

Ellen took a few steps forward, still reluctant. She looked at the floor but turned her face partway toward Gran.

"Trust me, baby."

She came into the circle of my arms. I lifted her onto my lap. I hugged her and kissed her forehead. She touched my face. Her fingers came away wet, the clay dissolving in my tears, smearing as she dried her fingers on her shirt.

"Gran?" she whispered, lost and confused.

I held her close. "She was very old. You know that, right?"

Ellen nodded. She pressed into the crook of my arm and my chest. I held her a little tighter.

"And you know she was sick sometimes."

"She hurt."

"That's right. Now she's gone to heaven, and she won't hurt anymore."

"I miss her, Mommy." Her voice ended on a high note, suggesting she'd be full-out crying any moment.

"She stayed with us as long as she could because she knew she'd miss us so much, and she knew we'd miss her. But God must've told her she'd done as much as she could, and she had earned a good rest."

"Can she come back? I want Gran back."

"No, sweetheart, but we can talk about her and remember her." I touched her chest and then my own. "She will always be with us in our hearts. You and I will take good care of each other like Gran taught us."

Ellen cried. I held her as I stood and carried her over to Gran's old rocker. We sat and rocked and cried together for a while. When we were done, I went back to the bed and pulled the coverlet up over Gran's face.

"No, Mommy." Ellen stopped me with a hand on my arm.

I looked at her, then decided to go with it. I pulled the coverlet back and straightened it around Gran's shoulders and arms, then tidied it down by her feet. I touched the blanket where it covered her poor swollen legs.

"Mommy?"

"Don't be afraid, Ellen. Gran can run and dance again. We'll miss her, but let's be happy for her, too, to be in heaven?"

"K."

I called Duncan Browne.

Gran had suffered so much loss. If she could hold up to that, then I could manage my own grief. It hurt, but at least this loss was natural in its timing. As I'd tried to convey to Ellen, I also told myself the same—this was a merciful kindness for a woman whose body hadn't been able to keep up with her spirit for a long, long time.

The sheriff's office sent a deputy, and the local funeral home sent a hearse. Gran had made her own funeral arrangements when she set them up for Grand. The funeral home provided the men and equipment to prepare the grave. I stood at the kitchen door and watched them working with shovels up at the cemetery. There was no way to get equipment across the creek and over the stone wall. It struck me that while progress brought many changes in the world around us, in Cooper's Hollow the graves were still dug the way they'd been for centuries.

The ground cried as it was torn open to receive one more of my loved ones. Another Cooper gone. There seemed to be strangers constantly around. However helpful they might be, neither Ellen nor I was used to company.

The sheriff's deputy helped me move the bed out of the living room. He was curious, I could see, as we moved the mattress and bedframe into the small back room, and I didn't blame him. I'd never really thought about it, but we were isolated—not only by geography but also by choice. Maybe we were objects of curiosity—those crazy people, those hillbillies. But we combed our hair, brushed our teeth, and wore clean clothing. Gran never tolerated a speck of dirt or dust in her house, either. After she was incapable of chasing down the dirt herself, she used me in her stead. Our furniture was old, but it shone with a century or two of regular polishing.

In preparation for the wake, I tidied the house again. I used the sweeper on the area carpet in the living room, going over it time and again. I gave myself permission not to clean under it. I didn't want to see those boards . . . the ones that didn't match. So I left the rug in place and moved Gran's rocker over to that space where her bed had been.

I wished I had more chairs. I remembered how it had been after Grand died. I'd been surprised by how many people showed up at the funeral. It had warmed my heart. Gran had invited those folks out to the house though the stress took a toll on her.

The pastor was happy to include my invitation in his eulogy. I spent a whole day cooking. Ellen was my helper. It was good to be performing these last duties in Gran's honor.

The next day, we held Gran's service at the Baptist church she'd attended for many years, until my mother died and Gran stopped leaving the Hollow.

The people who came to the service, and to the house after, were surprisingly familiar to me. I didn't really know them, not as friends, but in a friendly way—faces I'd seen through the years in high school and in the community. Even Mamie Cheatham attended, the Bridger relative by marriage who'd come to stay at George Bridger's place.

Ms. Cheatham was drawn to Ellen, and it unnerved me. Blood calling to blood perhaps? Of course not, I told myself. Half the people in the house were making over Ellen. In fact, excluding those who'd arrived in Louisa County in recent years, if we traced the family lines back a few generations, likely most of us around here would be kin to one another to some degree.

Ellen was subdued and patient at first, but the attention became a nuisance, and she was bothered, but I didn't know how to stop it. I'd just bid the pastor and his wife good-bye and turned back to the room and realized Ellen wasn't in sight. I dashed to look in the bedroom and the bathroom, then the kitchen.

Someone touched my shoulder. It was the sheriff. My heart yanked itself right out of my chest.

"Miss Cooper. I'm sorry about your grandmother. Miss Clara was a fine lady. It was our loss when she was no longer able to come into town."

"Thank you." I twisted my fingers together, anxious. "Have you seen my daughter? I can't find her."

He gestured toward the kitchen. "I saw her go into the log house out back."

"Thank you. Please excuse me. I need to check on her."

He nodded. "I think it got a little crowded in here for her." He shook my hand. "I'll let you see to her. I need to be leaving but wanted to express my condolences. If you and your daughter need us, call or reach out to my wife. She knew your grandmother well once upon a time."

"Thank you," I said again, and then slipped out the storm door.

Ellen was sitting at the potter's wheel. She hadn't reconnected the power and turned on the wheel, for which I was grateful. She was a small dark-haired girl sitting alone in a dim, dusty cabin surrounded by the smell of damp clay. It seemed a poor haven.

I knelt beside her, heedless of the dirty floor and the one and only dress I'd worn in years. I touched her cheek and turned her face to mine.

"My sweet Ellen."

Her lower lip pushed out. She shook her head.

"These people will be gone soon." I waited to see her reaction.

She wrapped her arms around me, over my shoulders, and clasped her hands behind my neck. She whispered near my ear.

"I'm sad, Mommy."

I whispered back. "Why are you sad?"

"'Cause I'm mad. So mad. Gran said not to be mad. Angry. She said I should smile."

"You have the prettiest, best smile in the whole world. I'm not surprised she wanted to see it often."

"Make them go home, Mommy."

"They will be gone soon."

"Gran's bed is gone."

I nodded. "It is. She needed it when she was sick. She hurt a lot. You know that. Now she's in heaven, my sweetest girl. She's happy, and she understands we are missing her, but she will think we're very silly if we are mad or if we stay sad a long time."

"But today is OK, right?"

"Today is a good day to be sad. Tomorrow we'll sing songs all day. Gran's favorites. We'll sing them loud so she can hear us."

Ellen nodded.

"I have to go back inside because we have guests. I'd like you to come with me, but if you don't want to be around those people, I understand. You can go into the bedroom, shut the door, and read. How would that be?"

She took my hand, and together we returned to the house my grandfather's grandparents built. This house had sheltered many, many generations, and it was where Ellen and I would continue to live—missing Gran, yes, but together for another year and a half—until fire drove us out of our home and away from our safe world in Cooper's Hollow.

CHAPTER SEVEN

Present Day

Roger told me they would widen the dirt drive and improve the grading in order to bring in heavy equipment. It would take a day or two to make the road adequate for their needs, and they were starting that work this morning. I didn't have to be there for the roadwork, but when the big yellow front-end loader rolled on-site to begin breaking up and hauling away the old house debris, I wanted to be there for that, no question.

"Should I come with you, Mom?" Ellen paused in the kitchen doorway where I was cleaning up the breakfast dishes.

"And ruin your perfect attendance?"

She shrugged and grinned. "After all these years, maybe I've earned a day off."

Ellen wouldn't want to mess up her record, though, so she must be worrying over me. I sought to reassure her.

"I'm meeting Roger out there. They're working on the driveway and a parking area today. That said, if you'd like to see the old place one last time before they clear away the remains of the house, I can take you out there after school."

Ellen set her backpack on the floor and walked over to me. She was as tall as me now, and when she hugged me, she was able to rest her face in the crook of my neck. I patted her back.

"What's wrong, sweetie?"

"I'm worried about you. I know you're doing this because I'm leaving for college soon. But Mom, moving back to the Hollow . . . I kind of understand it, but you're already going to be lonely without me. Won't you be even more lonely out there?"

I returned her hug, whispering, "Don't you worry about me. I'll be fine. I stayed in town for convenience, but it isn't where I belong." I smoothed her long, shiny hair. "Besides, it's not that far out. Certainly not like when you were little, and absolutely not like it was when I was a child. There's building going on all around the area, and you know what I'm planning for myself."

She stepped back but didn't break our hug. "You mean setting up your pottery studio in the cabin? I know. I can hardly wait to see it."

"And to try it, I'll bet. You have a lot of talent with clay."

Instead of her usual response, her dark eyes filled with tears, and she bit her lower lip.

I pulled her back into another tight hug, then eased away so I could stare into her eyes. I touched her chin. "Are you worried about my being on my own? Or more worried about going away yourself?"

Ellen laughed as she dashed the back of her hand across her eyes to catch a few errant tears. "Both."

"But you wouldn't change it if you could, would you?"

She shook her head.

"I'm glad. I never left home. There were good reasons for why I didn't, but still, I never did. I don't want that for you."

She smiled. "I was one of those reasons. Don't take this wrong—you are the best mom in the world—but one day I hope I'll find out more about my father. I want to learn about the kind of person he was and what we might have in common."

I stepped away and turned back to the sink to finish rinsing the dishes. "I'm sorry, sweetie. I know he doesn't feel real to you. I understand. I wish I could tell you more."

"You might not know a lot, but his family does."

It wasn't the first time she'd asked. I'd made up the stories about how he and I met, how we'd hardly known each other, and that he'd died before we knew I was pregnant. It didn't speak well for me, or my character, to have been intimate with someone I hardly knew. Nor, for that matter, did it flatter me to be able to lie so well in the present. The old stories worked because I had avoided details as much as possible. The story I'd told her of her father's death on vacation with his parents—caused by a misstep while hiking in the Rockies—was designed to be hard to research. I didn't like lying, but when the questions started in earnest several years ago, I was glad I'd thought it out ahead of time. More recently, she'd done some searching online. I knew because she'd left the computer browser up with the name William Smith typed in the search bar. Someday, Ellen might seek info more aggressively, but as long as I kept the details vague, what would she have to work with? Not much. Heaven forbid I should ever have to untangle the truth of her early life for her. I shivered. She wrapped her arms around me again, tighter.

"Mom, don't worry about me. I'll be in Blacksburg, not that far away, and with lots of my friends."

I nodded. Time to change the subject. "You'll need a way to get there."

"Bonnie's driving us to school today."

"I mean a way to get to Blacksburg."

She tilted her head, her eyes widening as realization set in. Then she waited, her breath held.

"Go check the garage. It's time to put your driver's license to good use."

She shrieked with joy and flew out of the room, her feet hardly skimming the floor.

I followed. "You can't drive it to school this morning. You have to get used to it and the controls and dashboard and everything. We'll go out together after school."

Ellen draped her body across the shiny blue hood of the car. "It's smooth, Mom. Sleek. She's beautiful."

"A note of reality here? Teens are high-risk drivers. You lost a class-mate earlier this year in an accident. This is a huge responsibility."

"Yes, Mom, yes, I know. Your parents died in a crash—I haven't forgotten. You'll see—I'll be the safest driver there ever was." She turned her face toward me but somehow still managed to keep her arms draped across the car. "Please can I drive it this morning?"

"I have an idea. You drive us to school. I'll drive the car home and then pick you up after, and you can drive us home."

"Mom." She groaned. "I can drive by myself."

"Not with this car, you can't. Not until you're familiar with it."

"I'll have Bonnie with me. She's an experienced driver."

"No riders. Not yet. Not until I'm sure you can handle it. Promise?"

Suddenly her frown was eclipsed by a huge smile. "Deal, Mom."

"I'll get my purse. You get your backpack. Call Bonnie and tell her you'll meet her at school."

She ran inside. Many of her friends already had cars. I'd held off for so long, but she'd earned this. Such a good student, perfect attendance, and full of dreams . . . I had to learn to let go, but not all at once. A little bit at a time, and maybe by the time she graduated from college and was truly an adult, I'd be able to trust her to live a good life and come home again on her own.

"Mom? Are you crying?"

I brushed the wet from my cheeks. "Not much." I laughed a little. "I'm fine, honey."

"Here's your purse. I've got my pack." She put her pack in the back-seat and tossed my purse over to the passenger side as she settled in behind the wheel and ran her hands around the circle of the steering wheel. "My own car. Oh, Mom, thank you very much."

There was a box on the dashboard, wrapped with a bow on top.

I nodded toward it. "You're going to need that."

She grabbed the box and tore past the decoration. She held up the key on its fancy fob. She kissed it, squealed softly, and plunged it into the ignition.

"Seat belt," I said.

As with everything she'd ever undertaken, Ellen managed driving like a pro—at least, once she was past the giggles and had managed to back out of the garage and down the driveway without taking out the mailbox. What had I been thinking when I parked it nose in, in the garage? But she did it, and I did my level best to keep my advice to myself all the way to the high school. For one thing, I didn't want to be the distraction that caused the problem. If she had an emergency, in a moment needing a quick decision, I didn't want her to hear my voice in her head causing her to second-guess herself.

Even better, from Ellen's perspective, was that two of her friends, Bonnie and Heather, were out in front of the school when she arrived. Her grin was a thing of beauty. It reached right up into her eyes as the girls ran up and exclaimed over the new car.

I got out and walked around to the driver's side. "Don't be thinking about this car. School's not done yet."

"Sure, Mom."

"Hi, Ms. Cooper." The other girl said, "Bye, Ms. Cooper." Ellen said, "Wait a minute." She handed her phone to Bonnie. "Take our picture."

Ellen pulled me over to stand beside the car.

"Relax, Mom."

So we leaned back against the car. Ellen put her arm around my shoulders, and I reciprocated. Our heads were together, our faces smiling, as Bonnie held up Ellen's phone and snapped our picture.

Before releasing her, I snagged a quick peck on her cheek. She ran off with the other girls and disappeared into the building. I drove home.

I was proud of my girl. It broke my heart to know I was losing her. None of the platitudes like "she'll be back; she's only going to college," or "she's earned your trust," eased the ache in my chest. Still subdued when I arrived home, I parked the car in the garage and went inside to prepare for the rest of my day. The best part, I suspected, had already happened.

I drove my SUV out to the old place. It was a sub-SUV, small enough that I could handle it, yet it sat a little higher than a regular car, plus it was good for hauling stuff around. Roger had a full-size SUV, and as I pulled up behind his vehicle, I realized it wasn't only a matter of grading the dirt driveway, but where would the workers park? How would the large equipment move safely around the work site?

Some of these trees would need to go, yet each one felt like a friend. This was going to be a day of hard decisions. I stiffened my posture. Sometimes tough decisions were what it took to move forward.

"Hi, Roger." I waved. He walked toward me, dressed in jeans but also in a collared, button-down shirt. Today's shirt was a soft blue. He always dressed neatly, and I imagined it was a hangover from his days in uniform. I liked it. We met beside his SUV.

He motioned toward the yard. "We have to talk about clearing some trees."

"I see the problem."

"The easiest way would be to knock down these trees here in the front, and a couple of those over there will definitely have to go—and should go because they don't look sound to me—and that will clear the way for parking. Frankly, you'll probably enjoy having access to an open grassy area after all the work is done."

"You'll grind the stumps?" I asked.

"Sure."

"I could use the area as a garden, maybe."

"Remember we're setting up garden beds for you in the backyard when we get to the landscaping. Let's walk around back. I put in some stakes to mark the layout of the house."

He put his hand on my elbow as if I might need assistance with finding my safe footing through this wilderness. I almost laughed.

"It's not exact, but only close."

Room here, room there, view, and so on—he gave me a tour. "After we've cleared the outbuildings—"

I moved abruptly; it startled him. He stopped speaking midsentence.

"Not the pottery cabin. Remember? You can clear out the old chicken coops and the shed. I'll need a new shed in whatever location you think best. Take the old outhouse, too, please. But I'm keeping the cabin. It needs some fixing up, and I know it's close to where the house will be, but I like that. It's convenient for my studio. It needs electric and water—"

"Hannah. Hold on. Relax. You already told me to keep the log cabin. As much as I'd like to incorporate those logs in the house, I understand why you want to keep it, and we'll work it into the overall landscaping layout."

"Did you know this was the original cabin? My grandfather did some work on it through the years, especially when he fixed it up for me, but it's still sound."

"Hard to imagine whole families living in a one-room, one-loft structure today."

"But it was perfect for my pottery and still can be."

"We'll rerun the electric and the propane lines. Water, too."

When I'd set up the shop in town, I'd had the old kiln moved there. Would I move it back? Or buy new? Maybe I'd want to go a little more basic, with a hand-built, hand-fired kiln. So much to consider. I touched his sleeve. "Thanks, Roger."

The remains of twelve autumns past had fallen here, the cold wet of an equal number of winters, and the perennial birth of spring and the lushness of summers, had all layered and mixed over and into the rich mineral soil. It created life within the dirt, and I'd felt that richness, almost like ground breathing beneath my bare feet, back when I'd gone barefooted, had grown up barefooted. When I'd followed the old paths and walked in the shallow parts of Cub Creek, and when I'd held a younger Ellen and had dangled her small feet in the creek and she'd squealed in delight.

My heart warmed. Life wasn't just about genetics and birth and loss. But that's where my ability to express it ran out. Verbalizing the connectedness I felt, of molecules intermixing and creating something new and beautiful, was beyond my ability to explain even all these years later.

"Hannah?"

I jumped.

"Sorry I startled you."

I smiled at him, perhaps too fondly because his lips smiled in return.

"I'm reminiscing. Remembering how it felt years ago."

We walked to the small bridge over the creek. I stood there at the rail, the water flowing under my feet, and looked back at the site, at the last vestiges of where I'd grown up. But the land—both Grand and Gran always said—the land remained regardless of whatever else occurred.

"It was a pretty bare existence from what I've seen," Roger said.

"Bare? No. Basic maybe. Yet very rich. People don't know how that works anymore. They live in their houses and put up glass and screens and yell if the door doesn't get closed all the way because the AC is getting out or the bugs are getting in. They have their yards and lakes and whatnot, but it's nothing more than a pretty picture seen through their windows. They don't live in it. *I lived in it.* The outside was my home, too. My living didn't stop at the boundaries of our four walls. It was virtually limitless." I added, "And loved. I was so loved, Roger. Sometimes it still overwhelms me. My grandparents were my people. Everything I am or will be is thanks to them. I don't remember my parents. It hurt my grandparents to speak of them. They loved their only daughter so very greatly that they took all their grief and multiplied it with their love and gave every ounce of it to me. Never failing."

"I hope you weren't hurt by any of the things I've said about the house and about this property."

"No. What you've said is reality. I'd be a fool to be offended. But what I do know is that the accumulated history of living hereabouts, including past generations, is the truth. And that can't be denied, either."

We'd moved beyond the bridge, and he held out his hand to assist me over the fallen tree. After a brief hesitation, I accepted it. I liked Roger very much. I could certainly do far worse than encourage a closer relationship with him. But not yet. For now, I had to concentrate on the tasks at hand.

First came Ellen and her graduation, and meanwhile my home would be under construction. I didn't need to be distracted by other decisions. I wanted my house built. After Ellen was safely off at college, I could consider me.

Roger and I had walked up the slope, and here was the cemetery enclosed in its walls. The stacked stones were mostly intact and about thigh high, but with no gate and no opening, as if reinforcing the idea of permanency.

"I should go. The shop needs my attention, especially since I'll probably be spending time out here at the cabin as the construction progresses."

"Which begs the question—you have Cub Creek Pottery in Mineral. Why do you want to set up a shop out here, too?"

I leaned against the wall, giving no appearance of wanting to go anywhere despite what I'd said. "I don't get much traffic at the storefront. I do more business with other businesses and private purchasers. Sometimes I wonder why I bother, frankly."

"Why? What's the problem?"

"It's uninspired, Roger. I've been making the same pottery and clay sculptures year after year. Maybe it's the best I can do. Sometimes I wonder why anyone buys it." I looked at my hands. There was no answer there.

"They buy it because they like it. Your clay work has always amazed me."

"Don't say kind things out of pity or consolation, Roger. I may not keep the shop once I'm back home in the Hollow; I'll likely let the store go."

Roger smiled. "Don't disappear on me. I don't want to complete this project only to find I've lost you to the life of a recluse."

I patted his arm. "Don't worry, Roger. You're important to me. I can't manage without you."

"Listen, Hannah. This isn't the first house I've built. For most people, a new home is a big thing for them—signifies big change in their lives—sometimes happy events, sometimes trauma, sometimes recovery—but always big. Even bigger when they're building from scratch. When faced with those changes, most have trouble letting go. Don't let a few outbuildings define what you want for your future. Don't panic or grieve over a pile of charred wood. You have the memories. They are in you, and that's the safest place for them."

He had effectively stunned me into silence. I knew exactly what he meant. I disagreed that it applied to me—my circumstances were unique—but I'd never known him to be so eloquent about emotional things.

I nodded. "I promise I'll try to be objective."

"By Monday we'll be ready to tackle the site clearing and prep. We'll clear the debris and put up the erosion control barriers. The barriers, the plastic swale, will also help protect those areas you're concerned about." He turned to me and put his hands on my shoulders. "Now put the worry aside and look forward to this as a new, exciting adventure. Have fun with it."

On Saturday evening, Ellen looked up from her schoolwork and saw me fretting.

"What's wrong, Mom?"

I shook my head. "Nothing. What about you? Sorry you didn't go out with your friends this evening?"

"Nah. Bonnie had to go with her parents to visit family this weekend. Now back to you, and don't change the subject this time. Are you thinking about the big day?"

I sighed. "Yes. Day after tomorrow. They're almost done widening the road, and the real show is about to begin. I hope . . ."

"What, Mom?"

"I hope I'm making the right choices."

"You always do."

What would she think if she knew about the choices I'd made through the years? Doubt tried to wrap itself around me. I needed to stop this now. I smiled at Ellen and teased, "Even when it comes to tattoos?"

"Please," she said with a groan.

Ellen was sitting at the island with her books and computer. She had a paper due. It was a big part of her grade, and she was serious about it though she already had college and scholarships all lined up. I smiled to reassure her, then resumed preparing our supper.

She said, "Why don't we go out there tomorrow after church? I haven't been to the Hollow in a while."

"You're smart to live in the present, not the past." I waved my spoon. "Totally normal for young people."

"Mom, to be honest, I don't feel guilty or anything about not going often. Like, if a huge storm came through tomorrow and wiped out the whole Hollow, I might be sad, but it wouldn't change anything. We are still who we are. Right?"

"True."

"But since it's about to change forever and we can go, why not? See it like it used to be, or close anyway. I'd like to." Ellen put down her pencil.

I leaned back against the counter. "What do you remember?"

"I remember the fire, but I don't totally remember how scared I was. Just that I was, you know, super scared."

"What about before that? For instance, do you remember the house? You were only five when our lives changed."

"I remember Gran. Mostly, I remember she was big and soft and smelled like lavender."

"Lavender. Funny. I hadn't thought of Gran and her lavender sachet in years."

"I remember the day she died."

"Do you?" I put my hand to my chest.

"Yes. Sometimes I think I remember Grand, but I can't, right? He died before I was born."

I was silent. Yes, Grand was already gone then, but not George Bridger.

She stared into a dark corner of the kitchen. "He was tall and thin and had a long white beard." She laughed a little. "For a long time I thought he was Santa, but a skinny one."

I forced myself to nod. I tried to control my face while I searched for words. But Ellen went on.

"I must've seen a picture of him and mixed it up in my memory. I do remember the house, or parts of it, anyway. It was dark, except for the kitchen. I remember a lot of light there. The house was warm. Felt like summer all the time because Gran was always cold, right? You and I shared a bed while we lived there, and I loved that." She stared at the wall, a wistful smile on her face. "I missed that the most when we moved here. I felt alone at night for the first time ever."

Her smile pushed away everything else. I realized I should let it go. Her recollections would continue to blend and change, and probably disappear as many memories did, like dreams, evaporating with time.

"The night of the fire, I remember how you woke me, scooping me out of bed in the dark. I would've been afraid, but it felt like I was flying in your arms. At least until I saw the flames in the living room. And then felt the cold outside. It was summer, right? But I remember it as being cold. I wanted my blanket and my doll. I looked at the fire coming out the window, and I was afraid. I wasn't afraid of the flames. Not for me. I was afraid I'd say the wrong thing, like 'I'm cold' or 'I want my doll,' and you'd run back inside to get it. I was afraid I'd lose you forever and it would be my fault."

"It would never be your fault. No matter what. You know that, right?"

"Sure. I was a kid, and kids think everything is about them."

I watched her face and was satisfied. I went back to cooking.

"So, is it a date?" she asked.

"What?"

"Tomorrow afternoon."

"Sure. Good idea."

After all that talk about the fire, not to mention old men with long white beards, I was afraid I'd be wakeful that night. The ghosts and regrets from my past were bound to climb into bed with me, but no, I dropped off to sleep as if I hadn't a worry in the world.

❧

I stopped in the same spot as always—the patch of dirt and gravel after the curve that gave us our first sight of the house. We'd huddled there in that spot as the house burned, as far away as safety required but where we could still see it. I'd pulled my young daughter into my arms, attempting to shield her, but I knew she was sneaking peeks through my fingers, and she was shaking. For myself, I couldn't take my eyes away—out of respect and grief? Or horror? Disbelief? Probably everything rolled up into one dreadful image—of flames through the windows, then erupting through the roof. I'd tightened my arms around Ellen, and we'd waited, knowing someone would see such a huge blaze in the dark of night and call it in.

Ellen said she remembered that night, that I had picked her up from our bed and carried her out past the flames into the night. I recalled that, too, but I also remembered waking up to the squeak of the springs as the mattress shifted. I'd opened my eyes to see Ellen settling back into bed beside me. I assumed she'd gone to the bathroom. I reached over to make sure she had the blankets pulled up over her—for a summer night, it was a chilly one—then drifted back off myself. Until I woke again. This time I knew in an instant that something had gone very, very wrong inside our home.

Ellen didn't seem to recall having gotten up in the night before the fire started, and I wouldn't remind her. Regardless of what she might have done, the fire wasn't her fault.

On this trip to the Hollow, I cast a sidelong glance at Ellen to check her reaction. How many times had I stopped here before understanding why? She blew out a silent puff of air from between her lips. I recognized that mannerism. It was her emotional response when she was confused or conflicted, so clearly she wasn't oblivious to the currents here, either.

I didn't try to comfort her and thereby prevent her from dealing with her emotions herself.

Ellen opened the door and slid out. She closed the car door firmly, cast a look at the work Roger's crew had already done to clear trees and widen the dirt road, and then set off down the driveway. She stopped at the porch, the charred black goo of long-flattened debris not far from her shoes. She pinched her nose.

"It still smells, I know," I said.

She removed her hand. "Not really. Not much. It's just that the smell reminds me of that night. You know?"

"I do." My fingers twitched. They wanted to grab my daughter's hand. I jammed my fists into my pockets.

She puffed out a soft breath again, then nodded and moved on. She walked around the remains of the house and headed to the backyard. I followed more slowly, curious about what would draw her attention most directly.

Ellen went to the old cabin. She opened the door and looked in. She squinched up her nose and backed out, sneezing. "Spiders?"

"Most likely." I laughed softly and touched the thick, rough logs. "Roger will fix it up. He'll get rid of them and the dust, too."

"I remember you working in there."

"And I will again."

Ellen crossed the yard to the small footbridge over the creek. She paused there for only a quick moment and then headed up the slope to the cemetery. As I hastened to catch up, she called out to me, "Looks good, Mom."

She stopped at the stone walls and stared at each of the graves. It made me nervous. Did her eyes linger on her father's grave? Maybe, but she didn't remark on any of them. Instead, she turned away, took my arm, and we quietly descended the hill.

After recrossing the bridge, she wandered farther down to the creek. I sat on a log, enjoying the sound of the creek and the spring feeding it. Ellen continued standing and staring straight ahead.

"Where does that go?" She was pointing at a path that disappeared up the slope into the woods.

Across the creek, and beyond the homeplace clearing where the trees took over again, the path was wide and clear, though it narrowed and almost disappeared in places as it climbed to the top of Elk Ridge. Or it had. I hadn't attempted that stroll in years. Was it still walkable?

"That's Elk Ridge up there. Our property follows the ridgeline."

Ellen opened her eyes wide. "Seriously?"

"Seriously. Of course, you can't see it from here because of the trees. The forest is thick up on the slope. Not much good for farming here. The land flattens out on the Bridger side of the ridge. The Bridgers used to farm over on their side. Mostly, Grand just hunted. Gran and I grew a few veggies. I vaguely recall an orchard. Grand tended that for years, but it took a blight or something—I hardly remember, it was so long ago—but otherwise, that was about it, as far as working the land. Grand was good with small engines and furnace repair and such. That's how he earned a living."

My voice was stilled as I recalled, from years ago, the attorney telling me my father's ashes had been poured into Cub Creek, destined to vanish. He was lost to the past, too. Erased? Not quite erased, but the aspect of him was changed. Gran had changed the truth of who he was into the memory of someone he'd never been.

My daughter, but not the daughter who'd carried the genes of my parents, paused on the bank where the creek narrowed, downstream from the bridge. I was about to call out to her to be careful, to remind her the banks could be slippery, when she jumped. Gracefully, as smoothly as a young deer, she flew over the water and landed on the far side. She started walking toward the path.

I stood. "Ellen. What are you doing? Come back here."

She called back to me, tossing the words over her shoulder. "Don't worry, Mom. I'll be right back. We have time, right? I want to walk to the ridge."

"Why? I mean, it's a long walk." I hardly recognized my voice. I reached forward, wanting only to pull her back.

Ellen nodded and left me.

Left me? *Get it together, Hannah.* Ellen was walking up to the ridge that I'd pointed out as being the property line. *Calm down,* I told myself. This didn't need to be a big deal. One step at a time, and before I knew it, we'd be back here on Cooper land where we belonged.

"Watch out for ticks and snakes! Spiders, too!" The warning was a feeble attempt to bring her back. Feeble and contemptible.

I hurried back across the bridge and angled toward the path to catch up to her.

"I remember Gran being sick," she said as we hiked up the slope.

"Yes," I said. "She had health problems, but until Grand died, she did well enough. She took his death hard."

"That's why you didn't go off to college."

"Yes," I said again.

"Instead, you met my dad while you two were in high school."

"Wait," I said. I stopped, and she did, too. "Is coming out here bringing all this up again?" I touched her hand. "I'm sorry you have questions I can't answer properly." I shook my head. "I remember once Gran saying a child deserved to have a daddy. I wish I could've given that to you."

Ellen spoke softly. "It's not your fault he died."

Not my fault. The death of someone who'd never existed but who served an important purpose in our lives nevertheless.

I drew in a deep breath that sounded a lot like a sigh and said, "After he died, his family moved away, and I never knew where they went. I wish I had something of his, perhaps a keepsake, for you. Maybe it would've made him seem more real." I tried to slow my lying heart, which was now racing. "We were young, sweetie. We went further than we should have. We should've waited, and then you would've had a real family. Remember that when you think you're in love. There's an order to things that shouldn't be ignored. If he hadn't died, we would've fixed that, but we never had the chance. Even so, I have never regretted having you. Never. You have been my heart and my sanity through all the craziness life has thrown at me. I've never regretted you—and if you believe anything, you must believe that."

She nodded. "I do believe it, and I believe his family knew how much you loved each other, and I remember that every time I think of them letting him be buried in the Cooper cemetery. They probably moved away because they couldn't bear to stay. If they'd known about me being on the way . . . Maybe having a granddaughter would have helped them heal."

I was stricken. This romanticized version I didn't know she'd crafted—of a stricken family and her deceased father—was my fault. All my fault.

What you sow . . . I had sown these seeds. These lies. I'd kept them watered and fertilized and pruned because I wanted to avoid an ugly, distorted reaping.

At that very moment, a nearby bird burst into song, filling the air with its warbles. The clear, delicate, earnest notes seemed to erupt from a grove of hollies, and the music soared and brought an expression of wonder to both our faces. Ellen smiled and reached out for my hand. She wrapped her fingers around mine, and for a brief moment, I saw the child with the creek-water brown eyes again who needed me, then she tugged, this child who now looked like a young woman and who was as tall as I was, and she pulled me up the hill along with her.

"Watch your step, Mom." She stopped. "Hold up. I've lost the path."

"This way." The brush had made a thicket here. "Are you sure you want to do this? You're likely to get scratched."

"Mom, please."

"OK, OK." I led her around the thicket, and we did pick up a few scratches, and then we climbed the remainder of the path now carpeted in fragrant pine needles. "These can be slick. Watch your footing."

Suddenly, there we were—atop Elk Ridge. The geography hadn't changed, as if the laws of time and nature had stayed their course, despite how greatly our lives had changed since I'd last taken this walk.

Ellen stood beside me, then abruptly moved on.

"Where are you going?"

She shrugged. "To follow the dirt road. I see an old house over there."

Beyond the fields, and in the gaps between the trees on the far side, the roof and chimney could be seen.

"The Bridger house. Mr. Bridger died years ago. A relative moved in there soon after. I met her, but I don't really know her. It's not right to trespass."

Ellen went a few steps farther, and then stopped. "I guess you're right about trespassing and all that." But then, despite her words, she resumed walking. "But we're neighbors, aren't we?"

The trees were thinner here, and the fields that used to grow hay were fallow, and thickets of sticker bushes and berries were overcoming them. There were other bushes, too. Planted bushes like abelias and butterfly bushes, and some I didn't recognize. Gran had loved abelias, and these were in bloom, covered in little white flowers.

Ellen ran her hand over a branch of blooms. It stirred the bush, and a few yellow and orange butterflies took flight.

"Oh, look, Mom!"

She stared, as did I. "I remember seeing butterflies here before. A long time ago."

"Ouch," Ellen cried out. She yanked her hand back and stuck the finger in her mouth.

"There are blackberry bushes in there."

She pulled the finger from her mouth and shook her hand. "It's too early for berries. Too bad. I'd love a cobbler."

I examined her finger. "A few seconds of pressure will make it stop bleeding." In truth, there wasn't much more than a pinprick of blood, but I knew how those thorns could sting.

She squeezed her finger.

"I used to pick berries when I was young," I said. "We'd can them. Also, Gran would make blackberry cobbler, and I'd walk it up here to Mr. Bridger. He was alone. A widower. He loved Gran's cobbler."

"Who lives here now, I wonder? You said a relative moved in?"

"A cousin, I think." I waved away a gnat. "It's time we headed back." I saw she was looking at her finger again. "We'll get that washed and put a little ointment on it."

Ellen tossed her hair again and smiled. "I'm not a baby, Mom. I can take care of it."

"Sure you can. Because I taught you how."

Before Ellen could answer, I heard my name called. I turned to see a plump woman walking briskly toward us and waving.

"Ms. Cooper? That you?"

The Bridger relative, Mamie Cheatham.

Just be polite, Hannah. Then you can leave. This is no different from meeting anyone else and being courteous. Take it one step at a time.

I waved at Ms. Cheatham and said to Ellen, "We'll have to say hello." We walked and met her midway.

The woman was wearing a straw hat over her gray hair that was pulled back into a ponytail. Her print dress, combined with sneakers, gave her the look of an eccentric.

I apologized. "I'm sorry we bothered you. It's been a few years since we last met."

"Certainly I remember you. It was at your grandmother's funeral, right?"

I touched Ellen's arm. "Yes, ma'am."

"I'd just come to live at George's place. What a mess it was." She put her hand to her face. "I shouldn't say that about family. Shame on me. I'm sure he did his best. Not easy for a man managing alone, I'm sure."

"Mom, does she mean Gran's funeral?" Ellen's face had lit up as if she'd made a connection, unexpected, but one that put her squarely into this conversation of memories. She'd been young, but not so young she didn't remember the funeral. She asked Ms. Cheatham, "Did you know my father?"

The woman looked surprised. I certainly was. I put my arm around Ellen, shaken but laughing politely. "Of course not, honey. We lost him long before Ms. Cheatham arrived in town."

Ellen blushed, embarrassed. "I thought because it was long ago . . ." Her voice trailed off. "My father died before I was born. He was hiking in Colorado."

"Oh my. How sad for you, dear."

I squeezed Ellen in a one-armed hug and smiled. "Ms. Cheatham, if you haven't already guessed, this is my daughter, Ellen."

She focused on Ellen, and her eyes were kind. "Well, I'm old, no doubt about that, but I didn't move here until a while after George died, so I couldn't have known your papa, sweetie. Call me Mamie, please." She smoothed her collar. "I remember meeting you at your great-grandmother's funeral. What a beautiful little girl you were, and now such a lovely young lady. I'm a cousin of the Bridgers through George's wife, Belinda. I hope you'll come visit me sometime. I miss having young people around."

She turned back to me. "I knew someone was here because the butterflies took wing. Magnificent, aren't they? My cousin Belinda planted all those butterfly-friendly bushes around the property when she came here as a young bride." She laughed. "Funny to think of butterflies as an alarm system, isn't it?"

"It was beautiful seeing them fly around like that," Ellen said.

"Oh, just you wait until July and August. They'll be thick like crazy. In fact, you put me in mind of her. Belinda, that is. Those dark eyes of yours and your hair. My cousin Belinda had that beautiful glossy dark hair." She continued. "Well anyway, I was about to drive into town. A Ladies Circle meeting at church, you know. Would you like to ride along? Or if you've a mind to visit, I can miss this one. Freda can catch me up later."

Stay for a visit? *Not a chance.*

Belinda, indeed. Dark eyes. Dark hair. It angered me, as if Mamie Cheatham was trying to assert some kind of claim based on hair color . . . My reaction was crazy. I was crazy. Not crazy, but I was guilty. I took a deep breath, trying to rein in my madness before I lost it on this poor woman. She looked so hopeful that I smiled, but regretfully, hoping my true feelings weren't obvious.

"We need to be getting back home. Ellen wanted to climb the ridge, but the afternoon is moving on, and, of course, Ellen has school tomorrow."

"I understand. Do come by sometime. I'm usually here."

Ms. Cheatham walked back between the fields to the house where her car was parked. Ellen and I moved back into the shade of the trees, but Ellen touched my arm, and I stopped.

"What?"

She had a funny, mischievous look on her face. I couldn't help myself. I responded with my own smile, curious.

The sounds of the car diminished.

"I want to see," she said.

"See?"

"The house."

My smile vanished. "I don't understand." I bit my lip rather than continue and perhaps drive the wrong questions.

"I want to see. Not do any harm. I heard about the Bridger house growing up. We're here now. Why not?"

"A quick look outside. I don't want to risk her coming back or someone else at the house seeing us and being embarrassed."

"Us or them being embarrassed?"

"Both or either."

"Just a quick look. I promise. I remember hearing about the stained glass window. One of the kids at school . . ."

Her voice trailed off as I followed her, trying to keep up. She wasn't running, but my legs felt especially heavy, and my feet dragged.

She stopped at the end of the field. The driveway was maybe twenty feet away, and beyond that was the house. My knees felt weak. It looked much the same, and yet different—better. Clearly Mamie had taken her caretaker responsibilities seriously.

The porch had been reinforced and hardly sagged at all. Instead of cartons and junk, there was a nice bench, chair, and table where George Bridger used to idle while he drank and spit. I imagined Mamie was more genteel in her porch-sitting habits.

"Look at it, Mom." Ellen was staring upward.

I observed her as she looked at the house and the window. Uneasiness stirred in me. If she'd ever seen the house from this view, she'd surely been too young to remember. But from the inside? That was more likely. She seemed fascinated.

The stained glass window was beautiful and perfect. When I'd seen it years ago, it must have been covered with a film of dirt that had diminished its quality—plus I'd had other things on my mind at the time. I moved forward and stood beside my daughter.

"Butterflies," she whispered. "Everywhere I go, I seem to run into butterflies. Are those monarchs?"

"I imagine so. Those are pretty common, right? And orange. Ms. Cheatham mentioned the bushes that attract butterflies. I guess the original Bridger who built the house commissioned the window. Belinda carried that further and planted the bushes. She must've been a real butterfly fan."

"It looks familiar."

My heart jumped. "Maybe you saw a picture or something."

"Did you bring me here? Maybe when I was very little?" She frowned slightly.

"Here? I don't think so."

Her frown changed swiftly to a smile. "I'd love to see it from inside."

"We'll come back one day and ask." The words seemed safe enough to say, since she'd be leaving for college in a few months. The passions and interests of teenagers could come and go in a flash. She'd forget.

"It's time to go home."

She put her arm through mine, and we walked to the ridge. There, we stopped. Or rather, she stopped, and I stopped with her.

"What's wrong now?"

She shook her head. "Nothing's wrong. It hit me that standing here, looking down the hillside and at the land below, at the tops of the trees . . ." She looked at me. "That's Cooper land. Cooper's Hollow—where we come from." She surveyed the slope and nodded. "I wasn't sure before, about you moving back out here to the woods. I didn't understand. Now I'm thinking it's a good thing. I don't know why, but it feels right. Like it was bound to happen."

"Like fate?"

"Or maybe destiny?"

"What do you know about destiny?" I teased.

"Only that we're supposedly shaping ours by studying hard and getting good grades and making good choices. That's what my English teacher says." Ellen laughed and began the descent.

"Watch your step," I reminded her.

Ellen chattered about butterflies as we negotiated our way back down the path to the Hollow. She walked with the grace of youth. I watched my own footing more carefully.

I loved the sound of her voice, its rise and fall, as much as I loved her smile and the brightness in her eyes when she was excited about something—even the down times, I loved them, too—and the sparkle of tears on her lashes when something moved her to compassion, though seeing her cry wrenched my heart.

After we were back home and Ellen was in her room working on her school paper, I sat on the back deck watching the night bugs trying to become one with the outdoor light and the fireflies played hide-and-seek among the branches of the fir trees.

Fate versus destiny. I wasn't a philosopher and hadn't studied those things. What I knew or felt was a sum of what I'd lived and learned and what Grand and Gran had taught me.

We reaped our fate by what we sowed. I had an idea that fate was predestined but that a thin line divided fate and destiny. Destiny was the result—hopefully the gift, sometimes the curse—that we might yet reap due to actions, or the lack thereof, that altered fate.

I understood now why I was anxious about Roger's people going out and hauling away the literal ashes of our history. The past was being erased, along with my ability to correct my lies and omissions—an opportunity I'd never considered an option.

I didn't think differently now. Was it my conscience that had hoped for a course correction? A restoration of truth?

That proved for a fact that a person's conscience didn't reside in his or her heart. I had lost the ability, the free will, to tell anyone the truth of the day that child had looked at me and said her name was Sweet Ellen. External circumstances might have prevailed—a parent might have shown up, Mr. Bridger might have returned home, Gran might have come to her senses and realized her error—and the truth could've been recovered with explanations, apologies, and little injury to anyone. But not voluntarily—not on my part. Not then and not now.

Some things were simply what they were. Some gifts must simply be accepted. With luck, or a favorable destiny, the payment could be avoided. If, in the end, fate ruled and the payment must be made, then the balance would be whether the happy interlude was worth the punishment. From my perspective, it was. Ellen might view it differently. I hoped I'd never have to find out.

The driveway had been successfully widened. The spot where we'd huddled during the fire already looked different, and the old lurch in my chest was so faint I could see the time coming when I wouldn't feel it at all but experience it only as a memory arising occasionally.

Bittersweet but encouraging words.

The road improvements were wonderful. As I rounded the last curve, I saw vehicles in the new parking area.

A large metal container was now in front of the old, burned house. The container had metal doors midway along the side. It wasn't what I considered a dumpster, though there was one of those, too, and it was nearer the drive. Easy access for the yellow heavy equipment, I presumed.

A dump truck was backed up to the house, and a backhoe was parked nearby. I pulled over to the parking area, parked, and got out of my car. As I walked toward the house and the dump truck no longer blocked my view, I was able to see Roger standing with a group of men on the far side near the pottery cabin.

He saw me approaching. He lifted his arm and waved me over. The other men moved away, apparently returning to work.

I'd dressed in jeans and old sneakers and an old button-down shirt over my T-shirt—to show I was prepared to get dirty. I eyed the blackened pile of boards and rubble as I walked around it to reach him.

This is the last time, I thought. *From here on, the new begins.*

I pointed at the metal container with doors. "What's that?"

"For what comes out of the toolshed. I've seen amazing things come out of old sheds out here in the country. You might have antique tools or objects you'll want to spruce up for decoration in the house or yard."

I was touched. "What a great idea, Roger. Thank you for thinking of it."

"Yes, ma'am. I aim to please."

Roger went on to show me how they'd erected the silt fences to protect the creek. "I have a man who's experienced with restoring old country buildings like the cabin and springhouse," he said. "They call that barnwood, by the way, in case you've seen those TV shows. He isn't here today, but soon. He's also a wood carver. I have something special in mind."

"What?"

He smiled. "Wait and see." He touched my arm and directed me away from the work area to a lawn chair in the shade. He pointed and said, "You sit here."

Frowning, I asked, "What are you talking about?"

"You can't be wandering and getting underfoot. It isn't safe for you or for the workers." He pressed the chair firmly down. The feet dug into the dirt. "So you sit and oversee from here. Please."

I sat, but I must've looked annoyed because Roger added, "I've instructed them to watch out for anything that looks interesting or salvageable." He glanced over at the pile, looked down at the ground, and shook his head. "We'll do our level best for you, Hannah, I promise."

As with many burned houses, the chimney remained mostly intact. Even the hearth had withstood the fire. The hearthstones had been blackened from use, permanently, I suspected, before they'd put a woodstove there.

The woodstove—I'd burned those news articles about my father in there. I'd flipped open the little door and tossed them in. Gran had watched me. I'm sure she had been wondering what I might say about the decisions she and Grand had made to keep the information from me and doubtless was prepared for the worst—as if I could deliberately hurt her, even in anger. But Gran hadn't been the only watcher. A pair of big brown eyes had watched, and her sweet voice had asked what Mommy was burning. I had dismissed the folder of clippings as trash I didn't need or want. She might've noted the bright-orange flames through the small window in the stove door, flaring up as they consumed the paper.

Who could know what might catch the attention of a child and percolate in a young brain? The night of the house fire, after Ellen had crawled back into bed, I awoke again sometime later, startled from sleep, knowing something was wrong. I'd run into the living room and seen the stove door open. Loose papers—they looked like pages from Ellen's coloring book—were on the floor near the woodstove, and the fire, somehow reignited, was skimming up the curtains and taking hold of a stuffed chair.

It was summer, but the day had been unusually cool and rainy, and I'd lit the fire briefly that evening to dispel the chill before bedtime. At most, only hot embers would've been in the belly of the stove, and likely, that's why Ellen hadn't caught herself or her nightie on fire when she opened the stove door. She'd been lucky.

I shivered even now, thinking of it. The pages she'd pushed onto those dying embers must've reignited the fire—if that's what had happened. A paper aflame, with the stove door open, could've cast off burning bits that lit the chair and wherever else they landed.

Or perhaps I was wrong. Gran and I hadn't kept things up properly after Grand died. I couldn't recall when we'd last had the woodstove pipe or the chimney cleaned. Or maybe the latch on the woodstove door hadn't caught properly the last time I'd closed it. Maybe. But those coloring book pages hadn't been there when we'd gone to bed. And I'd never failed to latch the door properly before.

In minutes, flames had leveled the house that had withstood the passage of so many years.

There was no point in identifying fault. What was done was done.

What had Ellen wanted to burn? I'd never know, and I'd never ask. I wouldn't risk planting the suggestion that she might be responsible for our loss. Moving to Mineral had been for the best. Sometimes our choices influenced our destiny. Sometimes fate stepped in and made those choices moot.

Back in the present, I watched the workmen move debris to allow access to the chimney. Among them was another expert—someone familiar with salvaging stone chimneys for later restoration. The expert numbered the stones as the chimney was dismantled and stacked out of harm's way. He wouldn't be able to access the hearth until more debris was cleared.

At first, the movement of the big yellow front-end loader's scoop, maneuvering to pick up the larger pieces on top, physically pained me. I pressed my hands to my chest over my heart. I couldn't help myself. The noise of it surprised me. The twanging and pulling, the sounds of forcible dismantling, rang in my head and tore at my heart. It forced me to my feet. Roger turned to look at me, grimaced, and then came over.

He put his arm around my back. "Are you upset?"

I nodded but bit my lip, holding back words.

He smiled reassuringly. "Lots of people feel this way. It will pass, I promise."

I must've looked unconvinced because Roger tightened his arm around me.

"Hannah, my experience has been that people cling too hard to the past, or they ignore it, or they try to obliterate it for their own reasons. This was a real thing here in Cooper's Hollow. Centuries of lives and living. For you, it also represents decades of memories. Yet, despite the fire, you managed to go on with your life and raise your daughter. You have earned this opportunity to blend the past and bring it into the future—not to leave it as ruins. You are taking something fire destroyed and turning it into a home with both a past and a future."

I leaned into his arm and chest and impulsively kissed his cheek. "Thank you."

The last large piece of tin twanged and vibrated like thunder as the front-end loader wrenched it from the pile and then carried it, along with the lumber that refused to detach—it looked like part of a wall—and dumped it into the truck. Roger was distracted by another worker and left me standing there.

When the area had been cleared around the fireplace hearth, the stone expert moved in to disassemble it, much like undoing puzzle pieces, and he marked them as he'd done with the chimney stones.

One of the men called out to Roger, and I saw them standing around, curious. I left my chair and joined them. Their attention was focused on the hearth, but I couldn't see what attracted their interest.

Roger motioned the front-end loader forward to push more debris out of the way, which cleared my viewing angle. They'd found a cavity beneath the stone blocks. One of the workmen reached into the debris as if to pull a board farther away and caused something to shift and send out a spray of ash.

"Move back," Roger called out, and the workers stepped away, except for the stone expert, who didn't blink. He leaned forward to stare into the dark space, then reached back to grab a small but high-powered flashlight from his tool belt. He shined it into the cavity.

"Hannah?" he called out. "Did you know there was a hiding place here?"

I shook my head. "No." But as I said it, another memory was stirring. I let it come to the fore while we waited to see what the hole would yield.

The stone expert, his hands still in the cavity beneath the hearth, grunted. He received the instant attention of every man there. He moved something in there, shifting it closer, so he could grasp it.

It was a small case. I was surprised it looked solid and intact. My heart thrummed. Suddenly my face felt warm. I supposed it was the thrill of adventure, of discovery, but it wasn't all happy. There was no one I would rather have shared this with than my grandfather. There was no one else to whom it would have held such meaning. I imagined him saying, "I remember my daddy talking about the lost box, or the hidden box," or some such thing. In a world where my Grand and Gran were still with us, one or the other would've known everything to be known about whatever was inside.

Roger carried the box over to my chair and then nodded toward the cabin. "Would you prefer to open it privately?"

Everyone was focused on that box and us. My initial response was to go ahead and open it, but now I hesitated.

The stone expert said, "Consider waiting and have an antique or archival expert open it. It's in pretty good shape—excellent shape, considering." He nodded at the box. "Could've been there for a century or more. You can see it's wrapped in an oilcloth to protect it, but the folds don't quite match up, so it could've been hidden but accessed at some time or other."

"My grandfather might've disturbed it in recent years. He died about twenty years ago."

"I don't think it's been disturbed for many, many years. Much longer than that."

"Maybe it was moved from the old cabin when this house was built. Maybe it was originally there."

"Old," he said.

He was right. This was a task best entrusted to the hands of professional archivists. The box might turn out to be empty, but I preferred to be cautious. This was about my family's history, the Coopers and Cooper's Hollow.

"That's a good idea. Could we put it in my car? It's probably safest there."

"I agree."

I tugged at Roger's sleeve. "There was another place. It was near the foot of Gran's bed. Probably about fifteen feet from the hearth. Gran talked about it being a safe spot, a hiding place under the floorboards. I have no idea whether anything was actually stored there. I'd forgotten about it, but seeing what was under the hearth reminded me."

Roger spoke loudly enough for everyone to hear. "There may be another hiding place here." He waved his hands, indicating a large area. "Be careful in case there's other personal property hidden under the floor that survived the fire."

He turned to me. "Keys?" He took them and secured the box in my car.

Soon after the hearthstones were marked and moved, the front-end loader was back at work. The driver had started in the front porch area and was working his way back. I think the earlier find made everyone more aware of the age of the house and of the possibility of finding other family treasure. Sure enough, about thirty minutes later, one of the guys called out. The driver kept the shovel up and unmoving while the young man who'd yelled picked up objects from the ground.

He held up several of Gran's spoons. She'd kept her silver in a case, and though we found no sign of it, it was meaningful to me to hold the sooty, tarnished utensils. I recognized the floral pattern as her mother's wedding silver.

Other items found their way out of the ashes, but they were mostly broken dishes and partially burned fabrics—nothing exciting. It was, in fact, rather depressing. There was no evidence of anything in the hidden space under Gran's bed, only a gaping hole into which the flooring and assorted junk had fallen.

I was standing there, wishing for a proper ladies' room and thinking about the mystery box, when a car came down the drive—a red sub-SUV—and Ellen climbed out. She waved at me, then spoke to the person in the vehicle, closed the door, and it drove away.

Arms wide, and despite my dirt and ash smudges, I hugged her hard.

"Was that Bonnie driving? What's up?"

"Nothing's up." She kissed my cheek. "I wanted to see what was happening out here. I knew you were still here, since you didn't answer your cell phone. Mom, seriously, how are you going to live where you can't get cell reception?"

Ellen didn't wait for a response. She was already waving at Roger. I noticed several of the work crew eyeing her. My temper rose. Ellen would never forgive me if I embarrassed her by instructing the workmen on manners. Still, if they didn't mind those manners, all bets were off.

She must've asked Roger about the worksite because he was walking the perimeter with her, pointing at this and that. She was always extra nice to Roger. I laughed, reminded that he was her pick for me. As I watched, he pointed across the creek toward the springhouse, then pointed again to where the front of the new house would begin.

Her smile stopped my breath. Even after all these years, she owned my heart. Would I have bothered with this project if not in the hope she'd come home again? And, in the future, bring her husband and children? I think I would have, but I would've put a lot less money and effort into it. The totality of it was for more than me—for Gran, though she was gone, and for Ellen and her children.

"Mom"—she was back at my side—"this is going to be fabulous." Suddenly a little embarrassed, she added, "Not that our old home wasn't wonderful, and not that our house now isn't, but this sounds amazing. Roger was telling me about the springhouse logs and the fireplace stone and all that. Gran's house, but with all the new cool stuff."

I hugged her again, pressing my face into her hair, so sweet smelling, but I didn't hold her for long. I guess we had a sort of bargain. I was allowed those grabs in public as long as they were quick and brief.

"I like how my room will face the back and the woods. I'll have a gorgeous view of the creek and the forest. Except I won't be here to enjoy it."

"By the time you graduate, the building should be well along. You'll have a good idea of the final product to take as a memory and to come back home to."

"Speaking of going away, I have some things I need. I've been working on that list for college." She smiled, her dimples showing.

"Oh really?"

One of the workmen shouted, drawing both of our attention.

They'd found another box. I ran with the others to see.

This box was bigger but flatter, and made of what appeared to be tin. Instead of being wrapped in oilcloth, a checked vinyl tablecloth had been folded around it and secured with twine.

I recognized that tablecloth.

"What's this?" a man's voice called out. "Ms. Cooper?"

Roger stopped me from climbing into the wreckage.

"I understand. I'll wait." I hadn't seen that tablecloth in years. Since before Gran passed. It had covered her kitchen table until it disappeared.

The vinyl fabric had decayed and softened. This box hadn't held up as well as the aged wooden box found under the hearth. The outside was filthy and corroded, but it appeared to be intact. Might the inside be water-damaged? I wasn't waiting to find out. Gran had wrapped this with her own hands.

Roger saw my excitement—how could he not? He carried the box himself, asking me, "Where to? The cabin?"

I nodded. Ellen walked with us and held open the door. Roger set the box on the wedging table. I practically pushed them aside.

"This was Gran's tablecloth." I could hardly imagine the effort it had taken for her to wrap this and hide it beneath the floor.

The twine holding the tablecloth in place fell apart at my touch. Forewarned, I eased the tablecloth from around the package. It was smudged with black ash, mud, and charred wood. My hands were soon as black and gritty as the vinyl, but the tablecloth had done its job. The box was intact, and a tiny latch held it shut. No lock.

Ellen and Roger were so close to me that I felt their breath on my hair as I reached toward the box. What sort of treasure would Gran put in here? I lifted the lid, saw a flash of pink, and realized I might be making a big mistake.

"What's that, Mom?" Ellen spoke with delight. "Is that my baby book?"

CHAPTER EIGHT

Eva had brought the pink book tucked in the side of the grocery box. I remembered that day clearly. She'd also brought the local newspaper listing Ellen's birth, which had prompted me to want to do better for my daughter than that bare announcement. I'd written my own version and drawn the pictures and had put those in the baby book.

After Ellen's death, I hadn't thought about the book. When I did, I couldn't find it. I was OK with not finding it.

Now I knew what had become of the baby book. Gran had hidden it here during our grief. What exactly had I written in it? Anything that might cause a problem?

Ellen reached for the book. I grabbed her hands. "Wait. It's probably fragile." I added, "You know, the fact is, I'm embarrassed. I didn't keep up the book. I didn't record first steps. No first teeth." I fumbled about in my brain looking for other excuses. "I had my hands full with Gran, you know."

"Mom, I understand."

Ellen couldn't quite hide her disappointment, and I could hardly blame her. I released her hands. "OK, honey. Be easy with it."

My daughter lifted the book from the box. There were a few smaller items in the box, but my attention was focused on Ellen and the baby book. She set it gently on the table. The page edges were slightly rippled, as if moisture had been absorbed, but when she opened the cover, the pages themselves were untouched.

"Oh, Mommy."

She hadn't called me *Mommy* in a while. Only *Mom*. *Mommy* was reserved for times of great distress or apology.

I saw the lock of hair in clear plastic. I recalled Gran snipping it for a keepsake. I'd forgotten the drawing of the infant Ellen. The tiny hand, the soft cap of baby hair, and so much more, that I felt the feathery curls almost under my fingertips again. That baby smell . . .

She read it aloud—that handwritten announcement on the cheap notebook paper. It had faded, but was clearly legible.

Something in my brain tried to split. The reality? The clash of realities? The young-adult Ellen reading the birth announcement of her predecessor? Roger put his arm behind me, around my waist. I'd forgotten his presence. Only when I felt his body alongside mine did I realize I was cold. My vision, which had grown unaccountably blurry, cleared, but a tiny vibration, no more than a shimmer inside me, caused me to shake.

"Oh, Mommy," Ellen repeated, then added, "that's beautiful." She turned the page, and there was my drawing of Gran holding our sweet baby Ellen. Ellen sighed, then laughed. "It says I was born with blue eyes! Imagine if they'd stayed that color?" She picked up a plastic bag. Within it was a keepsake—soft golden-brown curls.

Then it happened. I don't know exactly what. Roger was saying something about how lots of babies' eyes change color as they get older, their hair, too, but his voice faded, and then . . .

He was beside me. Ellen was upset and crying out. My head ached. Somehow, I was on the pottery cabin floor.

Roger's arm was around my back, and he was saying, "You're dehydrated. You've been out here all day."

"Mommy. Mom? Are you OK?"

I touched my face. It felt a little numb, and my skin was clammy.

"Get her some water, will you? There are bottles in the cooler in the back of my truck."

"I fell?"

"You fainted," Roger said, his voice calm. "Luckily I was right beside you."

"My head hurts."

"Dehydration." He lifted me to a sitting position. "How's that? Any dizziness?"

I saw the edge of the box on the table above and the book lying beside it.

"Hannah?" he prompted.

My nails were pinching him. I forcibly relaxed my grip, and Ellen came rushing back in, flushed and twisting the cap off the bottle of water. She tried to press it to my lips, spilling it down my shirt.

"Wait," I said. I sat up the rest of the way and leaned forward. I drank the water. It was cool and felt good going down. I closed my eyes and nodded. When I opened them, I saw their worried faces. "Help me up, please."

Their voices sounded around me. "Are you sure?" and "Take it easy. You might be light-headed." But back on my feet, I felt steady. I brushed at my wet shirt. "I'm fine, truly."

"Come sit out here," Roger said. "I'll drive you home as soon as I let the guys know. We can pick up your car tomorrow."

"What?" I shook my head. "I'll sit for a minute and drink the water, but I'm fine. I don't know what happened. Maybe it was dehydration, but I'm good now. No need to worry."

Roger looked doubtful. "Are you sure?"

"I am. I'm fine." I was grateful for the chair.

Roger brought a second lawn chair over for Ellen. She perched on the edge of it, only inches away from me, looking very uncomfortable and ready to grab for me at a moment's notice.

"Mom?"

"Yes, sweetie?"

"How are you feeling?"

"I was dehydrated, that's all."

"You scared me." After a moment, she said, "Thank you for drawing those pictures of me. I never had any baby pictures, and I understand why, because of the fire and everything, but now to have some and to know they were drawn by you is the most amazing feeling, Mom." She pressed a hand to her eye and sniffled, then made a show of shaking off the emotionalism. "I'm being silly."

"Not at all. I wish I had real baby pictures of you. I don't have any of me, either."

"Mom, let me drive you home."

I gave her a look.

"We'll knock off soon," Roger said. "I know you want to be here for the work, but you've had enough today. Besides, we've made good progress." He went into the cabin and returned quickly, holding the opened tin box. He stopped beside me.

"Hannah, what about the rest of these things?"

In all the excitement, we'd forgotten there were other items in the box. Ellen moved closer again. I picked up a small oblong box. It looked like a carved wooden jeweler's case, and I knew.

"My grandmother's pearls." Tears pricked at my eyes.

"They're beautiful, Mom."

I nodded. "She rarely wore them. They were her mama's before hers."

"Can I touch them?" Ellen asked.

I thought I'd lost them forever. I picked up the pearls carefully, fearful the string would break, and laid them on Ellen's palms. Ellen didn't speak, but after a moment she handed them back. Silently, I received them and returned them to the case.

Gran had managed to pack these away and then get herself down to the floor and back up again . . . during those dark few days after our baby left us. I didn't remember those days. Or nights. But that was the only explanation.

She'd tidied up loose ends—things that might hurt me and that hurt her, too. She'd tucked away the pain, hiding it with her treasures. I'm sure she intended to remind me someday that this box existed, otherwise what was the point of putting it in safekeeping? But something had interfered . . . had changed that plan, had perhaps even changed Gran's memory of it, as her reality had apparently rewritten itself on the day that a child showed up on our porch and restored her happiness.

I allowed Ellen to drive us home. I wanted to reward her for her kindness, to show I trusted her, and to give her another opportunity for practice and experience.

"I know you probably worry about me driving because of how your mother and father died." She looked over at me as she pulled from the driveway onto the main road. "But you don't need to worry. I'm a good driver."

"Keep your eyes on the road and your mind on what you're doing." I laid my head back against the headrest. *Because of how your mother and father died,* she'd said. Should I tell her the truth? Why? If not for Duncan Browne, I would never have known . . . unless some busybody someday broke that code of silence and told me.

My grandparents' withdrawal from social life, at least Gran's, was probably to avoid the gossip. Maybe also to reduce the opportunity for me to hear about it? And then time had passed, and the memory of it, surely hot when the crime happened, had dimmed and been pushed out of the limelight by new gossip.

We'd accepted Gran's ill health as the reason for her not going to town or church or socializing. I knew now it was more than that. She was doing what she could to control her world, her reality.

I guess my brain was still addled from the dehydration or the fainting spell, but it occurred to me that I could solve the problem of Ellen hearing about it from someone else. I said, "Actually, it's private family business, and I'd prefer to keep it that way."

"Like a secret? What?" She frowned.

"It's a very sad story. Are you sure you want to hear it?"

She glanced over. "Tell me."

"Eyes straight ahead. Pay attention to the road, please. Or better still, why don't you pull over at the next opportunity? The lumberyard is just ahead."

"Yes, ma'am." Ellen put on the blinker. She slowed and pulled into the parking lot, putting the car into park, and sat back. She looked at me, waiting.

The irony of discussing it here, in this parking lot where I'd read the clippings, wasn't lost on me.

"I found out as an adult that my parents didn't die in a car crash. Duncan Browne told me."

"Mr. Browne? Why?"

"Gran thought I should know but couldn't tell me herself, so she asked him to. In thinking back, I wonder whether Grand would've told me if it was up to him. I suspect Gran wouldn't let him."

"Oh, Mom. How did they die? *Did* they die? Are they alive?" Her voice was edged with excitement.

I dashed that strange, odd hope right away. "No, they're dead. They died soon after I was born."

"But not in a car accident?"

"No, sweetie. Sometimes people aren't who we think they are. People can wear pleasant masks, and maybe they mean well and would do right by the other person, but at some point their darker nature, sometimes their true nature, comes out."

I was proud of her, but a cautionary tale might not be a bad idea. Knowing the truth might have been valuable for me, too, when I was her age.

"A handsome young man came to town. Anne Marie, my mother, met him, and he swept her off her feet."

"A lot like what happened with you, Mom."

"Well, sort of, but not really. I delayed going off to college because of Gran and then met your father and had you . . ." I shrugged. "Well, maybe kind of like me." I smiled to reassure her. "But also very different."

I continued. "They fell in love and eloped. Mr. Browne said my grandparents tried, but they couldn't like him. When their daughter came home already married, they took the couple in, and everything was good for a while. She found out she was pregnant about the time he lost his job. He changed. He became suspicious and moody and eventually threatening."

She frowned. "He was really a bad guy after all."

"Maybe. I don't think it's as simple as that. Remember what I said about wearing masks? I think he knew who he wanted to be. I think he tried to be that person. But there was a sickness in his head. When things changed and the pressure got too rough, the darker part of his nature came out."

"What happened?"

"Soon after I was born, he killed her, and then he killed himself."

Ellen's eyes widened. Her jaw tightened, and she pressed her lips together as if she couldn't decide what to say or think. Finally she whispered, "Is that true?"

"It's true, sweetheart, and very sad." I touched her shoulder. "We'll never really know, but I think he realized and regretted what he'd done. I want to believe that." I shook my head. "But it was too late to take it back. He couldn't face it. He couldn't live with himself."

After several seconds of heavy silence, Ellen finally said, "You were lucky you had Gran and Grand."

"I was incredibly lucky. They were at the house when it happened, but Gran had me out in the yard with her and didn't know until they heard the shots inside."

Ellen's lips parted, words wanted to be said, but she seemed to have difficulty finding the right ones. Finally, she said, "How awful for them. For everyone."

I nodded.

She added, "Your parents. My dad's parents. I don't have grandparents." Her tone was pained. "Things like this affects the whole family, doesn't it?"

"It does."

"Does it make you sad?" she asked.

"I don't have any memory of my parents, so it's a little different in that way for me."

"That was a lot of people living in the one house. It was small . . . I'm sorry. I don't mean to criticize the house."

"Well, it's true, certainly. Maybe that intensified the pressure on him. Living with his in-laws and in close quarters . . ."

"Maybe it was good they didn't tell you. Every day you would've been thinking about how your mom and dad died right there in the house."

"Perhaps. And my knowing the truth would've made it impossible for Gran to pretend otherwise."

Ellen sat in silence for a minute, staring ahead. "Then you fell in love with my dad and he died. How awful it must've been for Gran to experience such tragedy all over again."

I let her words rest in the silence. As long as I didn't contradict the words or add to them, they were almost the truth. They were Ellen's truth anyway, as far as she knew.

So many lies. It had felt right at the time. The thing to do. The best choice. But more and more, I was feeling their weight.

"Let's get some supper."

Ellen put the car into drive and turned on the blinker before pulling back out onto Cross County Road.

"Dell's Diner or home?" she asked.

"Home, I think. How would you feel about bacon and eggs tonight?"

She smiled. "I'll cook."

"You?" I teased.

"Just like my mom taught me."

I reached out to touch her hair. "I'm proud of you, my dearest daughter. I can't imagine a greater gift than you in my life." There'd been another Ellen, the first Ellen. The two had long ago merged into one in my heart, and my head had had to accept it, and reaccept it, from time to time.

"Then I think we're both lucky, Mom. I'm lucky I was born to you. And I appreciate knowing the truth. I understand why you didn't tell me before, when I was younger and all, and I'm glad you trust me with knowing now."

That night, as I was locking up and turning off lights on my way to bed, I noticed the baby book was gone from the kitchen table. I'd placed it there when we came home. It had still been there when we ate our supper seated at the island.

Like Gran, like Ellen? Except that unlike Gran, who'd hidden it, Ellen had claimed it. When I walked past her room, I saw it on her desk, and it felt right. That night, I settled in my bed, cozy with the blanket over my legs, and wrote down a list of "firsts." First tooth, first steps, first birthday—not the actual events, but as I wrote them down, I imagined how it would've been in real life, and it almost felt as if they'd happened the way I described them. I even drew little pictures of the reminiscences. It was the best I could do for her. I was careful to note at the top that I couldn't be totally sure the dates were accurate, since I was recording the events long after the fact.

It was a small gift for Ellen. When I was done, I went to her room.

She was asleep. Teenagers slept like toddlers, except they hogged the whole bed. Adulthood would steal the ability to sleep soundly and heedlessly through the night. By the light of the hallway, I went to her desk and slipped the papers from my journal into her baby book for her to find in the morning. Then I stood near her bed and watched her sleeping.

Her eyelashes fluttered and she mumbled, "Is something wrong, Mom?"

I touched her hair. "No, all's well. Good night, my sweet Ellen."

CHAPTER NINE

It was as if the clearing away of the fire debris was a signal for time to fast forward.

In April I watched the foundation being dug, the concrete footing poured, the bricks rise, and the fresh gravel being dumped into what would become the crawl space. The floor joists were installed and plywood sheets were laid for the subfloor. The framing had begun.

We were suddenly in May, and Ellen's graduation was less than a month away.

I went out to the jobsite most days, but only for a short stay. I tried to refocus on my pottery and the shop, and I also began planning for the move.

The lights were out in the front room of Cub Creek Pottery, and the door sign was turned to **CLOSED**. There was little traffic anyway. I supplied pottery to gift shops in the regional area and to a few locations outside of Virginia, but for the most part, my clients were few and honestly, my pottery work was uninspired. When I saw the clay work being produced by others, especially online or in glossy magazines, I felt mediocre.

It would be different, I told myself, when I was back out in the Hollow. Working in Cooper's Hollow, away from this shop in town that had no history, no flavor for me, would provide the spark.

Ellen was consumed with preparing for college, talking about college, final exam nerves, and texting incessantly with her friends about all of it. I was glad she had friends to stress and de-stress with because it was wearing me down. They were going out tonight—she and Bonnie and a couple of their other friends. They were going to see a movie, as if this were the last movie they'd ever see . . . which it kind of was—it was the last movie they'd see as high school seniors and in a local theater and so on. Such high drama, and they reveled in it.

I'd protested that this was Sunday and she had school in the morning and not to be out late, and then realized that was likely the last time I'd be giving that admonition.

I pulled out the clay and did some wedging. I threw it against the table. I pounded on it with my fist. By the time the consistency felt right, the worst of my stress had eased, but I felt deflated again. Ellen would soon graduate and would leave for Tech by mid-August. Wedging clay didn't fix that. I wrapped the clay tightly in plastic, and washed up at the sink.

My cell phone rang. Roger.

"Everything good?" he asked.

"Sure."

"I missed seeing you today. Did you choose the light fixtures you wanted in the great room and in the kitchen?"

"Not yet. I'll get it done." I turned off the power switches as I spoke.

"Are you up for dinner?"

I stopped. "Tonight?"

"That's the usual timing for dinner. Or we can call it supper, if you like that better."

He was trying to lighten the mood. I tried to smile.

"Honestly, Roger, I'm not feeling so great. I'm a little headachy."

"Going out to eat might help."

"It might, but I don't think I'm up to making conversation."

There was a long pause, and then he said, "I don't need conversation. We're friends. You can be any way you want or need to be with me."

"Ellen is going out with Bonnie and some other friends this evening."

"Just girls? Or is this a girl-boy thing?"

My silence lasted longer than intended.

"I see," he said.

"No, really, it's fine. It's a group of friends. I hadn't considered . . . but she would've said if there was an actual boyfriend, right?" I sighed. Ellen was pretty and smart but hadn't dated much, and I was totally fine with that. I hadn't handled dating or love very well. My mother hadn't. I hoped Ellen, who was much more sensible and goal-oriented, would do better, but a little more maturity wouldn't hurt her, so going out with friends in groups seemed safer. Of course, there was no guarantee about anything.

My brain was too scrambled. Roger was right.

"Maybe I do need to get out and do something normal," I said. "Something pleasantly distracting."

"Five thirty?" he suggested.

"That will work. Where shall we go?"

"How about Italian in Louisa?"

"Perfect," I said.

Roger rang the doorbell at five thirty exactly. He gave me the once-over and said, "You seem better now."

"I am. I don't understand what's wrong with me."

"Do you want to talk about it?"

I shook my head. "No." As I snapped the seat belt into place, the words came anyway.

"Regrets, maybe. We all make mistakes, right? Some we can take back. Some we can't." *Or wouldn't even if we could,* I added silently.

"That sounds . . . philosophical. Or remorseful."

"Probably some of each."

"Want to talk about it? Things usually make a lot more sense and assume more reasonable proportions when shared with a friend."

"Not this, Roger. Trust me. Besides, everyone has done something they end up questioning time and again."

"Well, you're right. We all make mistakes or choices that go wrong. I've made plenty of mistakes in my life, and in every job I've had. If you're living, then mistakes are guaranteed. It makes the successes all the sweeter. That's life, Hannah."

He touched my hand. His hands were larger than mine. My fingers had been toughened over the years of manhandling clay, and I didn't get manicures often enough. His strong, square hands were well groomed; the fingernails were clean and neat. That seemed important to me. His were honest hands. Gently, I eased mine away.

We'd hardly been seated in the restaurant when my cell phone rang. Ellen's name was on the screen. I grabbed it and answered.

"Ellen?"

"Mom? It's OK. I'm not hurt."

Her voice was breathless. She sounded like she was crying.

"What's wrong?" I was already standing, looking around the room. *Where is my purse? My keys?*

"What's wrong?" Roger echoed my words.

Ellen continued. "They're taking us to the hospital in Charlottesville. But I'm fine. A couple of the kids were hurt. We hit a tree, Mom."

My heart rate ratcheted up even more. "I'm on my way. I'll meet you there." I added, "How are you getting to the hospital?"

"By ambulance. Please be careful, Mom. Don't rush. I'll be there soon, and I'm OK, truly."

I didn't want to disconnect. I wanted this phone connection to stay live all the way to Charlottesville, if possible, but Ellen said, "I need to let Bonnie call her parents. I'll see you soon, Mom."

She disconnected.

My purse? Where did I leave it? My hands clenched, and I realized I was holding it.

Roger was suddenly standing beside me, his hands on my shoulders. "Calm down."

"Calm down? My daughter is on her way to the hospital. I don't have time to think it through, much less calm down."

"I'll take you. You can't drive like this. Your daughter needs you to arrive in one piece." His eyes bore into mine. "Now take a deep breath and let it out slowly, then tell me what she said."

"She said she's not hurt. The ambulance is taking them to the hospital. A tree. They hit a tree, Roger." My voice went high as it hit the end of the sentence. I closed my eyes. "I need to calm down. You'll drive me there?"

"Of course. Besides, I care about Ellen. I'd like to see for myself that she's OK."

"That's what Ellen said . . . that she was OK. *OK* is such a big word, isn't it? A huge word, an awful word, a word that means nothing because it could mean anything." I forced my eyes to open. "Let's go."

In the fringe of the woods bordering the winding state road, wild eyes lit the night. Deer, of course, but the eyes of other creatures, too. My hands had been shaking since I'd gotten the call, and all those eyes seemed threatening. Anything that might delay me in reaching Ellen was unacceptable. I wanted Roger to drive faster.

Roger noticed my anxiety. He reached across the center console and grasped my hand. "She's fine, Hannah. She said so, and we'll see her soon."

I nodded. "Two of her friends aren't fine, though, and she could be downplaying her own situation. She could have an injury that doesn't show up right away."

"There's no value in worrying. Once you're there and you can see for yourself, you'll see she's fine, and you'll be fine."

"You're right, Roger. Thank you."

"That's better."

"I could've driven. I'm sorry to have dragged you out here."

"I volunteered. Besides, you're too distracted. Distracted, worried driving—it's not a good mix." He smiled at the night and the dark road ahead. "I'm glad you let me help tonight."

"I'm accustomed to being independent."

Roger took the ramp onto the interstate. Not much farther, though the Charlottesville stoplights and traffic slowed us down. The stop-and-start pace wreaked havoc on my nerves.

Roger spoke again. "You had to be independent. You took care of yourself, your grandmother, your daughter—all on your own. It's a good thing to be, but you have to know when and how to let others help you."

I could've told him that if you allow others into your life, then suddenly they want to know about you, and secrets have a way of getting out when people get too close. I didn't say that, though, and instead told him, "You're helping me. You're building my house."

"I build many houses. It's my profession. It's not the same thing."

"What about you?" I turned the focus to him. "You're also very independent."

Roger frowned. "It wasn't a choice. It's just how it worked out."

"It was the same for me. Not what I'd planned. Gran needed my help, so I put off college, only for a year, I thought, and then along came Ellen. But you know most of that already. We've talked about it before."

"I'm sorry I never met your grandmother. I—"

"How much longer do you think?" I interrupted.

"We're here. There's the ER sign." He touched my cheek. "You going to be OK?"

"OK?" I said, then caught myself. "What a word." We both laughed a little, and that helped. I felt stronger.

Roger dropped me at the door to the emergency room. "You go," he said. "I'll park the car." I nodded thanks, slipped out of his vehicle, and dashed through the automatic doors.

I blew through the sliding doors at the hospital, past the reception area, then headed straight back. I expected a security guard to grab me. I was confident I could give him the slip or drag him with me, but no one challenged me or tried to stop me from reaching my daughter. As if we each had built-in homing devices, I went straight to Ellen's cubicle and pushed aside the curtains. She was sitting in an ER bed but was unattended and, indeed, except for a bump and a bandage on her forehead, she looked fine. I dropped my purse on the foot of the wheeled bed and threw wide my arms. Ellen reached toward me. We hugged for one long moment. Ellen surprised me. Her grip was like iron, and she kept repeating, "Mommy, Mommy, Mommy . . ." over and over.

"Are you Ms. Cooper?" a man said.

I turned toward him as I tried to ease Ellen's grip. "I am."

"We did a head scan to be on the safe side. All her vitals are good. There are no broken bones. The bump on the head appears superficial. She'll need to take it easy for a couple of days. She may also feel some anxiety or emotional trauma. If that develops, be sure to contact your family doctor and—"

"Wait a minute," I interrupted. I kept my hands on Ellen but let some air come between us. "What happened?"

The doctor looked toward the desk, beyond where I could see from my vantage point with the curtain halfway pulled and blocking my view. "I'll let the officer know you're here. Meanwhile, your daughter can fill you in."

His words were colorless, but his face was kind, and the smile he offered Ellen was warm. That told me she was OK—OK as far as the police officer was concerned, too—I felt sure. There was nothing severe in the doctor's expression—at least not toward my daughter. He left.

I sat on the edge of the bed. "Tell me what happened."

"I don't know, Mom. Honest. We were on our way to the movie theater in Charlottesville. We were still out of town, out in the country, when . . . when it all went crazy."

"Who was driving?"

"Bonnie. She hit her head. Or the airbag hit her. I don't know, but she was bleeding a lot." Ellen touched her own head to indicate where Bonnie's head was bloody.

"Your head . . . Is that swelling from the airbag?"

"Um, no. I was in the backseat. Her car doesn't have side airbags."

I frowned. "Who was in the front seat with Bonnie?"

"Her boyfriend, John. You met him once, I think."

"How is he?"

"I think he hurt his shoulder."

"You were in the backseat?"

She nodded.

"With?"

"Braden."

It took all my inner strength to control my reaction, to keep my expression even. Her friend was in the front seat, driving, and Ellen was in the backseat with a boy. I tried to digest that and speak without sounding too suspicious or critical. "Do I know him?"

"No, I don't think so. His family moved back to the area last year."

"I didn't realize it was a double date."

"Mom. I'm a senior. I'm allowed, right?"

"Did you deliberately let me think this was just another group date?" I waved my hand, but gently, then straightened the sheet over her legs. "If so, I'd like to know why?"

"It's not a big deal, Mom. I feel like you don't want me to date. I didn't want you to worry."

"No worries. We'll talk about this more at home." I touched her forehead and smoothed stray hairs back out of her face. "And yes, it is perfectly fine for you to date. I want to know beforehand so I don't find out this way. But it's not worth you wasting even a moment of worry over it right now."

"Braden's hurt, Mom." She looked so young when she bit her lip. She was trying not to cry.

"Badly?"

"I don't know. His arm is the worst, I think. Maybe his head. He wasn't wearing a seat belt."

"Was he thrown from the car?"

"No, but he was thrown around inside the car." She touched her forehead. "I think this came from him. His elbow, maybe. It was crazy, Mom, like the scariest roller coaster you can imagine."

"It's over now, Ellen." I wanted to hug or shake the memory from her. She seemed trapped in it.

"It went on and on. The car kept moving and hitting stuff, and Bonnie was screaming. The windshield broke, and I saw the cracks spread across like it was in slow motion." She looked at me. "When I got out of the car, I couldn't believe we weren't all that far from the road." She shuddered.

I wrapped my arms around her again and hugged her while I pressed my lips to her hair.

A man's voice came from behind us. I turned, expecting to see the police officer, and saw, instead, the boy from my past, the first Ellen's father, Spencer Bell. The air whooshed from my lungs.

He was older, of course, as I was. His dark hair was thinning a little on top, but otherwise, time had been kind to him.

"Hannah? Is that you? Hannah Cooper?"

He moved toward me, and I used Ellen as an excuse to turn away from him—buying a short second to compose my face—and then stood and stepped away from the bed.

I smoothed my blouse and pushed my hair behind my ear. I didn't know what to do except to smile pleasantly as I said, "Spencer? What a surprise."

He extended his hand, and I had no choice but to take it. No reason to avoid it, really, I told myself. He was ancient history. He had no bearing on my present.

He shook my hand, then pulled me into a hug. Inwardly, I recoiled. What was going on here?

"Hi, Mr. Bell," Ellen said. "How's Braden?"

His mood was somber. "He's doing well considering. He's lucky he only has a broken arm."

I recognized his emotional struggle to reorient priorities and caring, to be able to say "only" a broken arm, and my incipient panic eased.

"It will heal well, I hope," I said.

"Mom, this is Braden's father."

I attempted a small joke. "I figured that out."

He pointed toward me and smiled at Ellen. "Don't tell me this is your mother? We're old friends from high school. Did you know?"

Ellen shook her head. "I didn't."

Spencer smiled. "Ellen's a wonderful girl. She and Braden are together a lot. I know you're proud of her, with good reason." His brow furrowed as he stared at me. "You and I . . . I don't think we've seen each other since the summer we graduated? Then I went off to college. That was when Braden was born. Melissa's son. You remember Melissa?" He forced a smile again.

I wanted to be sympathetic. He was worried about his son. But I didn't want to encourage this conversation.

"I hope your son has a swift recovery. I'm glad he wasn't . . . more badly injured."

He nodded. "Me too. Truly. I saw the car, so this is nothing short of a miracle." With that, he gave me a wry grin, turned, and walked away.

I was reminded of the boy who'd written my number on his arm and changed the course of my life. My head ached. I rubbed the back of my neck, telling myself to let this go. It meant nothing.

This whole experience was too much. But I was handling it, I reassured myself, despite the humming in my ears and the rush of heat in my chest and face. Then the officer walked up.

"Are you all right, ma'am?"

"Yes, I'm fine."

"Are you sure? Why don't you sit down? Would you like some water?"

"No, I'm fine, really."

"You're very pale, ma'am."

I forced a smile. "I've never done this before, never been in this position." I sat on the edge of the bed, and that seemed to satisfy him.

"Hopefully you never will be again." He nodded toward Ellen, who bit her lip. "Can you confirm her name, age, and your relationship to her?"

I did. He asked permission to speak with Ellen. I said yes, if Ellen felt up to it. Ellen said she did. But she didn't have much to offer.

"I wasn't paying attention. I don't know what happened. One moment we were driving along, and I was talking to my friend Braden in the backseat. Suddenly there was a bright light."

"From outside?"

She shook her head and looked at me, confused. "I don't know. Everything happened at once."

"Where were you coming from?"

"We'd been at Bonnie's house waiting for John and Braden." She shrugged. "When they arrived, we took off. We were on the way to Charlottesville to go see a movie. And that's it. If you're asking about drinking or anything—no."

He nodded.

"How are the others?" I asked.

"I'll leave the injuries to the doctors, but lucky. Very lucky. Your daughter came through the best."

"Mom always fusses about wearing my seat belt. I guess she's right."

"Moms usually know best," he said.

They released Ellen soon after. She insisted on going to see the other kids. Braden was with an orthopedist, and the other boy was getting stitches. Bonnie was bruised and subdued. Her parents were with her. Her mother's eyes were swollen and red. Her dad looked calm. I knew them, but barely, and we exchanged a few words, then I touched Ellen's arm and told her it was time to leave.

Roger was in the waiting room. I'd almost forgotten him. Ellen was delighted to see him. She brightened and hugged him.

"You brought Mom to me? Thanks."

"You look good." He smiled at her. "How do you feel?"

Ellen put her arms in both of ours. "Tired," she said, then added, "Take me home, please."

The doctor had given Ellen pills for pain. I was sure she'd be hurting come the morning. But she was young and resilient. I was a very lucky mom.

When we got home, I made us tea, and we had a small snack, but Ellen's eyelids were fluttering as she tried to stay upright and awake. Finally, I told her to get some sleep. She gave me a huge hug and a kiss on the cheek, and then went into the hallway. The light came on in her room and spilled back up the hallway. Within minutes it was off. Before I'd finished picking up the kitchen, she was sound asleep.

I stood in her doorway and watched her sleep. I wanted to smooth the hair back from her face and tuck the blanket around her snug and tight. I remembered when she'd made a much smaller bump in the bed.

She was grown now. A young woman. I was very proud of her. How close had I come to losing her tonight?

The temptation was strong to set a chair into the open doorway and watch her all night, but she didn't need me in that way any longer, and I wasn't as young as I used to be. I needed my rest. I moved on down the hall to my room, turned on the bedside lamp, and then closed the door so the light wouldn't disturb Ellen.

Now what? I sat on the edge of the bed.

Now what?

She hadn't asked about what Spencer had said about us dating years ago. I'd thought she would, and I was prepared to brush it off as meaningless ancient history. Sometimes trauma confused things. While she hadn't asked tonight, she might ask tomorrow. I needed to be prepared.

Prepared? What a sick joke. Ellen was dating Spencer's son.

Spencer Bell. He'd moved back to town, and I'd never had any idea. Small towns weren't so small anymore. People moved out here from the city all the time.

Lies were bound to unravel. One weak thread was all it took. I should've anticipated something like this. My shoulders sagged, heavy with the weight of it all. Was I overwrought? Possibly. But I might also be right.

I whispered a prayer of gratitude for Ellen and for her safety. She and Braden had been in the backseat together and so involved that Ellen had no idea of what preceded, or precipitated, the accident, but she'd been wearing her seat belt. Exactly how close was their relationship? Spencer said they were together frequently.

Was Braden planning to attend Tech, too? I would ask her, but not tonight and maybe not tomorrow. I'd have to see how tomorrow dawned for my daughter and me.

Sleep was elusive. When I did sleep, the dreams were chaotic and filled with warnings. The most memorable was a nightmare in which Spencer and I were arguing and Ellen, standing between us, had simply split into two pieces that collapsed onto the ground. I grabbed the pieces and hugged them to me, wanting her however she was. No matter what. Somehow, in the dream, she was still alive, and people gathered around, taking bets on who she'd be when we put her back together again.

A voice in the background was saying, "Change hurts. Metamorphosis sucks." And someone responded, "No one wants to be the caterpillar." Which made absolutely no sense to me and woke me from my sleep. I groaned, rolled over, and buried my face in the pillow, but I couldn't turn off my brain and find sleep again. I lay in the dark and let them play, both the fears and regrets.

Dreams. Were they prophetic? Probably not. At least, not mine. Without doubt, this dream represented my greatest fears. Hurting my daughter. Possibly losing my daughter. And my guilt.

Some misdeeds could be confessed with an apology offered. Forgiveness could resolve it. Not this time. Ellen would be hurt the most, and I was the one, the only one, with the knowledge.

I thought about those new DNA tests everyone was talking about. About heritage. About genealogy. About medical conditions. Ellen might take one. I couldn't stop her. She wasn't going to be under my supervision much longer. The accident revealed that I didn't know everything she was up to. But as long as I didn't take one of those tests, we were good. Our blood type was the same. So, in the end, as long as I didn't confess . . . I would rather, a thousand times over, bear the burden of my guilty knowledge and spare my child, and our relationship, from the truth.

Guilt, worry—the what-ifs were like the sheets that twisted around me as I tossed and turned, and like the pillows that shifted and grew hot and uncomfortable as I moved this way and that. Sometime after the pivotal hour of three a.m., my brain and body must've given up, worn out, and allowed me to pass out. I hadn't thought to set the alarm, and that was just as well.

"Mom." I was being jiggled. "Mom."

I opened my eyes.

"Good morning. I'm going to school. You don't need to get up. I'm all ready to go, but I didn't want you to worry when you realized I wasn't here."

I pushed up. My bed looked like a war zone. "School?"

"School. I didn't keep my attendance perfect to mess it up near the end."

"You're kidding, right? Go back to bed. You need to rest."

"I'm fine. If I don't feel good later, I can come home, but I'm going for now. Bonnie isn't going this morning. I'll drive myself."

"No. I'll pull on some clothes, and I'll be right there." I climbed out of bed, aching. I was moving like I'd been in the crash instead of Ellen. "Make sure you have money for lunch, or pack something. I'll be ready in ten minutes."

Life will. That was something smart people said. Life will out. Life will find a way.

I thought that meant life goes on and that whatever that basic, primal driver of life was, it won. Every time. It would push through and remind you, often with cruel strokes, that any pretense of human control was an illusion.

We were leaving for school, and Ellen was standing there beside the car. She presented me with a cup of coffee and opened the passenger side door for me. I paused, cup in hand.

"I have to get back on the horse, right, Mom?"

I settled in the passenger seat, almost relieved. "No accidents," I said. "I can't deal with it today."

She smirked. "No problem."

As we drove, I asked, "Did you hear from the others yet?"

"Bonnie and Braden. Bonnie's face is sore today, mostly from the airbag. She has tape on her face for the cuts—plus she has those awful bruises—so she's staying home."

"And Braden?"

"They kept him overnight. He says he's going home today."

"Did he text? Or call?" In my mind, there was a difference.

Ellen blushed.

Great.

We had arrived. Cars, buses, kids—they streamed around us and past us. End of school year excitement charged the air. I felt it, too.

"We'll talk later?"

Ellen grinned. My heart flipped.

"Go throw a pot or two first? Maybe wedge a little clay to work off some energy?"

"Tell me, are you in love with him?"

Her smile grew smaller and yet it deepened. "I don't know. I might be."

I nodded. Ellen falling in love—it was bound to happen one day, of course. It made me want to protect her even more. "Later, gator."

"Love you, Mom."

She was gone. I got out and walked around to the driver's side. She turned and waved. I waved back.

My heart was heavy. It seemed like all my efforts for Ellen and her future were seriously at risk. No matter what I did . . .

I drove home. I needed to stand under the shower, to let the hot water stream over my head and down my body to loosen the muscles. I diffused a mixture of lavender and lemon to surround myself with good-mood stuff. I regretted not having someone I could share my fears with and not worry about condemnation or betrayal. But I didn't. So I steamed in the shower and diffused the air and finished off my morning with another cup of coffee and a sweet roll.

The garden didn't require my attention. I'd only recently moved the seedlings into the yard. But I needed solitude, activity, and fresh air. I donned my gloves and settled down onto the kneepad. Any new weeds were too tiny to find, but I tweaked a leaf or two and crumbled small clumps of soil—performing little nothing acts to relax me.

The morning sun filtered through the leafy branches overhead at this hour. It was warm, but pleasantly so. I lost myself in the tasks. It wouldn't be long before I could replant these in the new beds. Roger was having semi-raised beds constructed for me ahead of the final landscaping so that I could transplant these before the heat of summer set in. The big issue would be watering. I was confident Roger would work that out. Meanwhile, this morning the breeze rustled the leaves over my head, and the squirrels ignored me. They were used to sharing this space with me.

"Hannah?"

I jumped, startled, dropping the spade, then scrambled for it again in some crazy idea it would serve as a weapon.

"I'm sorry, Hannah. I took a chance on finding you home. I hope you don't mind."

Spencer. *Why?* I asked the question silently.

"How did you know I was back here?"

He shrugged and smiled softly. "I knocked on the door. I was about to leave when I heard you singing."

I frowned. "Singing?"

He nodded. "Quietly singing. You have a nice voice. I didn't know."

"How is your son?"

"He'll come home this afternoon. The fracture was clean. They expect him to heal well." He shook his head. "Youth. It's prone to getting hurt, but it's also good for healing."

Finally, I smiled. "That's true."

"How have you been?"

I stood, pulled off my gloves, and gestured toward the patio. "Would you like to sit?"

"I can't stay," he said. "Maybe for a minute."

"Glass of tea?"

He drew in a deep breath. "Are you sure?"

"It's a glass of iced tea, Spencer."

"Then yes. Thank you."

"I'll be right back. Have a seat."

I paused in the kitchen to recoup my calm. His obvious unease gave me some confidence. I took two glasses from the cabinet, poured the tea over ice, and sliced a few lemon wedges. I carried it back out. He was still there. I almost laughed. What had I thought? That he might run away? But then, he had before, hadn't he?

He rose to his feet when I reappeared and held the door open for me. I set the tray on the table, and we both sat, took our tea, and then I waited to find out why he was here.

Spencer took a sip, cleared his throat, then said, "I was surprised to see you at the hospital last night."

I smiled and waited.

"I mean, it never occurred to me Ellen was your daughter. She's a sweet girl. Smart. Beautiful. My son is . . . has a crush on her." He looked away, shrugged, and turned back to face me. "Reminds me of us."

"That was long, long ago. Different times, different people."

"I guess you're right. I hope you don't mind if I skip the small talk?"

"Please do."

"Is there a problem with Braden and Ellen dating?"

My smile vanished. I waited.

"My mother told me long after the fact that you came to the house looking for me. She said you were pregnant."

I might've expected to feel distress, hurt, or maybe embarrassment. In the hospital the previous night, I'd been caught off guard. Now, though, with a cold calculation that surprised me, I ran my finger around the bottom edge of my glass. The condensation was already building up. With an icy, controlled anger, I set the glass carefully on the table.

"That was a very difficult time for me."

His face turned maroon. "I'm sorry, Hannah. I made some bad choices back then. For a while after that, too. I—"

"Ellen isn't your daughter."

"But . . . I mean I saw her birthday was . . . Braden mentioned her birthday, and I realized—"

"You thought you and I had a child together? There's been a lot of years between then and now, and I'm only just hearing from you?"

He shook his head. "Wait a minute."

I met his eyes ruthlessly, but I kept my tone cool and civil. "You aren't her father. I went to your house. I didn't tell your mother I was pregnant with your child. That was her conjecture."

"I—"

I interrupted, speaking as I stood. "I give you credit for not wanting your son to date his half sister, but I assure you the genetic pool is safe, and there's no legal or moral complexity here. We're good."

He stood. "I'm sorry, Hannah. I knew this would be awkward. I've handled it badly."

"I wish you well, Spencer, and I hope Braden has a swift and full recovery. Please give my regards to your mother." I held up my hand. "I do have one request."

"What's that?"

"I would appreciate it if you would encourage our children not to spend time together. Not because they are related, but because they both have plans for the future, separate futures, and I wouldn't want to see those plans sidetracked or interrupted."

He stared at me. "I understand."

"Well, then, I'd better get back to my tasks."

He waved his arms a bit, trying to work up something—I didn't know what. Courage certainly wasn't required. I couldn't offer him forgiveness. What would I forgive him for? I'd informed him he wasn't the father, right? And he wasn't. I was pretty sure I'd managed to avoid any specific lies. Small comfort. My intent and my honesty were very distant cousins here. I wanted him to leave.

"I'm sorry I offended you. I really did have feelings for you, I hope you know that. Any errors I made were due to immaturity and selfishness. I hope you believe me."

"I do. We both made mistakes when we were young, and we're bound to make a few more before we're done living. I want our children to get off to a good start. Maybe avoid some of our mistakes."

Spencer nodded. "I understand and I agree." He looked like he was considering offering me a hand or a hug. Instead, he pressed his hands together and said, "Take care, Hannah. Thanks for talking to me."

He walked away. I waited as he disappeared around the corner of the house. I was proud that I'd held it together.

I picked up my gloves from the table and knelt again in the garden. What had I expected? Potentially far worse. So that was good, right? I'd done well. But it didn't feel like I had. There'd been a tiny voice screaming in my head, yelling that I'd carried his baby. I would've been alone if not for Gran's help, and I'd given birth to his child and loved her with all my being. The tiny body had been buried, but the essence of that child, the memory, the feel and the smell of her were still bound fast in my heart. Even if I could have, I wasn't willing to share that with him. The memory, the feelings were mine alone. He had no place there.

The garden earth was rich and damp. I dug in my fingers, then realized I'd forgotten to put on my gloves. The soil sifted through my bare fingers and fell back to the ground. A tear fell, too. A single tear that hit my hand with force.

Someone moaned. I thought it was probably me.

The icy anger inside began to melt, setting loose the memories. This time I was powerless against them. I crossed my arms over my chest and leaned forward, eyes closed. Soon I was rocking back and forth. I was back on that porch caught in the fierce grip of old pain. And I gave myself up to it.

CHAPTER TEN

The house on Rose Lane had never been our true home. It was a nice enough brick ranch—an older house that needed fixing up when Mr. Browne found it for us. We were grateful to the pastor and his wife for taking care of us, but Ellen and I needed our own place again. We were accustomed to our privacy and not used to being surrounded by the energy, the noise, the needs of others. In that respect, it was probably a good learning experience for both Ellen and me—but we'd watched our home burn only days earlier, so lessons weren't sinking in for either of us.

Mr. Browne tracked us down the morning after the fire. He helped us get back on our feet. He found us the house on Rose Lane, worked out the rental details and then the sale, and introduced us to Roger, billing him as a guy who could fix anything. Roger then helped me make the house ours, and it had turned into a lovely home. We were comfortable there, and we had each other, but it was like a long-term settling in—not intended to be permanent. At least, not permanent for me. When I thought of Ellen and me, I thought of Rose Lane. When I thought of comfort, I saw, smelled, and experienced the old house out in the Hollow.

After Spencer left, the door to reality—or to facing reality and perhaps being destroyed by it—had cracked open. It was only a hairline crack, but the strength of the truth behind it shone through that crack in a blinding jolt. It was more than a confirmation of the unraveling I'd feared last night. My breakdown in the garden unnerved me. After I pulled myself together, I grabbed my purse and set out for the Hollow. I needed to think about the future and what Ellen and I were planning, in a place where I could also find peace.

I stopped at the usual place on the driveway, not in memory of the fire but rather in awe of the changed landscape. The shed was gone. The springhouse was still there but looked different. Someone had been doing something with it. The erosion swale blocked most of the view of the creek, but the cemetery was clearly in view up the hill on the far side, and the area around it appeared untouched.

The framing work was still in progress. Somehow, I'd thought that would move faster.

No other vehicles were in sight. I was alone here, and that suited my need- perfectly. The area to the left of the driveway had been leveled to allow for parking. I pulled in and parked.

When the construction was done, would this become an orchard? Was it sunny enough? Vineyards were becoming popular in central Virginia. I could grow a few grapes . . . Or not. Maybe I'd stick with tomatoes and cucumbers.

I walked up to the house and tried to visualize the final product. This corner, nearest the drive, was where the garage began. Beyond it would be the great room with the kitchen on the back at this end. On the far end would be Ellen's bedroom, a guest room, and a study for me. My bedroom and another guest room would be upstairs. All large, airy rooms.

Roger had cautioned me that people judge building projects by walls and roofs, that erecting the house frame was early days for a construction project and sometimes gave a false impression of progress toward completion. He'd said the majority of the work wouldn't begin until after the walls were up, and to please be patient. I would try.

I found a spot where I could climb into the house without too much effort, and then wandered through it, the wood sub-flooring feeling like a giant stage. No wiring yet. No pipes. Windows and doors were still in the future. I exited via the low spot and walked around back.

A short distance from the house was the cabin. It was the original Cooper home before it became my pottery cabin. Someone had cleared a downed branch from the tin roof, but otherwise, it looked the same as it ever had in my memory. The glass in the small front window looked cleaner, I thought.

Had someone been messing around in there? Roger had said they'd be fixing up the cabin, but I'd told him I wanted to be here, onsite, for any work like that.

I pushed open the heavy door, then paused on the threshold, allowing my eyes to adjust to the gloom and avoid the webs, both spider webs and cobwebs, lurking to catch in one's hair or face. The air felt clearer and fresher. I stared into the room, trying to discern what was different.

The cabin was about fifteen by twenty feet, thick logs and chinked. The fireplace hearth was at one end. At the other end was a narrow, enclosed corner stairway to the loft above. Grand had stored bushel baskets up there and old farm implements in the corners downstairs. There'd been other things stored there, too, most of which he'd moved out when he set it up for me and my pottery. In the winter leading up to Ellen's birth, the first Ellen, I hadn't been out here much. In those months after her birth, I hadn't had the energy. What little clay work I did during that time was while she slept, and mostly, I worked by hand on the kitchen table where I could stay close.

After she left us, though I did some work in fits and starts, it was too hard to give it consistent effort. After Ellen found the butterfly pot, I'd fiddled with the clay a bit, teaching Ellen and entertaining Gran. I hadn't gone back to the clay with any degree of dedication until after we'd settled into the house on Rose Lane and Ellen had started school. That's when I rented the storefront, mostly because I didn't have space for the pottery wheel and the kiln and the clay at the house. I'd set up the shop and thought I'd do great work with the modern facilities and lots of hours to dedicate to it, but I hadn't. I sold a few pieces to design agencies and such and gave some lessons. Not much to show for so many years.

It would be different when I was working in the Hollow again. In this cabin, I'd make the leap to more authentic creativity. But the building needed work. The old propane lines . . . everything—it all needed overhauling and updating.

Yet someone had been working in here. Cleaning it, and what else? The old half-finished clay pieces had been arranged neatly on the shelves—and the shelves looked sturdier. I went closer, noting the similarity of the pieces. A row of small figures, almost cherublike. Little girls. Some were more finished than others, but it was a strange lineup. All the stranger because I didn't recall doing this many. That would have been when we were grieving. I turned away.

The antique potter's wheel was still in its corner out of the main floor space, and it appeared unharmed. Someone had cleared out the old fireplace, the hearth—both unused for decades. Before my time, at any rate. A chair was situated by the hearth. Not the same chair Gran had used. This one was in better shape and well padded.

The mantel over the old hearth, the massive mantel, had also been cleared of junk. The few glazed pieces I'd left in the cabin were lined up there.

Roger. It must've been Roger. He touched my heart. He often did.

I owed him much more than I could repay. He offered support and steadiness. With minimal encouragement, he would offer more. There were times when I wondered if I could accept what he offered without feeling guilt. I would be short-changing him. He deserved someone with a ready heart. That wasn't me.

Standing there with a sigh fresh upon my lips, I heard a sound behind me.

Someone cleared his throat. I turned, startled, to see a man just inside the front door. Inside, but not moving forward. I was acutely aware I was totally alone here at the moment—well, except for this man. He made me instantly uneasy.

Dell's Diner. It had been more than a month. I'd seen him from the back and could hardly get out of there fast enough.

Years had passed since I'd seen this man face-to-face. He was older than me, and I hadn't been around him much back then. But I knew.

And I knew for sure that fate had put the final piece into play. That shimmery feeling was back in my chest. I fought not to cross my arms but lost the battle.

Liam Bridger.

He was a tall man with curly, unruly hair that needed a cut. He wore an oft-washed cotton shirt and jeans. His boots looked well worn, too. Other than the dark hair, which more than half the people on the planet had, there was nothing of Ellen in his appearance.

"You're Hannah Cooper, right?"

"I am."

"I'm Liam Bridger. I'm sure you don't recognize me."

I nodded. "I do. Or, rather, I was pretty sure. It has been a while. Years, actually."

"Yes, it has. I moved back a few weeks ago."

I tried to match his demeanor. "Welcome home. I spoke with your cousin, Mamie Cheatham, not too long ago. How long do you plan to stay? Or is this a . . ." I fumbled for a word. "Permanent return home?"

"For now. Beyond that, I'm not sure." He smiled, but only slightly. "Actually, I was looking for Roger Westray. His office said he might be here."

"I haven't seen him today."

He looked around again, up at the rafters, at the one-room framing that allowed the full view from one end to the other. "This is nice. I remember the cabin. Sorry about your grandparents and the house fire."

"Times change. Nothing lasts forever."

"I heard about the fire. Long after, that is. Many times I expected to get word that our own homeplace had fallen in or caught fire or something. Mamie has done a good job with it. The house is as stubborn as the Bridgers themselves, I guess."

"No interest in restoring it?"

"Takes money. Takes interest, too. Not sure I have enough of either." He nodded. "Well, anyway, sorry to have bothered you. I'll be on my way. If you see Mr. Westray, would you let him know I was here looking for him?"

"Sure." I couldn't resist. "Have you worked for him before? Or are you old friends?"

"No. I do construction work. Some specialty projects."

"I see."

"Looks good in here, I think."

"It does. Roger said he'd clean it up for me." I laughed politely. "I guess he did."

"Roger told me not to make any changes but to clear it out and make note of any bad wood or crumbling chinking."

I stopped and did a quick rethink. "You cleaned it up?"

"Yes. I was careful, especially with the pots and little sculptures. They're really good."

I felt like something was trying to communicate itself to me—but I was closed off and didn't want to receive it. Liam, or the miasma around Liam, was telling me more than I could bear to hear. I tried to sound civilized and reasonable.

"Thanks. They're old pieces. It takes me back to my childhood to see them. Happy memories. The place looks good."

"Thanks." He kind of half smiled. "That old treadle wheel? I don't think I've ever seen one that old. Weighs a ton. I left it in the corner rather than risk it pulling apart. If you want to move it—"

"No, that's fine. It was my grandmother's. Rather, her mother's. Grand surprised me with the motorized wheel when he set up the cabin for me to do my clay work. He bought it secondhand from a clay shop that was going out of business." I brushed my hair back behind my ear. "I moved that one to the shop in town after we got settled in Mineral . . . after the fire. Along with the kiln and other stuff."

He seemed very meek. My recollection of him was of someone brash and rowdy. Wild. Had problems. Nothing I knew about personally. It was probably what I'd heard my grandparents say, and even Mr. Bridger.

"Hannah?"

Roger was suddenly there at the cabin door, filling the doorway behind Liam.

Liam backed aside and nodded toward Roger.

Roger was clearly surprised to see me there, and he said, "I saw your car, Hannah, and a truck, too. I wondered who else was here." He took a quick look at my face, reading it, I thought, then he said, "Liam is our wood expert. He's checking on the wood we'll use for the porch, and I asked him to give the cabin a once-over." He turned to Liam. "How's it looking in here?"

"Good. Cabin's sound. I found a couple of places on the exterior, the shady side, but minor. I'll take care of them."

Roger nodded. "Right." He looked at me. "What do you think?"

"It's beautiful," I said. "It's never looked this good. I don't recognize the chair, though."

"Oh." Roger laughed. "I hope you don't mind. I came by it second-hand. Thought it would be useful out here."

"It's perfect." I wanted to hug him but felt constrained with Liam there. I didn't think Roger would've minded a public display of affection. It was just me.

"Glad you like it. Hannah, do you mind if we move on? Liam is an expert on old buildings and specialized carpentry. I wanted to go look over the springhouse with him."

"Mind?" I laughed. "No, indeed. You weren't expecting me to be here anyway. I dropped by on impulse."

He walked over to me and touched my arms. "Then it's my lucky day."

"Mine, I think. Don't let me get in the way. I'm daydreaming here."

"The cabin won't have power or water for a while yet. I have some ideas, too, about setting up the kiln and equipment that I'd like to discuss with you."

His tone sounded far more tender than the literal meaning of the words, and I was conscious that our sweet little exchange was onstage and happening in front of Liam.

"I'm looking forward to it. Please carry on."

Roger dropped his hands, saying, "I'll see you later," and stepped away. He nodded toward Liam. "Over this way. Did you take a look at it yet?"

He and Liam walked out beyond the end of the swale and doubled back to the bridge to cross the creek to the springhouse. Our plans for the front of the house depended on being able to utilize the wood from it. I hoped it was in better shape than it looked.

I turned and went back into the cabin. I took one more look at the shelves, at the swept hearth and the glazed pieces on the mantel. Above the mantel, on a hook that had been empty for years, hung an old picture. I could only guess that Liam had found it amid the junk stored in the corners or in the loft. It was a piece of battered tin, but not randomly or accidentally battered. The marks and dents and hole punches were precise. As I stared at it, the marks and shapes merged into a picture—a landscape. The creek. The trees. It showed the springhouse at one end and the cabin at the other.

It was a thoughtful touch to hang it here.

I went to the window and looked outside. Roger and Liam were still down at the spring, barely visible through the trees from this angle.

While the men were busy, I slipped away. This visit hadn't gone quite as I'd planned.

I tried to relax as I drove, but Liam had compounded the unease resulting from Spencer's visit, which I'd come here to escape. It seemed to me that no matter how many improved roads or cleaned cabins I distracted myself with—at some point, my nerves would stretch too tightly, and then what would happen? Would I explode? Would that be any better than simply telling Ellen the truth?

The car swerved. I nearly left the road. Where had that thought come from?

No, that was never going to be a possibility. The truth was the truth, and the actual truth was that Ellen hadn't been born to me, that she had come to me in a very different, but no less genuine, way, and after so many years, excellent years, it couldn't be undone. No matter what.

❧

I was back onsite for the final dismantling of the springhouse, and a few days later when the logs were put into place for the new house. The porch would integrate with those logs. I tried to target my visits for when the crews were gone so I could stand where the deck would be and consider the view. Sometimes I sat in Roger's lawn chair, put my head back, and listened to the old familiar songs of nature. How different would this be from what I'd grown up with? Not very. It gave me comfort.

On the other hand, the perspective from the back deck would be different. It would be wide and span most of the back of the house. What would I see? The cabin, of course, and also the creek, the cemetery, and as far up toward Elk Ridge as the forest would allow. It would be perfection.

I was at the jobsite when the stonemason reerected the chimney. I'd taken the mystery box that had served its owners like a safe-deposit box under the hearth to an expert in Richmond to be opened. We discovered old documents, along with some ancient cash, plus the original survey plat of the land and an old will. I was having a copy made of the plat, which I'd frame and hang on the wall by the fireplace.

Per Roger's advice, I'd been picking through the metal storage unit in the front yard and had found some antique tools with decorating potential.

The main room would be large and open across the back of the house where it met the back deck. The kitchen would be on the south side of the house. On the other end would be bedrooms and a study. The master suite would be upstairs, again with an outstanding view of Cub Creek, Elk Ridge, and the glorious woods in which I'd grown up.

A beautiful house with a beautiful view. I didn't want to live alone, but if that's how it ended up, and it looked like it might, then so be it. I'd have my pottery cabin and continue my business from here. I didn't need the storefront.

All those years of growing up barefoot and living on a meager budget had been unnecessary, and I didn't understand why my grandparents had chosen that lifestyle, but they had, and I respected that. While I didn't like excess or waste, I had never embraced an unnecessarily parsimonious lifestyle for Ellen and myself. As long as I had the choice, I never would. In fact, had I not needed to clean those houses for cash—that first loss, the greatest loss, would never have happened. How might that have changed how Gran and I responded to the gift Mr. Bridger left on our porch?

These thoughts flitted through my head as I watched the progress, the changes, occurring in Cooper's Hollow. Framed and roofed, the house looked huge, vast and echoing. Almost churchlike? Solemn. A work in progress teetering on the edge of the future.

Suddenly, doubt hit me. I stood at the wall of window openings that overlooked the back. The toolshed was long gone, the springhouse was gone, the pottery cabin was looking better, and the cemetery in its peaceful setting seemed almost eternal. It wasn't, of course. Nothing lasted forever.

From the corner of my eye, I saw a shadow. A small shadow atop the cemetery wall. Perhaps an animal?

I stared at the cemetery and at the hill. The only shadows were those cast by the trees. Anything else was born of my imagination. Reassured, I smiled and looked down. Eventually the deck would be finished, but for now it was about a three- or four-foot drop down to the raw, red dirt and I needed to mind where I stepped.

I drove home but couldn't rest. The baby book was still on Ellen's desk. I didn't want to touch it. It was an emotional bomb for me. Or was it a warning that things—my life as I knew it—were about to change beyond my own plans, beyond my control, beyond all recognition?

Could I take counsel with Duncan? He was still my attorney. I didn't doubt his discretion. But anything, once told, was subject to be repeated or written down or to be divulged in some way whether on purpose or accidental.

It was a huge risk. I'd lived in this bubble for the last few years, had grown comfortable and almost complacent, but with Liam in town, it was as if my chickens were—more than metaphorically—coming home to roost. What I'd sown might have to be reaped after all. Did my original intent matter? Not in the face of the actual choices I'd made and acted upon.

There was no one I could speak to about it.

I could talk to Liam.

No. The idea sent a jolt, a painful, burning jolt, throughout my body. No. I rejected the possibility of it. Despite . . .

Despite how he'd looked, standing there in the low light, in the echoey openness—a tall man dressed in old jeans and a cotton shirt, his hands hanging at his sides—I sensed a need in him, something missing. *Did I sense it because I knew about Ellen? Or was that my conscience speaking?*

I knew nothing about him, really.

He could be a worthless drunk for all I knew.

Regardless of right or wrong, or of what it might do to me, I couldn't risk exposing my daughter to so much unknown.

I'd done what George Bridger had wanted me to do, hadn't I? And he'd certainly known his son better than I did.

I set my small cooler in the area that would be the kitchen, and I could clearly see how that would look now, and then carried a crate of peat pots out to the raised garden beds Roger had constructed. He said the rest of the landscaping could be managed around them. This act, the first round of transplanting of my plants, seemed like an official event. The first step of the actual move. Now I needed the house to be finished. *A minor point,* I joked silently.

It was encouraging. We were still in May, but the latter half. I appreciated that he'd gotten this done ahead of schedule. I spaced out the pots. The soil looked amazing. Roger had promised, and he'd delivered. I sunk the plants into the ground but kept the rim of the pots a fraction above the soil level. Then I took a water jug I'd brought and gave each a drink. Roger had cautioned that the water wasn't running there yet, but I liked the idea of transplanting in stages, so I'd decided to proceed regardless.

When I was done, I took off my gloves and pulled out the hand sanitizer. I grabbed my lunch bag from the cooler. It had seemed like a fun idea to have lunch out here, but I was realizing the flaw in my plan. The only restroom was a portable toilet.

Better than nothing, but if I had the option, I'd drive the two miles down the road to the gas station/convenience store.

As I walked through the house, I saw movement outside. Liam. He was standing on the ground, below the level of the porch floor, and he'd been half-hidden by the porch posts. His truck was parked near my car. I hadn't heard a thing.

Was this a problem?

Hadn't I handled Spencer? Only a few unseen emotional scars had resulted from that. Nothing I couldn't live with. What about Liam? He had even less reason to be curious about Ellen. Yet he had more reason to be told.

From the open doorway, I said, "Hello there."

"Hannah. Hi. I hope I didn't disturb you." He waved a hand. He was holding woodworking tools. "I'm starting the posts today."

The porch posts were special. I didn't know where Roger had obtained the pieces, but the wood was fine-grained and the diameter was impressive. Like showpieces-to-be. Art integrated with function.

I stepped out, over the threshold, onto the porch. "What do you have in mind, if you don't mind my asking?"

He smiled a shy, secretive smile. "Make them distinctive. That's my plan."

Clearly he didn't want to say more. It was as if he were protecting something . . . His art? I did the same when I was working my pottery and other clay projects.

"Hungry? I have two sandwiches." I held up the bag. "I wasn't sure which I'd want. I made two and figured there'd be someone here willing to eat the other."

Liam averted his eyes. "I apologize."

I frowned. "For what?"

"I don't know," he said, looking up at me, "but I know there's something bothering you, and I think it has to do with me. I see it in your eyes."

"Not at all." I tried to shrug it off. "That's ridiculous."

"I might think so if I hadn't seen you talking to others and then seen . . . that change when you see me. If I've done anything to offend you, I apologize."

"Hey," I tried to joke, "I just offered you food." I shook the bag. "I wouldn't do that if you'd offended me in some way."

He nodded. "Glad to hear it." He looked at the tool he was holding, then stared again at my face. "If it's about my father, I understand. I know your grandparents disapproved of how I was gone so much of the time. They worried about him. Maybe some of that influenced your opinion of me? I couldn't blame you—or them, for that matter."

I didn't know what to say. "You were gone by the time I was in my teens. I hardly knew you, but I did know your father. I don't blame you, though. How could I? I have no idea what was between the two of you." I waggled the bag again. "Look, these aren't improving with age. Want one? How about chicken salad? Or, if you prefer roast beef, you can have that. I don't have a strong preference."

His face relaxed. His mouth curved up in one corner, and he shook his head. "Chicken salad sounds good."

He stepped up onto the porch and I held the sandwich toward him.

"Homemade," I said. "The cooler's in the kitchen. Be right back with the drinks."

"The cooler?" he asked. But I was already moving. I took two water bottles and closed the lid again. I returned to the porch and gave him one.

I sat in the open doorway to the porch, cross-legged, and set my water bottle beside me so I could unwrap my sandwich.

"So, where were you?" I asked.

He was sitting down himself, and he looked at me, surprised. "You mean all those years I was gone?"

"Do you mind my asking? None of my business, right?"

He held the sandwich and looked at it for a few moments before speaking. "I went off to school first. That didn't work out. I got married. That didn't work out well, either. I joined the service for a while but didn't re-up. It wasn't for me."

He unwrapped the sandwich and took a bite.

"Somewhere in there you learned to carve wood?"

"Irony." He shook his head. "Ready for it? I learned how to carve before I ever left home. Not with my dad but from an uncle. He was an artist, though he would have decked you if you called him that. 'Craftsman' is what he called himself." He took a drink, then set the bottle back on the porch floor. "So, here I am, years later, back where I started, doing what I love, and wondering why I ever left in the first place."

"Sometimes, I guess you don't know until you're gone, right? It's good you figured it out before it was too late." I looked at my porch posts and Liam's tools and smiled. "I've seen something on TV where the guy carves with a chainsaw."

"Not me. Although I've been known to do the rough cuts with a chainsaw."

A large, long, beat-up red tool chest was on the porch.

He pointed at it. "I have what I need in there."

"Do you make a good living at it?" I added quickly, "I'm sorry, really sorry for asking that. That's very personal." I laughed. "I throw pots and do some clay sculpture, and I have some regular customers, but I can't make a living at it."

He looked around at the growing house. "You must be doing good."

"This? No. I couldn't afford this if I didn't have some money from my family."

"I guess that's true for me, too, though I could make better money if I was willing to travel more, but I've lost the taste for it. You've met my cousin? Up at the house?"

"I have. I met her several years ago, but I've seen her only a few times."

"Mamie's talking about leaving here and going to live with her daughter. She's not getting any younger, as she says, and she's got a grandchild now. I have to decide. Do I stay? And if I stay, do I stay at the house? I'm there now, but I don't have a lot of good memories."

I sat, chewing and sipping and thinking. George Bridger was set in his ways and could be a little odd, but I'd never seen cruelty in him. If there had been, my Grands wouldn't have had anything to do with him.

"It sounds like you two didn't get along. Too different, I guess."

"Likely true."

"If we're lucky, we live long enough to work out our differences— that's what Gran used to say. I remember Mr. Bridger saying shortly before he died that you were coming home to see him. I'd taken him up some cobbler. He was looking forward to the visit."

"I didn't make it. I tried. My wife and daughter were going there, but then she went missing. I was overseas."

The word *daughter* felt like a slap. What conscience I had left in me recoiled. I hid it as quickly as I could and must've done it well because Liam kept speaking.

"By the time I was able to look for her . . . We'd had problems. I didn't think she was in any sort of danger or anything . . . only that she took off. I couldn't locate her. I didn't know it was over between us. At least, not as soon as she did. So, when I couldn't contact her, I came back to our home, but she was gone. I went on a wild goose chase trying to find her and Trisha."

"Trisha?" I said her name deliberately, like a test of myself. Like when a tooth hurts and you keep checking it to see if it's still tender. "Did you find them?"

"The police found her first. Her car had washed away in a flash flood. They found Sheryl downstream. They never found Trisha. The child seat and some toys were in the car, but they don't think she was strapped in. Never found." He was staring at the empty wrapper, crumpled in his hand, as if it might have answers.

Who had answers? I did.

I pressed my lips firmly closed, tightening my jaw muscles, clamping my mouth shut.

"It was a long time ago," he said. He lifted his gaze and stared at me. "I'm sorry. I said too much. I didn't mean to go on. As I said, it was a long time ago."

I nodded. Still not able to speak. The words couldn't form; I refused them. Let him think I was overwhelmed with sympathy at his sad story. Let him believe I was a better person than I was.

He stood in one movement. "I'd better get to it. Roger contracted with me to do these posts. I hope you'll like them. I'd rather not discuss the ideas, though. When I try to put my ideas into words, sometimes they evaporate. Better to let the wood guide me and trust the cosmos."

His remark shook my jaw loose. "The cosmos?"

"Sure." He grinned, but ruefully. "Our better angels. God. Eternity and infinity. Where ideas come from. You feel it, too. I know you do. When you're working with your clay?"

I nodded again. "I do. I'm sure I'll be delighted with whatever you carve."

With a grin, he said, "I hope so."

The timing was right to walk away. I stood, gathered my trash, brushed the seat of my jeans, and went inside. In the house, with the dim light and the smell of fresh-cut wood mixing with that of nature and the swaying pines outside, it felt otherworldly. Like a blank slate. A page not yet written on in which all things were yet possible and no wrongs had been done. I wished I could live in it this way—at least until the cold arrived. Winter would come in its time. Rain would fall and blow in through the open spaces. Raccoons and squirrels would come and go at will. Half-done, the house might feel special at the moment, but it wouldn't do in the long term. Would the same happen in my head? With my conscience?

I turned around and saw Liam running his hands along the post. He might get splinters. All actions yielded a result, right? Sometimes we got lucky. Maybe he would.

Hopefully he knew what he was doing, since I'd have to live with what he carved.

Sooner or later, my choices would yield results that couldn't be hidden or ignored, and my position would become untenable. Was this denouement something I could control? By driving it? By altering the current path to avoid an outcome I didn't want?

It was up to me. It was my information and my choice. It was inevitable that my decisions would impact people. Likewise, I'd been the recipient of impacts from the decisions others made.

They had their paths to follow, as I had mine.

A day later, I dropped by the jobsite and discovered Ellen and her friend, Bonnie, hanging out on the porch. They weren't alone. Liam was there.

I stared, trying to take in everything and determine what was happening. Liam was older than the girls by almost thirty years, I estimated, but he'd kept much of his good looks. And that hair of his, longish and curly, lent him a certain quality . . . something that hinted of danger and tragedy. Unworldly, romantically charged teen girls might find that intriguing.

Graduation was close now. These kids were all heady with it, high on life. It was exciting for them but scary for a mom.

Clearly, the girls had been chatting with him for a while. Bonnie's car was parked nearby. Bonnie was shifting her position with a movement that reminded me of a model's hip thrust and then leaning against the wall in a languid sort of pose. Liam seemed not to notice but was listening to something Ellen was saying. Ellen was seated on the edge of the porch, her legs dangling. I saw nothing in her posture to worry me, but their direct communication certainly did. Liam was dividing his attention between the conversation with Ellen and his woodwork.

Ellen saw I'd arrived. She lost her relaxed slouch and tensed. What did that indicate? A guilty conscience? She said something to Bonnie, and they waved at me.

As I reached the porch, I asked, "What's going on?"

"I wanted to show Bonnie the house. You don't mind, right?"

"What about school?"

"We had an early release today. Did you forget?"

"I did forget." I looked at her face closely, then at Bonnie, and decided it was all good. "It was fine to show Bonnie." I turned to Liam. "I apologize for the distraction. I presume they introduced themselves?"

He grinned, and I knew he was reading my mind. He knew what I was really asking.

"No problem. They're nice young ladies. They were interested in the carving."

"I'm sure. Thanks." I said to the girls, "Time to move on. Did you see what you wanted?"

It was probably my fault for phrasing it that way, but Bonnie giggled. Ellen elbowed her. I tried to keep my facial expression neutral.

"Come on, girls. Let's get out of his way." I gestured toward the cars. "Ellen, why don't you come with me? Didn't you have some shopping to do?"

Bonnie moved to her car but didn't get in right away. Ellen came close to me.

"Mom, can't Bonnie and I go together? I think I made you angry, but I don't know why."

"Yes, you can go with Bonnie, but listen carefully. I'm serious about this. Neither of you is to come out here without me present. Understand?"

"We didn't do anything wrong."

"That's not the point. This puts Liam in an awkward position, especially if—never mind what. Just know it isn't fair to put a man who's only

208

trying to earn a living into a position where someone else could see you out here with him and suggest something inappropriate is going on."

"That's crazy, Mom."

I cut my eyes over to Bonnie, then back to Ellen. "Are you sure?"

Ellen pressed her lips together and looked down at the ground. She shrugged, then shook her head. "No. I guess I see what you mean."

"And that includes you. Promise?"

She nodded.

"Serious promise?"

"Yes. I promise."

"What do you promise?"

"Mom, please. I promise not to come out here without you. Is that good enough?"

"It's perfect. Thank you. You can take care of that shopping now. Use my card. But be home in time for supper."

Her downcast look shifted in a heartbeat, and she smiled and hugged me. "Thanks, Mom."

The girls drove away. I was tempted to speak with Liam again, but I took my own advice instead—have respect for a man who'd already had enough trouble in his life and give him a chance to get his work done. Never mind my own worries about his being here and Ellen hanging around.

I waved. He waved back, and I returned to my car and drove away. I didn't get far before I pulled over and checked the location GPS on Ellen's phone. The girls were already miles away. With a sigh, I put my phone back in my purse and drove home.

I couldn't quite ditch the feeling that things were moving well beyond my ability to control them.

Soon, graduation. Two and a half months after that, Ellen would leave for college. I would miss her, but that was normal. We'd be back on track then, and this feeling of imminent dysfunction, this uncertain period, would be behind us.

CHAPTER ELEVEN

Roger dropped by the house on Rose Lane. I'd been clearing out the closets and making big progress. One pile was for donations. The other was bound for the dump.

I opened the door. "Don't mind the mess, please. I'm moving soon, you know," I joked.

He held a folder of papers and wore an expression I couldn't read. His eyes skipped right over the boxes and general disarray, and I knew his mind was on something other than our project.

"What's wrong?"

"Here's the paperwork for the fixtures. Please take a look at it. It's past time to get this all ordered."

"Roger?"

He shook his head. I pushed him toward the living room.

"Please sit down. Can I get you something to drink? Maybe tea?"

We made it into the living room, but he refused to sit. Instead, he moved his hands as if trying to find the right words, words that were eluding him.

"Just say it, please, Roger. Whatever the problem is, tell me."

"Liam."

"Liam?" Instantly, I thought of my secret. I thought of Ellen. "What about Liam?"

"The other day you seemed very friendly with him. Almost . . . cozy. Today, one of the workmen mentioned you'd been out there a lot, and he insinuated you were spending a lot of time on the porch."

"On the porch? Does that mean with Liam?" I almost laughed. It was too close to what I'd warned Ellen about the day before. This was crazy. This was me. "What am I missing here? Am I not allowed to be friendly with other people? Why are you annoyed about Liam Bridger? You hired him, and I enjoyed talking to him. What's the big deal?"

Roger's expression was grim, his jaw tight. "You know I care for you. I have for a long time, but you've always kept me at arm's length. I've tried to accept it."

"Hold on, Roger. I have always appreciated your friendship, and I care about you, but you've had a few girlfriends over the years. I recall you were engaged to one."

"It's not a joke, Hannah."

I drew in a deep breath before responding. "No, it's not. I'd never want to hurt you. You must know that. But my first and most important job has been to take care of my daughter."

"I respected your feelings early on, but I thought it would change. But the wall—the wall you built between you and the rest of us mortals— got taller and more impenetrable with each passing year."

"Wall? We see each other almost every day."

"As friends of a sort. And for business. I know Ellen approves of me. She's told me. But you, Hannah Cooper? Sometimes I think you keep me dangling on the line, in case one day you're desperate enough to need me. You don't want me, but you won't let me go."

"Won't let you go? What are you talking about?"

"I'm talking about how whenever you need something, or something needs fixing, or you want to discuss something, you call me. You bring me back into your life." He shook his head. "Don't get me wrong. I'm happy to help. But between being summoned into your life, I start finding my own way, meeting other women. If I don't have the same feelings for them that I have for you—then neither do they have the power to hurt me by treating me like a hired hand."

My jaw moved, my lips worked, but no words came out. I didn't know what to say. But the silence lasted too long, and finally, Roger said, "Let me go, Hannah. Turn me loose. Tell me you'll never have that kind of feeling for me, not enough to make it worth your while to take down the wall and give us a chance."

"Roger." He wasn't asking for a lot. Honesty and unselfishness. But I couldn't give him even that, not when I had so much to protect.

He closed his eyes for a long second, then opened them as he shook his head. "See you later, Hannah."

I let him go. Roger deserved better. I understood he suspected Liam was claiming some piece of my heart he'd never been allowed to touch. How could I explain my heart, my whole heart, had already been claimed long ago when a sweet, tiny newborn's fist had seized my finger and held it tight?

Roger was barely out the door, and I was still struggling to deal with what he'd said when Ellen rushed in.

"What's with Roger? He didn't say hi or wave." She sounded breathless. "It wasn't about me, was it?"

"No. He and I had a chat, that's all." I frowned. "Why would it be about you?"

She stared at me with her dark-brown eyes, and I saw when she accepted what I'd said. But something more was troubling her.

Her voice trembled. "Oh, Mom, it's Braden. Or rather, his father. He told Bonnie's father that you and he used to date."

"Yes, we went on a couple of dates a long, long time ago. We talked about this at the hospital, remember?"

"Sort of. That night is fuzzy. But the point is that when he told Bonnie's dad about it, it started everyone talking."

"Everyone?" The shimmery sensation returned. I touched my chest, wishing away the odd feeling, and reached out to a nearby chair to steady myself.

"My friends. Their parents . . ."

It was just gossip, I told myself. Maybe Spencer's pride had been a little wounded after the way I'd spoken to him.

"Sweetheart, I can't see that they have much to talk about. It was nearly two decades ago."

I moved into the kitchen, forcing her to follow and to give myself a moment to anticipate where this was leading.

"It was weird," Ellen said. "And awkward. You know Spencer wasn't married to Braden's mom, right? At least not until a few years later, and then they divorced, so it was a mess, but Braden's mom and Bonnie's dad are cousins."

"I still don't see what's bothering you. People date. It's small-town drama." I gave a little laugh to show how meaningless it all was. "It'll blow over."

"It's not funny, Mom. This is about my father. I want to know about my father. When the others are talking about their parents . . . There are times when it's wrong not to have your own info to share, like today, when people started making their remarks." She looked away. "Did you know I make things up?"

I had no words. It was as if she were speaking a foreign language. I struggled to comprehend.

"I make up stuff about my dad. I tell the other kids about things he did, like being good at sports and how he was smart and all that. I've been doing it for years, Mom. I don't want to keep doing it. I don't like lying. Plus, it's hard trying to remember what I've said and to whom. You never want to talk about him because it makes you sad. But Mom, when the other kids and parents are talking . . ."

I put up my hands. "Wait. Calm down, sweetheart. Let me catch my breath and you do the same?" I gripped the counter. "Take a seat in the living room. I'll get us both iced tea, and we can talk."

Ellen sat but stayed perched on the edge of the sofa cushion, her hands on her knees.

I placed the glasses on the coasters, sat next to her, and put my hands over hers, squeezing reassuringly.

"I can sympathize. My grandparents never wanted to discuss my mother and father. Of course, in later years I found out why, and now you know the story, too. I never wanted to do that to you. Never. I apologize for putting you in the same situation."

"So tell me, Mom. Why don't you want to talk about him? I know you weren't together for long, but you must know more about him. However little, I need to know."

I focused on the light filtering in through the glass panes in the door. The bright rays pierced through the bands of dust motes and touched the foyer table and the wooden floor. This was the same sunlight that touched every surface and every person in its turn, in its own good time.

"His hair was curly and unruly. Dark brown like yours. You got his hair color and my lack of curls." I forced a soft laugh and smiled. "How I envied those curls."

Ellen smiled in return.

I took a deep breath and let it out slowly, reminding myself that sometimes it was more important to craft the story right than to speak the truth.

"I met him on a sunny day when I was at the river with friends."

"The river?"

"The South Anna. We were down there for a barbecue."

"Who was there?"

"Some friends. Friends of friends. Most of them I hardly knew, and they've all moved on now. People do, you know. But he was there that day and so was I, and we met."

"Like a blind date?"

"A coincidence. No one was trying to set us up. But we hit it off right away. He was athletic, but I don't recall we ever discussed . . ."

Her excitement, the light in her eyes, dimmed.

I added, "Wait a minute. He ran track in high school. I'd forgotten. So you and I must've discussed that before, since you mentioned he was good at sports, right? You remembered without realizing it."

Her eyes lit up again, and I continued.

"Remember, we didn't attend the same school for very long. He grew up elsewhere, and his family moved here, but they didn't live here for more than a few months."

"He died on a family vacation in Colorado."

"That's correct. He tripped on a hike and fell. It was an accident. No one did anything wrong."

She nodded. "And they moved away after he died?"

"That's right."

"They didn't know about me?"

"No, honey. I tried to find them. I should've tried harder, but I had my hands full with Gran. I intended to try again, but time passed. I asked Mr. Browne to help find them, and he tried, but to no avail." The lies slipped past my lips so easily, and yet I felt a prickling along my hairline, as if I were about to break into a sweat, and my face felt a little wooden. I was practiced at avoidance, at misdirection, and when all that failed—outright manufacturing of lies. Lies and details were risky. The more there were, the more likely they were to fail.

I added, "It's such a common name. It was hard to trace."

Ellen said sadly, "I looked online, you know. I searched for him, for William Smith. But there were tons, everywhere I looked."

I leaned forward and put my hand to my forehead. I had brought her to this. Who had those lies been intended to save? To protect?

"Mom? I know this is hard. You still care for him all these years later." She wove her fingers through mine, then eased them apart. "I'm sorry."

"Don't be, sweetheart. You have every right to know."

"If you remember anything, please tell me. One day, I'll search for them properly, and I'll find them. I promised my father."

"What?"

"I mean that sometimes I talk to him, you know? It's silly. I know it is. It doesn't mean that I'm not grateful for our life. You understand that, right?"

"I understand." This was impossible. I wanted to end this, at least for the moment. I had to think. I pulled her close. "I'm sorry, Ellen."

She smiled up at me despite her tearful eyes. How did I ever deserve this child?

"You're right, Mom. You always are. I'm going to wash up. My face feels all teary. I'm going to read over my speech again, too."

"You're perfect. Your face and your speech both, but I understand. What would you like for supper? I'll get it started."

"A salad, maybe? I'm not very hungry."

Ellen went down the hall to her room. I heard her moving around, shuffling back and forth, resuming her life. The storm had blown over. For her. Not for me. Everything was closing in around me.

I was chopping lettuce when Ellen came into the kitchen carrying her phone and wearing a sheepish expression.

"What's up?" I paused with the knife held in midair.

"Bonnie texted."

"Oh?"

"She wants me to come over."

I looked down at the lettuce, at the knife, at the fridge, but there were no answers anywhere, only doubts and misgivings.

"Ellen, stay home this evening. I don't like the idea of you being around these people right now, even if it is silly gossip. What they're doing is mean."

"No, Mom. You taught me to be brave. Besides, it'll just be Bonnie. Her parents are going out tonight. She'll be home alone. We'll hang out and watch a movie or something."

"Why don't you invite her over here? I'll make myself scarce, I promise."

"Please, Mom. I want to talk to her. I'm going to tell her that my family business is my own, that the gossip and teasing hurt my feelings."

"I still don't like it."

"If you insist, I'll text her back and say I can't."

My sigh started at my toes and worked its way up to my lips. My stomach churned. Every instinct I owned warned against this, but the mercurial drama of teenager-hood mixed with the irrepressible recovery of youth was more than I could sort out tonight.

"It'll be good, Mom. I'm an adult now, right? I should be able to handle things."

I didn't know what else to do. I put the knife in the sink. "OK. Fine."

She planted a quick kiss on my cheek. "Thanks. Bonnie's picking up something for our dinner, and she'll swing by and get me."

"Wait." I turned toward her. "Don't you want to drive yourself? That way you can come home when you're ready."

"But she's already on her way. No worries, Mom, right? It'll work out, right?"

"Of course it will." But as she closed the door behind her and they drove away, I knew better. Some things you just knew in your bones.

※

I lay down on the bed fully dressed. Prepared. I hoped I would feel foolish yet relieved when my sweet Ellen walked in before midnight, her usual happy self.

My apprehension probably wasn't even about Ellen but a result of the day's accumulated stress. I felt the way an emotional punching bag might. Had it been only a couple of hours since Roger had come by and basically broken up with me? Is that what he'd done? Or was it a sort of ultimatum? Or simple honesty, maybe.

I hadn't had the opportunity to process what he'd said before Ellen came home begging to know more about her father.

I sat up in bed, pushing the pillows back against the headboard.

How dare these people put Ellen on the spot? Shame on them.

Despite the worries running through my brain, I dozed off, upright and all. I awoke to the sound of rain and a very distant rumble of thunder. The only light was from my phone screen, and as I noticed the time was eleven thirty, it rang. Ellen's ring.

She was either on her way home or telling me she'd be late.

I picked it up and answered.

"Mom?" she said. Her voice sounded wrong. Shaky.

"Where are you?"

"I'm walking home. Could you come get me?"

"I'm on my way. Tell me where."

"A few blocks from Bonnie's house. I walked up to the main road to 522."

"Stay off the road and don't look like you're hitchhiking. I'll have my interior light on so you can see it's me coming. I'm on my way."

The rain dotted my windshield. It was a warm night, and the rain was light, but whatever had happened to Ellen had resulted in her fleeing into the night, reduced to calling her mom to come get her.

Unconscionable. Someone should pay for this. No one had the right to treat a young person this way, especially not my daughter.

Then the fear started. Suppose I drove and drove and didn't find her? Young people vanished . . .

Not Ellen. I wouldn't allow it.

If she wasn't there, if I didn't find her, there'd be no limit to what I'd do. I'd move heaven and earth.

Thankfully, she stepped onto the road and waved. She was near the tall neon sign at Dell's Diner. I pulled into the parking lot. She'd walked farther than I thought. Sad. Bedraggled-looking. She seemed in control, though. For me, however, it was all about anger. Sometimes anger was hot, sometimes icy. Tonight it was both. I grabbed the blanket I kept in the back and wrapped it around my child and ushered her into the passenger seat.

"Are you all right?" I asked.

She nodded. "Just wet."

"What happened?"

"Can we go home, Mom?"

"I want to know."

"I want to go home."

Once we were back on the road, I tried a different tack. "Is Bonnie OK?"

"She's fine." After several moments with her eyes averted, she finally said, "I didn't know John and Braden would be there."

"Braden . . . but he has a broken arm."

"Yes, but he came with John anyway. Bonnie bought enough food for all of us, so she knew they were coming, though she pretended she didn't. And then her parents got home early, and they got mad at Bonnie. And then, for some reason, Braden's dad came over. He'd been drinking. I could smell it. And he acted like it. Next thing I knew he was saying stuff about Braden and me staying away from each other."

Ellen stared at me. "He said you told him we shouldn't be together. Did you?"

I gripped the steering wheel so hard I was sure the dents would be permanent. "Sort of, but only in terms of not messing up your college plans."

"Well, he made it sound like something else, something dirty. They all started talking about my father again. Like how they didn't remember him being in high school with them. I told them. I told them what you said about his running track and all that. About how you met him at a party at the river."

"Oh, honey." I closed my eyes, but I couldn't keep them closed. I had to focus on the road.

"Braden's dad started laughing."

"He's an idiot. A self-important, drunken idiot. I'm sorry, Ellen."

She was silent for a long moment, then she spoke softly. "I want to go home, that's all," she repeated.

As much as I wanted to punish Spencer, and Bonnie's parents, too, this was my fault.

"At first, I didn't understand," Ellen said. "There was a lot of winking and laughter . . . You know the kind of laughter where other people know the joke, but you don't? And you laugh politely because you don't know that you're the joke?"

"Yes."

"Braden's father was joking about how Braden and I were . . . might be . . . related. Like brother and sister, except we weren't . . . Braden's father said, according to you. He asked Bonnie's dad if *he* was my father. Like it was a big joke. Because somebody was, he said, and nobody knew who the lucky daddy was." She gave a sob and clapped her hand over her face while she regained control. "I wasn't going to tell you all that, Mom. I'm sorry. Braden was embarrassed. He left with John. He left me there, Mom."

Another long moment of silence followed, then she resumed. "Bonnie was going to bring me home, but her car was blocked in, and I wouldn't wait because . . . I couldn't. I'm so sorry."

"You're sorry? None of this is your fault. It's my fault for my decisions. Spencer Bell's fault for being the jerk that he is. Shame on Bonnie's parents, too, for letting him say such things. They know you. They should've kicked him out instead of encouraging him."

She shook her head. "I don't want to be angry, Mom. Not at anyone. What they or anyone says shouldn't, doesn't change who I am. I know that. But I can't help it, Mom. It still hurts."

I reached over and stroked her hair. Ellen was now living with the results of the decisions I'd made fifteen years ago, and decisions made before that when I dated Spencer. If I hadn't accepted the job with Babs . . . If Grand hadn't passed . . . If I'd gone on to college after graduation.

If I had, I wouldn't have Ellen, and I couldn't regret that. But I would do everything I could to ensure she didn't repeat my mistakes.

We pulled into the garage, and I helped her out of the car.

"I'm fine, Mom. Or I will be."

"I'm sorry, sweetheart. I'm sorry I did things in the wrong order and that you lost your father and never got to know him. I'm sorry it's made you uncomfortable, ever, even once in your life." I opened the door into the house. "And I'm sorry that left an opening for idiots like Spencer Bell to intrude."

"Mom. Please don't say anything to anyone. Not to Braden or his father or to Bonnie's parents. No one. I can handle this. If you get involved, it will be worse."

"I hear what you're saying, Ellen. I'll have to think about it, though. I understand about not talking to your friends. I know it will blow over with them. But these adults? They should know better."

"Don't say anything. Promise, Mom?"

I fixed her a mug of hot chocolate. She was already in her room and dressed for bed when I brought it to her. I set it on the nightstand. She was subdued, which I understood, but it worried me. I turned to leave.

"Mom?"

I stopped in her doorway. "Yes, sweetie?"

"I don't want to go to graduation. It's too fresh. People will still be gossiping. There won't be time for it to blow over and be replaced by other gossip."

Ellen was valedictorian. She'd been practicing her speech for weeks. Ellen had perfect attendance. Everything she'd worked for since we moved to Mineral after the fire, the dedication she'd put into her school pursuits, her life out of school—it was all wrapped up into this culmination at graduation that was happening in two days—and she wanted to stay away.

"I understand, Ellen. But I don't agree. People will always gossip about one thing or the other. Most won't have any idea about any of this, and the ones who do . . . well, they know you and care about you." I sat beside her. "If you don't go to graduation and give the speech, you'll always regret it."

Her expression was sad yet stubborn. She ignored the hot chocolate and rolled over, turning away from me.

"Graduation is in two days, Ellen. Your speech is ready, and you'll be brilliant as always, and all this nonsense will be in the past."

She looked over her shoulder at me, doubtful.

"My sweet girl, we'll talk about it in the morning. After a night's sleep, we'll both feel more objective about it. Sleep in and I'll get you up for breakfast. We'll have all our favorites."

"OK, Mom."

OK. Such an inadequate word. Tonight, it was probably the best I could hope for from my hurting child.

"Good night," I said softly and closed her door, but not all the way.

How could I go to bed and sleep as if nothing had changed? I wandered back to the kitchen. It was neat. Not a speck of dust. No item was out of place. The soft light over the sink lit the granite counter and the pewter fixtures. All was well. But it wasn't. I stood there at the counter, and I'd never felt so alone in my life. If I'd wanted to go to Roger for advice, perhaps for comfort, that was now out of the question. It would be like confirming I wanted him only when I needed him. I knew that wasn't true, but he didn't.

During the night, I peeked into Ellen's room, and she appeared to be sleeping. The baby book was lying open on her desk. I didn't know what that meant, but it made me inexpressibly sad.

In the morning, I arose early, checked again on Ellen who was still asleep, and grabbed my shower. As the water streamed over me, I practiced what I might say to her. First was the graduation problem. I wanted her to attend, but I could accept her decision not to, if that was truly her choice. Beyond that, I had tougher decisions to make.

I lured her out of bed with eggs, bacon, and cinnamon toast. She came to the kitchen and picked at the food. She left quietly, and I heard the shower running. When she returned to the kitchen, she seemed more like herself.

I took a chance and asked, "Did you hear from Bonnie?"

"She texted and apologized. Same with Braden."

Braden. Who knew what impact he'd have on our lives? Certainly, when Eva Pullen had mentioned Melissa's baby all those years ago, I hadn't.

But Ellen seemed to be working things out with her friends. Whether I liked them or not, I saw that as encouraging.

"That's good, right?"

She shrugged. "Maybe." She leaned against the island as I rinsed the breakfast dishes. "Mom?"

Here it comes, I thought. The graduation conversation. "What, Ellen?"

"I'm going to stay home."

"From graduation? You don't want to miss that. You'll regret it."

"No. I'm not going to graduation and not to college, either."

I spun around. "What? What are you talking about?"

"I don't want to start college under these circumstances. Bonnie and Braden and all our friends will be there." She pushed her damp hair out of her face. "I'll delay a year. I'll go somewhere else. Maybe to a school in California or somewhere."

My throat and mouth had suddenly gone dry. I only croaked a noise and then coughed.

Ellen tried to smile, but her puffy red-rimmed eyes betrayed reality. "The good thing, the good news is, I'll be here to help you move out to the new house. I'll go home to Cooper's Hollow with you, and I'll figure it all out later."

"No!" The word erupted from me. "No, Ellen. I don't need your help. I can manage on my own."

She turned pale. She looked stricken.

"No, sweetheart." I moved forward to touch her arms, but she shrank away. "You'll see this is no big deal. It will pass quickly. You'll stick with your plans. You'll graduate and you'll go to Tech. Nothing else is acceptable. Trust me. Everything will be fine."

She crossed her arms and turned her face away. "No, Mom, I don't think anything will ever be fine again."

She walked down the hall. I heard the soft noise of her door closing.

Without the kitchen counter to hold me, I would've fallen. The world spiraled around me in a series of errors repeating and sins recurring. I closed my eyes and focused. This would not be. Ellen would go to college. She would face this down. A tempest in a teapot of a small town . . . She was too young and vulnerable to understand how swiftly this would blow over if she could manage to ignore it. Her world, our world, would right itself, and I intended to proceed on that basis. It had worked thus far. We would soon be back on the right trajectory. My personal universe had had a number of resettings. It had worked for me.

The butterfly—one of the butterflies Ellen was always collecting and sticking here and there—was held by a magnet on the side of the refrigerator. I pulled the colorful paper butterfly from beneath the magnet and held it to my cheek. I closed my eyes and saw George Bridger's stained glass window with the butterflies and lilies entwined.

Lilies for death and butterflies for rebirth. It stunned me. *Where had I heard that?* I had no recollection, but I knew what I had to do, no matter how painful.

My daughter's hurt had far more power to destroy me than any hurt or fear of my own. Except for once, long ago. Only then had I experienced pain that could never be exceeded. At least, not be exceeded and survived.

If I lost my daughter again, would it destroy me? Life as I knew it, probably, but there would be life beyond it as long as Ellen was alive and happy in this world. My child. My heart.

As far as I knew, Gran, as Clara, had married my grandfather willingly. They were happy together and depended upon each other greatly for the years I had borne witness to. Yet they'd had only one child, and she'd been born late in life. I didn't know if there'd been others, miscarriages or lost infants. Gran had never discussed it with me. But that one child, the one they'd poured their love and hope into, had eloped and trusted her love to a man who didn't deserve it. She'd loved unwisely, and it had killed her and damaged both Gran and Grand, and me, too, although I hadn't really understood until this moment. Gran had passed the damage on to me by her silence. Was she protecting herself or me by not telling me the truth? She'd worked hard to keep me from knowing and to protect herself from having to encounter the remarks from nosy people in town.

How it must've hurt her when I seemed to be repeating the same errors . . . and yet, she'd been afraid I would leave. I'd known it and hadn't blamed her, but I'd made sure the same issue wasn't true for Ellen. I'd gone out of my way to encourage her in school and the community. I did everything I could to make sure she'd go on to college and not be held back by me.

Yet my biggest error had been made back when she was left on our porch and I decided not to tell the sheriff. There was no righting it. I wouldn't go back and change it if I could because I also believed it was the only decision I could have made, error or not. Wrong or not.

But to allow the error to continue to shape Ellen's future was wrong.

How could I fix it? How could I stop the error from continuing infinitely into the future?

Only by acknowledgment and confession.

The distress in my heart, the pain in my head, it all eased. I breathed deeply. Only the right decision could bring this feeling of relief.

I would do this. I would do it well. All wasn't necessarily lost.

Honesty, sincerity, and love were the essential keys. I would tell her the truth. We'd work through it together.

With fear, but also with newfound peace in my heart, I went down the hall toward Ellen's room.

I should've known somehow. The air in the house should've changed with her departure, but I hadn't felt it. As the curtains blew into the room, billowing on the late May breeze, my brain struggled to understand its meaning. The window was open, and the screen had been removed. I saw the screen, haphazardly propped against Ellen's dresser.

The bed was disordered. The pillow was out of place. The bedspread had ridges and valleys left behind by a restless or distraught young woman. One who was no longer present.

I went to the window, stared outside, and tried to think. The curtain wrapped around my face. The other panel draped itself on my shoulder. Her car should have been in the driveway. It wasn't.

Who? Where? Why? The questions spun in my brain. *Had she gone to see Bonnie? Braden?*

Her phone. She'd have it with her. I ran for my own.

Our phones communicated locations. I could find out immediately where she was.

No location found. She didn't show up on my phone.

No cell service.

She was in Cooper's Hollow.

Whatever my daughter was doing out there, I needed to reach her before she moved on. I grabbed my purse and keys. I ran to the garage and my car.

I controlled myself until I was out of the Mineral town limits and then opened up my speed on the winding road. I knew the road well from many years of driving it or as a passenger with Grand.

It was almost as if he and Gran were there with me, urging me forward.

❧

Her car was there in the new parking area. Only hers. I was grateful. I closed my eyes and bowed my head to my hands, gripping the steering wheel. I wanted to do this right. With the least damage. To me, of course, but more especially to my daughter. To Ellen. I didn't know what the right words were or whether such words existed in the universe. I felt alone. Absolutely alone.

Everyone must pay his or her debts eventually. *This must be my turn,* I thought. But I had hope. Our love, our bond, was so strong I believed we'd make it past this. Regardless, this was Ellen's life, her future. I would pay any price necessary to make her happy.

Cooper's Hollow looked different now with the construction far along and blocking the old views, including the view of the pottery cabin. The huge storage container still sat in the front. It was a construction site, and that's what it looked like. The house was well along, but it wasn't home yet.

Where was home anyway? Here in the past? On Rose Lane in the present? Or was it where our loved ones were? Not those in the grave, of course. We carried them with us in our memories. For them, the cemetery was not their home but only a memorial. As much as one might miss them and respect them, it was hard to hold a cold memorial and feel the love returned.

"Ellen?" I waited. When she didn't answer, I stepped up onto the porch.

The ground was rough around the porch, churned and clay-red. The roof was on the house, and the plywood was up for the exterior walls. It was far from being finished but full of the promise of what it would be. The porch post showed preliminary notching and shaping. Liam's work, of course, but no tools were in evidence, and there was nothing fresh like wood shavings or a coffee cup or whatever to indicate he was around. I paused in the doorway and called Ellen's name again.

Most of the interior walls were only framed—very little drywall was up—so the view from the front door to the back array of windows was open, yet it was dim inside. Ellen was standing at those back windows, facing the woods and cast into dark silhouette by the outside light.

She hunched her shoulders forward but otherwise didn't respond when I called her name.

I stopped near her. "Why did you run away?"

Ellen didn't answer. She crossed her arms and kept her back to me.

"Sweetheart, we need to talk. There are things I haven't told you, or anyone, that you need to know."

She shook her head. "I've made up my mind." Her voice didn't have an echo when she was facing outside, but when she turned toward me and spoke into the interior of the building, each word hit the surfaces above and around us and rebounded.

"I called Braden when I went to my room. He said his father doesn't want us to see each other. He said he confronted his father about the stuff he'd said."

I shuddered. "Let's talk." I nodded toward the corner, to the one room with walls. "Less echo in there."

She didn't move. I walked over and put my hands on her shoulders. She didn't pull away.

"I know you are hurting right now, but believe me, it won't be long before this will be a distant memory. You'll have a different perspective and life experience to add to it." In my heart, a tiny hope bloomed. If she would respond to reason, then perhaps the rest need not be said.

"I wanted him to meet me here. For us to run off together. Get away from this town. He was all for it. He said John would bring him."

Inside, I trembled. Outwardly, I forced myself to show calm. "Ellen, this is unnecessary. Such a mistake. Is he coming?"

"No, he called me back while I was on my way. He said he couldn't go. That he'd thought about what his father said and that it wasn't right for us to be together."

I bit my lip. My hands were still on her. I felt some sort of deep energy, something more than distress or tension, like a deep-seated earthquake whose reverberations were about to rewrite a region.

"Is it true, Mom? Mr. Bell said he was my father despite what you'd said. He told Braden you'd denied it but that my birth was nine months after . . . The timing was too exact . . . That he'd known you'd never . . . That he was your first." She shook off my hands and stepped away. "Mom, I know what you told me about Mr. Bell, but is it true?

Did you lie to me? Is Spencer Bell my father?" She nodded toward the window, casting a quick look past me toward it. "Who's buried in my father's grave?"

She'd been staring out there when I'd arrived. At the cemetery. The deep emotion shaking Ellen rushed into me, through me, and my teeth rattled. I made a last effort to control myself, to keep my voice low and calm.

"Spencer Bell is not your father. I promise you. I swear it to you, Ellen."

Her hands continued covering her face, but her posture sagged. I tried to pull her toward me. Her hands came away from her face. Her eyes looked haunted, but she held her ground.

"Why would he say such things, Mom? Why would he tell Braden that?"

"Come with me." I tugged her arm again. "We can sit in here. I see Roger's chairs in there, and the echo isn't so bad."

Ellen walked into the room, but as I entered, I stopped. An object had been set in the sill of the framed window opening—the butterfly pot. Below it, on the floor, was an open duffel bag and a backpack, both belonging to Ellen.

She saw me looking.

"I packed a few things, but I don't . . . won't . . . Do you think maybe I can camp out here? Or maybe in the cabin until the house is done?" She picked up the butterfly pot from the windowsill and hugged it to her.

"This is your room, sweetheart, but it's not suitable for living in yet. We can go home and talk about decorating it. I was going to surprise you when you came home for the first college break, but this is a better idea."

"That's over. Everything has changed. I'm not going."

Roger's lawn chairs were leaning against the wall. I opened them and placed them near the window.

"Sit here."

I was out of options. That last suggestion about discussing decorating had been silly and pointless. It wasn't going to be simple, and I knew it. No matter how difficult, no matter the cost, I had to do this for my daughter.

She sat in the chair, moving like she was in pain. Given time, her youth would restore her. It couldn't help but do that because it was the nature of youth and health and regeneration. I sat in the other chair. I didn't know where to focus. On Ellen's face? The present and future? Or out the window to the past, to my history?

Someone was sitting on the cemetery wall . . . a small figure. I gasped.

I blinked and saw it was a trick of the light. A cloud perhaps, a moment of darkness, but then the sun was bright again. A breeze rustled the branches overarching the cemetery. When the true shadows moved, it became clear no one was up there. But the butterfly pot was now back in the open window space.

"Mom?" Ellen touched my shoulders.

My hands were pressed over my heart, and my chest hurt.

"Mom?" She shook me. My head jolted, and she stopped. "Sorry, Mom. You scared me. You weren't breathing."

I gulped. "I'm fine. I'm breathing." I dragged in a deep breath to prove to both of us I was all right.

Ellen retrieved the pot from the sill and took her seat again. "We're both having bad days, I think." She gave me a small, brave curve of the lips that barely qualified as a smile.

I stared at her, memorizing her face, and thinking I'd rather die than . . . I'd heard it said a hundred times at least. I'd rather die than— fill in the blank. Today I understood it could be a real thing—not light words for drama queens or throwaway party conversation. Because, in my cowardice, I would rather die here on the spot than say aloud, "There was a child. Spencer Bell was her father. I lost her when she was five months old. I wanted to go with her. But someone had to stay here and take care of Gran."

Had I said the words aloud? I thought I might have. I'd tried to watch her face, but there was a big blank space in my memory. Had her expression changed? I had no idea. It was all a blur. Beyond her, the cemetery pulled at me like an irresistible magnet that overruled all other attractants. The shadows played across the stone where the cemetery was perched on the hill. That figure again. Small. Childlike. I leaned toward the window, touching the opening. There it was. I was on my feet now, and the wood beneath my fingers evaporated. It was just gone and I was stepping forward . . .

"Mom!" Ellen yelled.

I snapped back. I was still seated. I hadn't gone anywhere. The wall was there, and solid. Ellen was in my face, her hands pressed hard against my cheeks.

"I have loved you from the first moment I saw you," I whispered. "So did Gran. Please always remember that."

She dropped her hands and stepped away. "What did you say?"

"I have loved you—"

"Not that. Before. A moment ago you said something about losing a child." Her voice sounded harsh. Her words were like slaps. Incomprehension and disbelief clouded her eyes.

I cleared my throat. I had to do this because I loved my daughter. I had to do this one thing and then I'd be done. I could move on then. But first, this.

"I was planning to go to college, but Grand died." I faltered, coughing. I tried again, doing my best to sound sane and reasonable despite the pounding of my heart and the ringing in my ears.

"You know I couldn't leave Gran because her health was poor, and she needed my help. I didn't know the truth of how my parents had died, but now I understand why she avoided people, town, and society. Others knew and might ask questions. She wanted to avoid that."

"You said something about a baby. About a baby dying."

I closed my eyes. How could something hurt so badly after all these years?

"Yes, we lost her," I said. I forced the words out. "When she was five months old. SIDS, I think. She didn't wake from her nap. That was all."

"A sister? I had a sister?"

She was struggling to understand, to put the pieces together in a way that made sense. I shuddered. "Her name was Ellen."

My daughter grabbed my shoulders and shook me, then she dropped to her knees and forced me to meet her eyes.

"Her name was Ellen? She died? Then who am I? Did you name me after her? Was she older than me? How could that be? Mr. Bell said—" She pushed away from me. "I saw the baby book. The sketches. That's me, right? Tell me, Mom, that's me?"

I shook my head, and the room seemed to spin ever so slightly, each movement delicate, slow, and infinite. Not with the brute force of an earthquake but with the deceptively delicate movement of butterfly wings whose fluttering could ultimately impact global events, the words I had guarded so carefully for so many years were about to reach into our world and change it forever.

"No," I said.

Ellen stumbled and reached for the chair, and the butterfly pot fell with a crash, the blue shards scattering and beyond repair.

CHAPTER TWELVE

Emotionally and physically devastated, I tried to explain, but each word I spoke was strained and stretched as if pulled from the lips of the condemned.

"You were left on our porch with a note," I started. Then the words came out in a rush, tumbling one after the next . . . That I hadn't wanted to do the wrong thing . . . That I was simply trying to protect her . . .

But there was no way to explain it that didn't sound self-serving.

"You're not my mother?"

I stared at her and patted my heart but couldn't speak.

"Mr. Bridger left me at your house? I was staying at his house—the one beyond Elk Ridge? My parents left me there?"

I nodded. "I tried to find Mr. Bridger, but he was already deceased by the time I located the hospital. I didn't know where to find your other blood relatives . . . or your father or mother. I was afraid if I went to the authorities, they'd take you away and put you in foster care or . . . Meanwhile, Gran . . . and I . . . we had such emptiness in our hearts . . . and you . . . felt like a gift from God. People assumed . . . and I let them."

"I knew I'd seen those butterfly windows before." Her voice dropped to a whisper. It sounded more like a hiss. "I knew I remembered them despite what you said."

"You might have. You were young, but . . . it's possible."

With the force of an overzealous prosecutor, she said, "Liam Bridger. The man who's working on the porch posts. He grew up at the Bridger house. Does he know my parents?"

"He's Mr. Bridger's son."

"His son," she said as she paced.

"His only son."

"Are you saying he's my father?"

I looked away.

"Does Liam know?" Her voice rose higher with each word. "Am I the only one who doesn't know the truth?"

I opened my mouth to respond, but other words entered the room before mine could.

"Do I know what?" Liam said. "What's wrong?"

Ellen turned to look at him. Surprisingly, I felt grateful relief. Now he could take over.

"Do you have a daughter?" Ellen asked him.

His voice, still coming from behind me, sounded hesitant. "I did. Her name was Trisha. She died many years ago."

She came up close to me and asked in a breathless voice, "What have you done?"

"I don't know what's going on here," Liam said, "but you shouldn't talk that way to your mother."

Ellen shouted, her tone ugly. "She isn't my mother! And you . . . Why didn't you take better care of your daughter?"

I wanted to intervene. I tried. I raised my hand, but my arm seemed to be moving within a different sphere of time from everyone and everything around me. My hand dropped back into my lap, giving up. Outside, through the window, the shadow had re-formed on the stone wall.

From a distance, Liam's voice said, "My daughter died in a flash flood in New Mexico. She was with her mother while I was . . . away." He paused. "Why are you asking about Trisha?"

"Because it seems like maybe she didn't die. It seems like maybe your father left me on the Coopers' porch fifteen years ago, and Hannah Cooper decided to keep me because she'd killed her own baby."

"Killed . . ."

She shook her head and waved her arms. "Not killed, then. Not killed. Lost. She lost her baby. Lost, lost, lost. Like it's misplaced. How do you misplace a baby? But I guess you can, because my parents lost me and she"—Ellen pointed at me—"got a do-over." She stared at me. "What did you think I was? Some kind of toy? A doll you could play pretend with and never need to tell the truth?"

Ellen backed away from both of us. She was hitting her fist against her chest. Her dark eyes were flashing. "I just found out my life is a lie, and I don't know where I belong. Do I belong anywhere?" She pointed at me. "Because it can't be with the woman who stole me from my real family."

Liam finally moved into my view. I saw his boots, his jeans. His T-shirt. I stopped looking when I reached his chin. I looked away, to stare at the floor. He bent over and picked up a blue glazed fragment from among the many scattered on the floor. He turned it over, examining it, then knelt in front of me.

"Hannah? What's happening?"

His eyes were kind. They were dark. Dark and warm like the eyes of my daughter, Ellen. I tried to smile in reassurance, to touch his cheek, but nothing moved. Not my lips. Not my hands. I shook my head. That was all I could manage.

I'd handled this poorly. Back then and again today. Well intentioned, but badly done.

I turned away to look out the window again. Ellen might be lost, but so was I. Lost.

Ellen. Trisha. Hannah. Even my mother, Anne Marie, before me.

Focusing on Liam, I said, "I don't have your father's note. It burned in the fire."

He frowned. "What note?"

"No, it didn't," Ellen said. "It was tucked into the baby book. Stuck between the pages. I didn't understand it. I didn't think it had anything to do with me."

Not me. Gran must've put it there.

I put a hand on Liam's arm and stood. My fingers hurt. They felt torn. Like when I'd dug up the concrete block and rolled it up the hill and into the cemetery to secure the grave. I examined my fingers, but there was no dirt and no blood. I faced Ellen.

"No matter how you feel right now, you are still my daughter. You will always be my daughter. What you choose to do is up to you, but it won't change what's here." I touched my heart. I turned my full attention to Liam. "I owe you an apology I can never give. Your father put Trisha into my care long ago. Maybe I should've made different decisions, but nothing can change that now. I regret you didn't have her in your life. She's been a blessing to me. A gift."

The expression on his face, though silent, shouted of shock and confusion. Soon there would be anger.

"If you choose to speak to the police," I said, "I won't blame you. I probably broke several laws not reporting her as abandoned. Anyway, I'll be easy to find if they want to arrest me."

He waved his arms. "Hold on. What are you telling me?"

"Liam, Ellen needs a place to go. She won't want to come home with me."

His frown was deep. The lines carved in his face seemed to have no bottom.

"I'm sorry." I tried again. "Ellen needs a place to stay for a while. I thought you and Mamie . . ."

"I can't believe you're doing this . . . saying this . . . ," Ellen whispered. "You think you can steal my life and then give me back and walk away?"

I faced her. "Then come with me. We'll work this out when you're ready." I held out my hand.

She pressed her lips together so tightly, they almost disappeared. Her shoulders hunched up around her neck, and her arms crossed in a defensive posture. Her hands were tucked securely out of my reach.

I moved toward her, and she began shaking. I stopped.

"Hannah," Liam said, apparently waking up to the possibility that his daughter lived. "Is this really Trisha?"

I kept my focus on Ellen. "Roger will be happy to put you up for a few days. You know he thinks of you like a daughter. But I recommend you go to Elk Ridge and take this time to get to know your father."

I turned to Liam. "Yes, she's Trisha." I closed my eyes, unable to look at Liam's face as the truth dawned on him. "I know you will, but as her mother, I have to say it anyway—treat her well or you'll deal with me."

I walked away, yet I watched surreptitiously from the corner of my eye. Liam moved a few steps toward Ellen. He spoke softly. Her arms relaxed, her shoulders dropped, and she stood taller. She nodded.

I left.

I didn't remember the drive home to Rose Lane.

Suddenly, I was just there, sitting in the car in my garage. The keys were in my hand. My purse was in the passenger seat. I grabbed it and hugged it to me. My arms felt empty.

Had it been right to leave her there? Did I have a choice? No.

In the house, I sat in the dark kitchen. Food and drink had no appeal. I went to the living room hoping to find comfort in the pottery made by my grandmother and her mother and hers. They were still beautiful pieces, I acknowledged as I stared at them, but when I touched them, I found them cold—made of old clay and antique glazes—and empty, literally and emotionally.

Rest. I needed rest. I tried lying down on my bed but couldn't settle, so I wandered. I no longer felt connected to any of this. To anything. I puttered around the house. My nerves kept me from being able to relax, and by midnight I accepted Ellen wasn't coming home and no one was going to call. Had I really thought she might? Apparently, because my disappointment was sharp and real.

Fitful dreams, nightmares, in which I admired the posts that Liam was carving, rocked my attempt at sleep. As I touched the figured wood, the abstract shapes reassembled into butterflies. Liam laughed, and suddenly, Ellen was there beside him, laughing, too, as Liam said, "Surprise, Hannah! It's all about the butterflies!" They haunted my sleep. Not surprisingly, I left my bed and didn't return.

This house had been for Ellen and me, our home together, after we'd fled the fire.

Ellen was at the Bridger house tonight. Liam had his recently discovered, long-deceased daughter, Trisha, back with him. Maybe together they could find some healing. Mamie was there, and Ellen had met her, so that was good. I was pretty sure Liam and Ellen wouldn't be eager to spread the story. But Mamie? Only time would tell.

Was that why I threw a few things in a box? Was it because I couldn't stand being here alone? Or was it because if the sheriff was going to roll up in his cruiser to arrest me, I didn't want it to be here where neighbors would come out and stand in the street to watch and be concerned and curious?

I loaded the box and a pillow and blanket into the back of my car.

Ellen had always liked a nightlight. Me? I'd never been afraid of the dark. Sometimes darkness felt like protection, especially for the secrets dwelling within me.

I parked in the cleared area. Dawn had preceded me by an hour, but the trees blocked much of it, and the light was dim. Still, a couple of workers had gotten an early start as some trucks were parked in the lot. Not Ellen's car.

Looked like today was another drywall day. I stepped out of the car. Bright lights were hooked up inside. The noise of the stapling was loud, and the rhythmic punctuations filled the air. I took my box from the back and carried it around behind the house and to the cabin.

Once inside, I could collapse. The sleep I hadn't gotten during the night slammed me. I put the blanket in the corner chair. The chair was large and well stuffed, and I curled up in it. I thought briefly of securing the door, but it was only a half thought that briefly brushed my consciousness but then lost its grip and flitted by.

❦

"Hannah?" Roger said.

His tone was hushed. I'd slept through whatever construction noises penetrated the cabin walls, yet Roger's whisper woke me. I sat up abruptly, touching my face and brushing my hair aside. I put my legs on the floor but was tangled in the blanket and couldn't stand right away. My neck hurt. The position had been awkward. My brain was fuzzy.

"What happened?" he asked. "Is something wrong?" He knelt at my feet, helping to work the blanket free.

Was something wrong? It all rushed over me, and I put my head back, unable to stand.

Roger pulled a stool next to the chair. "Talk to me, Hannah. Tell me what happened."

I coughed and cleared my throat. Roger handed me a bottle of water I didn't remember having. I'd brought it from the house? Or no, it had been in my car. Now, somehow, it was in the cabin with me.

"I . . . I . . ." I shook my head. "I don't know where to start." I tried to sit up, to lean forward, and my head spun. "How do you know something happened?"

"Well, you're sleeping in a chair in a cabin on a construction site when you have a nice house in Mineral." He tried to grin, but it was brief and grim. "I saw your car, and no one had seen you, but Liam . . . He suggested something had happened but wouldn't say more. I thought this was the place—if you were here and you must be—then this was where I'd find you."

"Liam's here?"

"He was, but he didn't stay."

"Was Ellen with him?"

"No." His eyes narrowed. "Why would Ellen be with him? Did something happen with Liam? Should I fire him?"

I shook my head. "No, I don't know how to start telling you."

"You can tell me anything."

I wanted to laugh, but it didn't come out that way. It sounded like I was choking instead. Roger handed me the water bottle again. I tried to focus on him, on his face. Had his anger with me passed? Was he still angry? I couldn't think clearly enough to figure it out.

"How long have you been here?" he asked.

"Only since this morning."

"Maybe we should go get a bite to eat. It's noon."

"I'm not hungry."

"I'm really worried now. You always have an appetite."

I knew he was trying to normalize the moment, to inject some levity, but he didn't understand how far we'd traveled since yesterday. This was a strange new world.

He said, "What about graduation? Does Ellen need a ride there or is she meeting us?"

Roger was confused. He was the least likely person I knew who'd ever be confused, but this time there was plenty of reason. I had to explain this to him.

"I won't be attending."

Roger started to argue and I raised my hand to still his voice.

"Let me tell you why. Ellen and I had a talk. She heard some nonsense from her friends, and the parents of her friends, that Spencer Bell was her father."

"I remember him from the night of the accident."

241

"Yes, him."

"You've never been willing to talk about Ellen's father. Not that you seemed particularly stricken about the loss—it was long ago, and you're a very practical, levelheaded person. But you didn't want to discuss it, and I didn't think it was my business unless you wanted it to be."

"Spencer isn't Ellen's father." Poor Roger's world was about to change, too, through no fault of his own, but because he cared about Ellen and me. Roger was yet one more person I'd wronged, at least by omission. It hurt so much that I felt numb, thank goodness. Otherwise, how could I bear it?

"Spencer was the father of the first Ellen. We, Gran and me, I mean . . . we lost her when she was still an infant." I watched his face. He was speechless now. "Ellen, the present Ellen, turned up on my front porch when she was two years old or a little more, courtesy of old George Bridger."

He pulled his hand away. He moved back and sat straighter.

"I didn't intend to keep her, but Gran . . . Anyway, one thing followed another, and before long . . . we had our Ellen back." I clenched my fingers together. "When all this came up with Spencer Bell, I told Ellen the truth. It was time. I didn't want her to derail her life, her future, because of my choices, my lies."

Roger was all about integrity. The woman he knew as Hannah Cooper had lived a well-constructed life. Practical and levelheaded, he'd called me. But herbs and vegetables—good things—started life in the mud. Why should people be different? The messiness of it, the lies, would trouble Roger, and I knew that. Perhaps that was part of the reason I'd always kept him at arm's length emotionally.

"I'm sorry, Roger. I don't know what will come of this. I understand you might not want to be my friend, but please finish my house."

He blinked. His jaw moved, but it was a long moment before he got out the words. "All this, and you're worried about the house?"

"I need the house. Regardless of whatever else happens, a half-built house does me no good at all."

Did I sound too practical? Every trait had a good and bad aspect. The same was true for Roger, though likely his sins had been less heinous than mine. He frowned, trying to process what he'd learned. I wished I could smooth those lines away, but I was busy growing my own, and to touch him would be like making promises, perhaps suggesting bargains that would hurt him.

Roger stood. Without a word, he went to the door, opened it, but then he paused. He faced me, the light behind him throwing his own face into shadow, and asked, "The first baby. What happened to her? Where is she?"

A familiar darkness closed in. It shielded me and allowed me to speak. "She went to sleep and didn't wake up. I buried her in the cemetery."

He closed the door behind him as he left.

I started shaking. Whole-body shaking. An earthquake that I alone felt. I gripped the blanket, holding it tightly around me, but I wasn't cold. The blanket was for holding me together lest the many parts of me go flying, scattering into the world to be lost. My body wouldn't need a burial. That was a good thing, as there'd be no one left on this earth who cared enough to dig the hole.

I'd shattered once before—that night in the cemetery. Suddenly, my fingers began stinging again. I held out my hands. They were clean, and yet the dirt was still there, staining my flesh for all to see—all who knew the truth. Now there were more who knew. Word would get around. Soon others would ask.

If I was lucky, I would lose my daughter for the second time, but I'd still have the Hollow. It was a strange world in which I could consider such a loss to be "lucky." But if Ellen was safe and well and moving forward with her plans, I could accept it. I could live an acceptable life alone with minimal interaction with the world. In fact, it might be a nice change to live without my heart being torn between hiding the past and wanting to live and love in the present.

Once upon a time, I'd dreamed about the future. For years, I'd imagined how my life would be after Ellen left for college. Accordingly, I built my plans. Now I tucked them away forever. The best I could hope for was a completed house and that the law would allow me to stay in Cooper's Hollow.

I remembered the broken pot. Later, after all the workers had left, I crept out of the cabin and into the house to retrieve the pieces. They were all gone. Swept away, and gone with the trash. Not one tiny piece remained.

Days had passed since I'd told Ellen the truth. The windows and exterior doors were installed and the remaining drywall was hung, taped, and mudded. Each day, after the workers left, I emerged from my cabin and walked through the emptiness.

These looked like rooms now. I could see how the furniture would lay out and the colors I might choose for the walls. There was a part of me that still cared. Still hoped. I hated and loved that part all at the same time and didn't try to do otherwise. I was in limbo, and I was content with that because I knew it could change for the worse at any moment. As of now, Ellen could return to me. Liam might forgive me. Roger would build my house. I was home again in Cooper's Hollow. So long as I was here, there was a sliver, a tiny window of hope, that things would come right again.

I paused and looked across Cub Creek to the cemetery. It remained untouched by the changes in the Hollow or the recent events in my life. None of the construction crew had been near it, not for a shady lunch spot or to recline on the wall. Why had I ever thought they might? People did vandalize old cemeteries, but what was I protecting? I'd been protecting Ellen from the truth, but the cemetery? Gran and Grand were gone.

Ensuring respect? Yes, that was part of it. But not of the empty graves. They'd served their purpose. But of Ellen, the first Ellen, my precious baby Ellen . . .

I hadn't seen the figure on the stone wall again. After all the years of tender care I'd given the cemetery, now I wanted to avoid it. I was almost afraid of it.

I was also clearheaded. I'd slept myself out despite the awkwardness of the chair. First and foremost, I needed food and a shower. I would pick up fresh clay at the shop, then return to Rose Lane after dark. Clay—I needed to dig my fingers back into it.

My fingers burned and stung from phantom abrasions, memories of that night long ago. The clay, cool and moist, would soothe them.

At the house, I closed the blinds and kept the lights turned down low while I cooked myself a proper meal. I slept for a few hours on a real bed where I could stretch out. I awoke before dawn. While the coffee brewed, I added more candles and water bottles to the box in the car. I watched the sun rise as I drove back to the Hollow.

I'd picked up a bucket and filled water containers at Cub Creek Pottery the evening before. That would be my best option for handwashing after working with the clay. I could've worked at the shop. For that matter, I could've slept at the shop at least as comfortably as I could at the cabin, and there I had a proper sink and toilet. But in the shop, nothing stirred me. Never had. The work I did there felt utilitarian, an occupation to show the world I was useful, had a purpose, and could earn some money, because otherwise the world got curious and then suspicious.

Making pottery and managing the store had been part of what I'd done to occupy my days while Ellen attended school, worked her hourly jobs, participated in after-school activities. Together, we'd attended church and involved ourselves in activities there and in the community, and I'd made plans for my future and the return to Cooper's Hollow. I'd thought I was waiting for Ellen to graduate, for us both to be ready to move forward to this next stage of our lives. Maybe I hadn't been honest with myself. Everything I'd done, all the efforts to rebuild and move back to the Hollow, seemed to have had the opposite effect, zeroing in on the core problem, almost tempting fate.

I unloaded my car and set up the bucket of washing water with a bag of rags handy in the corner. The clay went on the table, with my tools next to them. But then my resolve flagged. It was early in the morning. I didn't think anyone was on the jobsite yet. I picked up my cup of coffee and walked over to the house.

From the cabin door, the view of the back of the house was nearly unobstructed. The full-length windows were arrayed like a gallery across the central portion of the back wall, and in their midst was a four-panel French-door arrangement. The deck was nearly completed now, except for the steps. I stole a quick look across at the cemetery, but then turned away and touched the side of the building to brace myself for the big step up.

I wandered through the rooms knowing each by heart. The study here. Beside it was Ellen's room. The kitchen was on the far side of the great room. And so on. Gran wouldn't have known what to do with all this space, but I thought she might've enjoyed trying to figure it out. I stopped by the fireplace hearth. The fireplace was like a marker, the one corresponding feature between old and new, like an anchor holding steady in the same spot. A few feet from here was where Gran had her bed, and around the corner from there would've been my room. Most of the original house would've fit in the great room.

I'd never felt cramped in our small house. In the new house, no one could feel cramped. Space, or the lack of it, mattered not at all. It was who you were with, or weren't with, that made the difference.

This house, under construction, felt like a waiting space. A space that was growing and becoming but that hadn't arrived in its own time yet.

I stopped short. The front door was open. Liam was standing on the porch with a chisel, seeing me as I saw him. He must've noticed my car and known I was here somewhere, and when he'd opened the door, he must've realized I was inside the house, not hiding in the cabin, yet he'd stayed. Did that mean anything?

"Hannah."

"Liam." I cleared my throat. I couldn't stop myself from immediately asking, "How's Ellen?"

He scratched his jaw. He looked freshly shaved. When he stared at me, I could see Ellen's dark eyes focused on me through his.

"She's good." He stared down at his boots and then slowly raised his face. "I don't know what to make of any of this. Why, Hannah?"

About twenty feet separated us. It was so early the light outside didn't really penetrate, and I knew I must be in shadow, a silhouette at best, to Liam. I moved toward the door, toward Liam and the morning light.

"You don't look well," he said.

There was something different about him. He looked like a man who'd gotten very good news. He stood taller, his hair was neater, and his shirt was tucked in. Little things. Small touches that contributed to the overall impression.

"How is she?"

"I told her she should talk to you. She isn't willing yet. But soon, I'm sure." He went silent, and his jaw tightened. He hit his fist lightly against the post he'd been carving. "I don't understand this, Hannah."

"You know most of it. What specifically do you not understand? That I kept your daughter as my own?"

He leaned against the post. "Actually, no. I've got that figured out. Don't misunderstand, you were wrong to hide the truth for as long as you did, and it was wrong of you to keep Ellen away from her family and me."

"Ellen. You called her Ellen."

"That's what she wants."

"I see." A tiny spark wanted to light in my heart. I tamped it down. Too soon.

"What I don't understand is why, after all these years, you told her."

His question stopped my breath. I thought I was prepared. Apparently not, because my knees gave way, and Liam was there, suddenly, with his hands on my arms, supporting me.

"Steady, there," he said.

I touched my face. It felt numb.

"Sorry," I said. "I thought I could do this."

"Do what?"

"Face you."

"Well, sit down before you fall down."

There was no chair or stool, so Liam helped me to the floor, the front door threshold. I leaned back against the lintel and clasped my knees.

"Sorry, I'm not usually such a delicate flower. I seem to faint a lot these days. I really created a storm, didn't I?"

Liam shook his head. "Part of me is angry, but at the same time, I'm almost grateful to you. I was . . ." He sighed, then looked at me. "I was in jail, picked up for a parole violation just before Sheryl brought Trisha—Ellen, I mean—to my father's house. I was headed back to prison, and Sheryl was angry to be on her own again."

"Prison," I echoed.

"So she dumped Ellen at the house with my old man, who'd never been a good father to me, in a house I can't begin to imagine the state it was in."

"He did his best by her, I think. It was over the winter, and we didn't know she was there. He didn't bring her to us until May."

"Sheryl left her there in November."

I nodded, my heart twisting. I wouldn't tell him the toddler's skin had been chapped and her body was filthy. I couldn't do that to Mr. Bridger and worsen the memory his son already had of him. "When I went up to the house looking for him," I said, fudging the facts a bit, "it was messy—you know how he kept house, I'm sure—but her clothing was clean and folded and her room was tidy."

"That so?" He looked away and pressed a knuckle to his eye. He wouldn't look back at me. Because I was such an accomplished liar and owed him more than I could ever repay, I added, "She looked good. Well cared for."

He nodded. He blinked and pressed the back of his hand to his eye. "I can't tell you how glad I am to hear it. I always believed Sheryl took our daughter with her when she left. No one knew Trisha wasn't with her. Not me, that's for sure. I was doing time when they told me my father had died and when Sheryl's car was found."

"Prison," I said again. "Not overseas."

"Not overseas. 'A polite fiction' is what they call it, right? No, I was never in the service. I was in the States and incarcerated. I had a drinking problem. Made poor decisions. DUI. Breaking and entering. I'd rather not go into it further. I'd hoped no one here would ever need to know."

"No one does, and they won't hear it from me."

"I never learned to be a grateful or a peaceful man, but when I understood my daughter hadn't died in the flooding . . . I thanked God, probably for the first time in decades."

"I kept her from you . . . not deliberately, but by keeping her as my own."

He shook his head. "For the first time in years, I was even grateful to Sheryl. I'm sure she ditched Trisha because having a child along was inconvenient for her lifestyle. Too much partying and drugs. Yet if Sheryl hadn't left her behind, or if the flash food hadn't killed her, then our daughter would've grown up living as her mother did. By the time I was released, our daughter would have been . . . well, I don't know, but I can't be sure I wouldn't have made it worse. It's taken me several years to find my way back to a decent life.

"If you had notified the authorities, Trisha . . . Ellen, I mean—" He shook his head with a wry grin. "She surely would've gone into foster care. I thought my daughter had died. That was bad, yes. But instead, she was loved and cared for. That was good, for her and for me."

"Do you think she'll ever see it that way?"

"Honestly, I don't know."

Birds flew overhead, and we watched them pass. *Have patience,* I told myself. *There is hope in patience.* In the silence, I heard the distant sound of the creek and of the leaves in the nearby trees rustling.

"I have another question," he said.

I braced myself.

"If I'd come back sooner, say several years ago, would you have told me then?"

In a quiet voice, I said, "Yes. If you had returned, and if I wasn't worried about her safety or well-being with you, I would've told you."

"What if I'd been messed up and not managing? You wouldn't have come forward?"

Images flashed in my mind of what that would've meant. Handing over Ellen to a stranger with a drinking problem or worse? I held my breath and shook my head.

He nodded. "I believe you. It confirms what I thought about your reasons."

"Liam, you asked why I told her now. I want her to go to college. I still want that. I don't want her to make decisions based on fear, or hurt because her friends said thoughtless things. Will you encourage her?"

"Yes, but I won't force her, Hannah. I don't know if I'm ready to lose her again this soon."

"No, please, Liam. Encourage her to go. She'll return. Don't make her like me. Or like you. We don't want her making decisions that will haunt her and hold her back for the rest of her life." I stood gingerly and touched his arm. "Don't you see how wrong it would be?"

He put his shoulders back, drawing away. "I see both sides, but I've only just found my daughter." His gaze flicked away. "I've got work to do."

We weren't done discussing this, but before I could tell him, I realized Roger had arrived. His car was stopped partway down the drive, and I knew he'd seen us. I turned without another word and went through the house, out the back, and into the cabin.

I nearly barricaded the door but didn't. I forced myself to stand and wait.

I'd kept my secret for so long, too long. By the time I did tell, I hurt people. I'd confessed the truth to halt further damage to Ellen's life. And now? What purpose had any of it served? Ellen had been Trisha Bridger in the Bridger house; now she was Ellen, perhaps still a Cooper, too, and I'd given her all I could, including the truth. And now she was back there again, at the Bridger house, perhaps to stay.

Perhaps never to leave.

Could I step away from it? Let it go? I'd done what I could. This, in a very real way, was no longer any of my business.

Yet, would I have a choice? Someone somehow would pull me back in. I had no fight left in me, and I didn't want to do any more damage.

When the thick door began to move, Roger called out, "Hannah? Can I come in?"

I gulped and couldn't speak. He pushed the door the rest of the way open.

Roger stared, his eyes adjusting to the dim interior light. "Hannah? I went to the house, I went to the shop, I have looked all over town. Why are you hiding in the cabin?"

"Because I don't want to see anyone," I whispered.

Roger eased the door closed. He turned back to me. "Like Liam?"

"I didn't know he was here. When I did, I wanted to find out how Ellen was."

"How do you *think* Ellen is?" He sounded angry.

"Have you spoken to her? How is she?"

"I did, but only briefly, then I went looking for you. Where have you been?"

"Here, and at Rose Lane, and at the shop."

He looked around, and his tone changed. "Are you living out here?"

I moved around to the far side of the table. If he hadn't noticed the clay and the tools before, he did now.

"Rose Lane is where I live with my daughter. I don't want to spend time there right now."

"Are you hiding?"

"I want to be away from . . . People talk. Right now, until I know how things will . . . resolve, I don't want to be an object of . . . however people will view what I've done. They don't know my family or me or why. I can't stop people from talking, but I won't add to it or give them the opportunity to butt into my life. I don't care what they think."

"If that were true, then you wouldn't be hiding and moving around town under cover of dark." Roger leaned forward, his hands on the table. His words slammed into me. "Did you do the right thing fifteen years ago? No. But let me ask you this: Do you regret it? Would you do it differently if you could go back?"

Would I? I already knew the answer in my heart. "I won't lie. No, I don't regret it. I couldn't do it differently. I am sorry people were hurt, though."

"But you'd hurt them all over again if time rewound?"

I nodded.

"Then step out there. Don't hide as if you believe you did something wrong."

"But I did. I did do something wrong."

"Make up your mind, Hannah. Stop hiding."

Hiding. I had made the choice to hide. In many ways I'd been hiding since the day a toddler was left on my porch. Or maybe since I'd lost Ellen the first time.

"That's why you never married," Roger said. "You never let anyone else get close because you had a secret to hide." He shook his head. "I thought the problem was me. It wasn't, was it? You wanted to protect yourself."

"Wrong." Suddenly, I was on my feet, shouting, "I protected my daughter. I gave my life caring for my daughter. Who are you to judge me? I always knew you'd condemn me if you knew the truth. You are so much about right and wrong. Everything for you is simple. My life looked simple on the surface. It wasn't, but it was blessed. That child saved our lives—both Gran's and mine—and I did my best to make sure she benefited from it. I was a good mother to her. I still am. She was repeating the mistakes I'd made, that my mother had made. I stepped up and told her the truth. I know she may never forgive me."

Roger's voice dropped low. "What about your other daughter? The first one. Have you forgotten about her?"

My arms crossed, protecting my body, the vital organs in my body, from the sharp pain, but the pain was inside, always inside, reawakened for the moment by Roger's callous words. I closed my eyes and tried not to fold. "I'll never forget her."

He came around the table. He put his arms around me. I stood like a statue and refused to accept or reject his embrace. He whispered, "Hannah, you are so focused on Ellen—and don't think I don't know you're hiding from more than public gossip—and I don't know how it will work out. That's yet to be seen, but the reality is that you buried your deceased child in the family cemetery without consulting anyone—not a doctor, not police, not authorities. I'm sure that's against the law."

Blindly, I shook my head. My face brushed his shirt. "My daughter. She went to sleep. She didn't wake up. I couldn't hand her over . . . I couldn't say the words . . ."

"What's to prevent the authorities from accusing you of harming her, even accidentally, like a shaken baby situation? They could say you buried her to hide your crime."

I pushed against him, trying to shove him away and hitting him with my fists, all at the same time. He tightened his arms around me.

"How did she die?" he asked.

My hands managed to work themselves up to cover my face. "She went to sleep. Her midday nap. A storm came up, and when I went back inside, both she and Gran were sleeping. I checked on her, but she was gone. Already gone."

The blackness tried to move in on me again, darkening the edges of my vision, both literally and in my head. I ceased struggling and was grateful his arms held me, kept me from falling. Somehow his breath was on my hair, and I pressed my face against his chest.

He spoke softly. "I've made mistakes. Done things I regret. Some I was able to fix. Some I couldn't. That's true for everyone." He touched my hair. "Now you, you made a big mistake and, if I'm being honest, in your situation I might've made the same choices. I won't judge. It's up to Liam and Ellen. But it's possible there could be legal involvement—for both daughters, for both Ellens."

His hand touched my face, my chin, lifting my face up, and I met his eyes.

"If that happens, Hannah, you'll face it. Make up your mind right now. Don't be frightened; don't run away. Face it and deal with it as it comes. Be prepared. You won't be able to hide here in Cooper's Hollow, and not on Rose Lane, either. If you are questioned, make sure you don't speak to the police without an attorney present." He added, "It's real life, and real life has consequences that you can't solve by hiding. I know this isn't what you want to hear right now, Hannah, but it's important."

I pushed at him again, and he relented and released me. Suddenly, I felt alone. That was what I'd wanted, right? Maybe not entirely. Not at this moment.

"How do you know what I want to hear?"

"It's simple. You want to hear Ellen say she understands and forgives you and loves you and wants to come home."

"Close. Mostly I want her to move forward with her life. Go to college. Not to get stalled like I did, like my mother and grandmother did. If she can do that and can also forgive me, then that would make it all worthwhile. That would be a happy ending I could rejoice in. If Ellen or Liam wants to press charges, I won't fight them. I deserve whatever comes my way. I've already hurt her too much."

"You're right. It's not just about you," he said.

Roger stared at me with his brilliant blue eyes, but I couldn't read them. His face wore a blankness whose meaning eluded me, and he left. Left me there alone.

Face it, he'd said. Be prepared. What did he mean? This was in everyone else's hands now. There was nothing more for me to do except wait while Ellen worked her way through this. Worked her way through it alone? No, she had Liam. Her father. A man she hardly knew. A man who'd lost his own child years ago and now might not want to let her go. I knew how that worked. But at some point, even the Cooper women, strong-minded though they were, had to take a chance and give the good and bad the opportunity to fight it out, and have faith that the outcome would be the right one, no matter if it meant leaving oneself defenseless and leaving one's loved ones to figure it out on their own.

A few days passed. Each night I said a prayer for Ellen and for healing, and each morning I hoped, and feared, to see her. True to her decision, she had stayed away from the graduation ceremonies. I knew because the high school principal called me. My response to him was regretful but deliberately short on details. Ellen didn't visit me, either, but I chose to find hope in that. I saw Liam a couple of times. I was amazed he continued to work at carving the porch posts. But he didn't seek me out to speak with me, and I returned the favor.

By the end of a week, I'd established a routine of sorts incorporating trips to Rose Lane and the shop with my continued, and increasingly extended, stays in the cabin. On a lovely Saturday morning, when the workmen were off enjoying their weekend, I decided to tend to the cemetery. I had avoided it since those hallucinations. They'd been caused by the extreme circumstances, and I couldn't get them entirely out of my mind. I decided the best way to erase them was to replace them with more familiar memories of when I'd tended to the cemetery through the years.

I carried my bucket of tools and my gloves up the slope and climbed over the stone wall. I sang softly as I pulled the new weeds from around the headstones and the crosses. I picked up the small branches storms always culled from the trees and left behind where they fell. The empty graves . . . For my father's grave, I left the stone Grand had created. My mother's name was on it, for one thing. For another, though he'd committed murder . . . still, my mother had loved him, at least for a time. I could believe only that mental illness had caused their tragic downfall.

I touched the cross and hoped he'd found peace. There was some kind of symmetry in seeing his marker, even knowing he wasn't here, but instead washed in the sea and absorbed back into the earth. The other empty grave—the one for the man who'd never existed—I removed that marker and set it aside for disposal. That fiction was over and done with.

Grand and Gran, Grand's parents, my mother, plus there were unmarked graves. The one I couldn't deal with was the tiniest.

My Ellen. The first Ellen. My sweet baby. I wrapped my arms around my knees and put my face against them. That pain, the old excruciating pain, came back, cramping in my belly and in my heart, and I understood that while the arrival of the second Ellen had given me another chance, it didn't resolve the first loss. Nothing could.

All the darkness came back, sweeping over me as if it had abated but had never gone away. The tide was now coming back in and with a vengeance.

At some point, I'd stopped singing, and my vocalizations wanted to become a high-pitched wail. I struggled to keep the sound inside. I leaned forward, almost convulsed with the effort. The ground was against my forehead. I bent farther and felt the dirt and sticks against my cheek and my lips. Earth's leavings. Nature's gleanings. Birth and death. Birth and rebirth. But my baby was still gone, and I wanted to scream at God and beat my fists at the earth.

"Is that where she's buried? The first Ellen?" a familiar voice said, my daughter's voice, but she sounded hard.

I knew I could rise, if I tried hard enough. I could stand, perhaps blush a little at my extreme emotionalism. I could ask my daughter how she was. I'd tell her I was glad she'd come to speak with me. Except I couldn't because I was huddled, kneeling on the ground with my arms over my head, and I knew tears and dirt covered my face and made it impossible for one Hannah to hide the other, the one who could not be consoled.

Did it matter? Ellen had her father now. She was strong enough. I'd heard it in her voice. Strong enough to move on without me.

I dug my fingers like claws into the earth on either side of her small grave.

"Hannah." A man spoke with a warning note in his voice. Liam.

My daughter spoke again, saying, "Stay back."

She came over the wall. I heard the sound of her clothing moving against the stone. A stick cracked where she touched ground, and then she was near me. I felt her hand on my back.

"Mom." Her voice was low at first, but then she spoke more loudly. "Mom."

I eased my grip on the earth. I pushed against it and rose a few inches. I was being forced to return to the present, not by Gran's need but by my daughter, who was speaking to me and calling me *Mom*. She put her hands on my shoulders and pulled me gently upright.

This young woman, Ellen, knelt beside me, then reached past me to touch the concrete block covering the first Ellen's grave. Her fingers played over the quartz and mica fragments arranged along the edges.

She asked, her tone soft now, "This is her grave?"

A ragged breath, a sniffle—it was the best I could do before my shoulders moved inward again.

"I always knew it must be an infant's grave, but I never suspected . . . Why, Mom?"

I blinked.

"Why?" she asked again.

I brushed at my lips. They felt numb, and bits of dirt fell from them. "We lost her—"

Ellen interrupted me. "You didn't *lose* anyone. She wasn't an umbrella or a book. She was a baby, and she died."

"She died." I echoed her words. "My baby died." I gasped. I'd never said those words together before. As if they belonged to one another, in a sentence together. It hurt with such exquisite sharpness, I could hardly bear it. "She's dead." The pain burst from me in a high moan. My hands rushed up to cover my face. My fingers dug into my cheeks and forehead.

Ellen grasped my hands and pulled them away. "I know. What I'm asking is, why are you still so upset about it?"

Startled, I looked up. She was staring at me, examining my face.

"I thought it was me you were upset about," she said. "About my finding out what you'd done, about me being hurt and angry."

I nodded. "I was. I am."

"I believe you, in part, but I don't think that's what upset you the most."

"I'm sorry. Truly. I should've done it better, made better decisions. I wanted to protect you."

"Who were you really protecting?"

Her voice was so harsh, so angry, I was desperate to stop it.

"You. Gran."

"No, Mom. You were mostly protecting yourself."

"I wanted only to keep you safe. I've never cared what the world thought of me."

She stared into my eyes and repeated, "You were protecting yourself. You were desperate to avoid acknowledging her death." She shook her head. "As long as you *protected* me from the truth, you could protect yourself from having to face your own truth."

"For me, the truth is that finding you on the porch made all the difference to us. You and Gran were my truth."

"No, Mom. The truth is that Ellen died."

"She died," I said again, hearing the words more than saying them, feeling the pain, still there but diminished. I looked away from Ellen and brushed my hand against the stone slab. "I put her here."

"You have to let her go."

"I thought I had . . . when I found you." I closed my eyes for a few long seconds, then opened them again. "There's something I need you to understand. I'm not making excuses. Just hear me?"

She touched my cheek again, brushing at something clinging to it. Not leaves. Her hands came away wet. She nodded. "I'm listening."

"Gran thought you were her. Our baby. Our Ellen. When she saw you on the porch, she thought you'd come home to us. I let her have her fantasy while I tried to figure out what to do. And then . . . and then it was too late. Too late for both of us. For all of us."

Ellen shook her head. "What you did was wrong. But my father told me about his life at the time, about my mother and her problems. I don't know what my life would've been like if you'd told the authorities, whether I would've been stuck in foster homes. I'll never know. In a way, you stole that from me, too, but I think you also rescued me, even if it was done with lies." She put her hand to her forehead. "What you did wasn't right. I'll never say it was. I think it was dumb luck that it worked out."

Or destiny, I thought. Maybe it happened just as it was supposed to.

"I understand," I said. "I don't blame you for being hurt and angry. I'm glad you have your father after all these years, and I'm glad he has you. I know it will be a good thing for both of you, and I'll always be here for you. Please believe how sorry I am."

Suddenly I saw myself through her eyes and knew I was covered in dirt. Muddy tears were smeared across my hands. I could feel them tightening and drying on my face.

"I'm sorry, too, but this isn't something that can be forgotten like it never happened." Her tone had harshened. "I came to tell you—"

"Ellen," Liam said.

We both looked up. Over the stone wall, I had a clear view of the slope. A man in uniform, a deputy, was crossing the footbridge across the creek.

Swiftly, I looked from Liam to Ellen and back again. Hope could uplift, but it could also hurt. One never understood how painful hope could be until the last shred of it was ripped away.

Now wasn't the time for forgiveness. My debt must be paid. But come what may, I was done with lying. I wasn't afraid. No matter how long they kept me away from here, one day I'd come back. Roger would finish building my house, and I'd come home to Cooper's Hollow— because I'd never really wanted to be anywhere else.

From the corner of my eye, movement on the right caught my attention. I turned to see Roger. He came from nowhere, crossing the woods and the slope, waving at the deputy. He moved at a relaxed but fast clip, almost an eager pace. They met midslope and stopped to talk, and then Roger pointed toward the cemetery, and suddenly the officer was looking directly at me.

So they'd told the authorities after all.

I meant what I'd said to Roger about deserving whatever punishment might come my way, but my courage fled. It evaporated. My last hope was gone.

CHAPTER THIRTEEN

Liam grabbed my arm. "Don't run away," he said.

I met his eyes. "I've never been one to run, and I'm done hiding from the truth, too."

Ellen had gone over the wall, as if to join the deputy and Roger, but she stopped a few yards from them. She was watching them and waiting. For something.

Liam dropped his voice, speaking softly. "Ellen came to confront you, to have it out with you. I explained how her life might've gone if it had all happened differently, but she said, 'What might have happened doesn't justify what was done.'" He looked down at his boots before he returned his gaze to me. "When she saw you here at the grave, I think she understood something she hadn't before."

"What's that?"

"Something I tried to tell her. That sometimes there are no rules for life."

"There are rules. Laws."

"Laws are things politicians write down to make you do what they want you to do. I'm talking about rules. Moral rules but also common-sense rules. Most laws don't have much common sense built in." He looked away. "People want black and white, up or down, on or off.

They want it spelled out. I'm saying life doesn't always lend itself to clear, easy choices."

I sighed. "I appreciate that, but wrong is still wrong. I would do it the same way if it happened again, but I should've tried harder to find you. It's just that by then . . . I couldn't bear to lose her."

"But you were ready to give her up now, regardless, when you saw how she was hurting and about to make some big mistakes."

I looked back down toward the house. Roger and the deputy were walking away, heading back toward the parked vehicles. Ellen, never having joined them, was almost back to the cemetery.

"What's going on?" I asked as she came back over the wall. I nodded toward the deputy and Roger. "Why was he here?"

"The deputy? He came to see Roger about something, I think. One of his workers had a problem."

"I thought . . ." I coughed. "The deputy was looking this way, pointing, and I thought—"

"You thought I reported your crime?" Ellen said. "Or should I say crimes?"

Nothing could soften the hurt her words caused. I cringed and started to turn away. She grabbed my arm roughly.

"Do you really think I'd turn you in? That I'm capable of doing that to you?" She released me. "Let's go," she said to Liam.

Confused, I said, "But you were going down the hill to meet him, right?"

She threw me a scathing look and repeated, "I'm leaving now."

"Go ahead," Liam said to her. "I'll be along shortly."

Ellen hesitated, then tossed her hair back over her shoulder and climbed across the wall again, leaving us there.

We watched her go.

"I don't know how much is Bridger," Liam said, "or how much is due to the Cooper influence, but she's formidable, isn't she?"

I nodded, finally remembering to breathe. "Yes, she is."

"Actually," he added, "I think she was afraid that the deputy was here for you. I think she was heading down there to stop him, but Roger got there first, and she realized that wasn't why the deputy had come. She'll walk it out and calm down. She was scared."

"Scared? For me?"

"Sure." He picked up a loose pebble from atop the stone wall and examined it. "Something else I think you should know. Roger spoke to her. To us, too, including Mamie."

"How is Mamie?"

Liam smiled broadly. "It's been like a miracle for her—that is, once she got over the shock. She loves having a young one around. She was talking about going away but now says maybe she'll stay and housekeep for me if I'll stay, too."

"How are you with that?"

"It might be a good plan."

He stopped. I waited.

"About Roger. He said not to mention anything to you about his speaking to folks, but I thought you should know." Liam added, "It's good to have friends."

"I'm sure that's true."

"One more thing I need to tell you."

Now what? My nerves were wearing thin.

"I'm not sure how you'll feel about this."

"Please, Liam. Just throw it at me. Get it said." I felt tears trying to form. I didn't want to cry again, and certainly not here in front of this man I'd wronged.

"It was Mamie's idea." He waved his hands. "I'm sorry, I'll say it plain. Mamie says people will talk about Ellen being at our house, and she's right. Mamie suggested that maybe we could hint around—just that, a few hints carefully planted—that I'd been home briefly eighteen years ago or thereabouts. Sort of a hit-and-run visit, and that's why no one had seen me—and you and I had hooked up and . . . well, you can imagine the rest. Then I took off and married Sheryl. You kept your counsel about who your baby's father was to protect Ellen and our families, but now I'm back, and I know about Ellen. And my daughter and I are getting to know each other."

I gasped. I wanted to laugh, but there wasn't enough oxygen left in me to fuel it.

He continued. "If you're OK with it, of course. It makes the most sense, I think. I hope you're not offended. Mamie reads a lot of romance novels." He scratched his head. "So, if you don't mind the story, I'll run it by Roger? I know it might not look good for your reputation . . ."

And I did laugh then. It felt good. Delightfully so.

During June and July, and the early days of August, the house was finished—down to the last detail. Roger came and went. We didn't speak except to confirm a choice of electrical fixtures and other things related to the project, but gradually the tension eased between us. I had lived mostly in the cabin with my clay, except for when I was at Rose Lane organizing things for the move. Alone.

Ellen stayed at Elk Ridge with her father. She didn't come to see me again. It was a different kind of jail that she'd put me in, I guessed. Liam finished carving the porch posts. They were works of art. Each evening, after he left, I examined the progress. Leaves, rough tree trunks were well defined, and that's what you saw immediately, but as you looked, as your fingers strayed over the shapes and textures in the wood, you began to discover the small animal faces—a squirrel, raccoons, and others—emerging from hiding. Near the base where he'd shaped tall grasses was a rabbit's nose and one long ear, edging out from between the thin blades.

After Liam was finished with the posts, he came over the ridge a few times, mostly to let me know Ellen was doing well. On one visit, he told me she was, indeed, going off to college in mid-August. He didn't speculate on the future, and he offered no reassurance. His manner was kind, if reserved, and that was appropriate. I'd given him a daughter—one he'd lost who was now returned to him. Though perhaps I'd kept her overlong.

They were getting to know each other. He had discovered Ellen had a mind of her own. She would do what she would do. Of course, she was that way. I'd taught her myself, hadn't I?

In the second week of August, Ellen called to say she was leaving for Tech. Hearing her voice on the phone set my heart to racing. She said she was coming by on her way out of town, if I didn't mind.

"Yes," I said. "I'll be here."

I walked out to the porch to watch for her car, my hands resting on Liam's posts for comfort. She drove down the widened, updated driveway and paused a ways from the house, ironically not far from the spot where we'd huddled in the face of the fire, before pulling the car closer to park. That spot had lost its hold on me. Now it was as Ellen had once said—she remembered being very afraid but not the actual fear. That memory had been superseded by other, sharper events. Because that's what life was—a series of changes, some painful but sometimes garnering greater beauty despite the pain.

She came up to the porch, carrying her duffel bag. We hugged, not with the enthusiasm of old, but I reminded myself that sometimes life was about baby steps.

"On your way?"

She nodded.

"Thanks for coming by."

She paused and lifted the duffel bag. "Actually, I wanted to drop off a few things. I want to leave them here, if you're good with that."

Breathe in, breathe out, I reminded myself. "Certainly. Absolutely. Do you need help?"

"No, I've got it."

"Can I fix you a sandwich or a glass of tea?" When she didn't answer, I added, "I can wrap it up for you, in case you get hungry on the road."

She breathed out a small puff of air. "Sure. Sounds good. I'll take it with me."

I busied myself in the kitchen. I sensed she wanted privacy. Was that good or bad? I didn't know.

She carried the duffel bag to her bedroom and then went back out to the car, returning with a couple of large plastic bags. Clothing, I guessed. Seemed like a good sign, then. She stayed in the bedroom longer this time. When she came out, she paused in the main room, her hands deep in her pockets. She faced the French doors for a minute or two, apparently taking in the new deck and the landscaping; then she turned around to examine the main room, and her gaze paused on the hearth. Her eyes slid past it, then back, and she walked over to the stone fireplace.

I thought she might be memorizing the new house. How much of the old homeplace still remained in her memory? Most of it had probably being pushed out or overwritten long ago. That seemed to be the fate of memories.

Ellen cleared her throat, then spoke but with hesitation in her voice. "You aren't the only one who made a mistake. The night the house burned . . . I never told you, but I messed with the woodstove. I promised I wouldn't, but I did anyway. I was cold. I took some of the pages from my coloring book and put them in the stove to feed the fire. I knew I was breaking a rule, but I did it anyway." She stared down at the unburned logs in my lovely new fireplace, but that wasn't what she was seeing. "I never told you because I was afraid I'd . . . that if you found out it was my fault that the house . . . caught fire . . ."

With all the honesty I could put into my voice, I said, "It wasn't your fault. I woke up when you returned to bed. I went to check on things and found the stove door open. I closed it. That's not how the fire started."

She turned toward me swiftly, her eyes full of unshed tears. "Seriously?"

My love was honest even if my words weren't. "Seriously. The fire was caused by a clogged flue pipe."

"Are you sure?"

"Yes, sweetheart. I'm as sure about that as about anything. It wasn't your fault. None of it was your fault."

Ellen rested her hand on the mantel, almost as if it were holding her up, and then I saw strength and confidence returning to her as she stood taller. She stepped away from the fireplace, but as she did, she stopped again, staring at the pots on the mantel.

My latest pots. The glazes were glorious, if I were to say so myself. The textured patterns in the clay and in the glazes kept drawing my own hands toward them, wanting to touch and hold them, as if each time I saw them anew. A while back I'd told Roger my clay work was uninspired. No longer. Over these past few months, I had changed. So had Roger.

Ellen reached slowly toward the pots. She turned to me, wonder in her eyes, then looked back at them again.

"These are beautiful, Mom."

Mom. My heart fluttered. Was it hope, perhaps? I bit my lip. I remembered how cruel hope could be.

She frowned. "Is it the new kiln, do you think? What else is different? Maybe a new clay? Or the glaze?"

She seemed to be speaking to herself, not really expecting an answer. I cried, but quietly.

Ellen was kind and pretended not to notice the tears on my face. Then the clay figure near the end of the mantel, slightly in the shadow of a larger pot, caught her eye. She reached toward it and captured it, cradling it in both her hands.

It was the child figure, the tiny girl on a stone wall, with butterfly wings coming around from behind her, spilling over the stone on which she sat. The membranes of the wings were fingerlike, curving inward protectively, yet the tips of her wings soared up above her body. She'd been fired for durability, but she remained unglazed, unfinished, and always would, of course.

"Is she me?" Ellen whispered.

I smiled and felt new tears squeeze out from my eyes. Was it Ellen? The first Ellen left us—she died—and the new Ellen came into our lives. Did the figure represent the first or second Ellen? Was it me? I knew the answer but didn't speak it aloud.

It was three. All three. All different, yet inextricably entwined. Beautiful, but never complete, never perfect. Never truly finished.

Ellen stared at the floor and shuffled her feet slightly. "I was thinking . . . I don't know how you'll take this . . ." She looked at me directly. "I don't want to hurt you."

"Go ahead," I said, ready to accept whatever was coming my way.

"I was thinking that lots of kids split their time between their parents when their parents divorce. Do you think that would be appropriate? I mean, I know this isn't exactly the same situation, but I thought I could spend some time here with you and also with my father at Elk Ridge."

Spend time here with me? Was this a step toward mending bridges? It was a *big* step. My heart fluttered again, almost as if it had grown tiny, delicate wings.

"Yes, I think that's a splendid idea."

"Good." She set the figure back onto the mantel. "I left some things in my room for when I come home again." She made a quick grimace. "If you don't like how I left them, you're welcome to rearrange them or whatever."

I was busy marveling at how easily she'd uttered the word *home* and almost forgot to respond. "Excellent, but I'm sure they're fine," I said. "I painted your room lavender. Are you OK with that?"

"It's beautiful. It makes me think of sunset and sunrise. And Gran." She walked over to the kitchen counter. "Is this my sandwich?"

"Yes."

She picked up the bagged sandwich and the bottle of sweet tea. "I'd better get going. It's a long drive." She paused again. "Labor Day weekend, I'll be back. Then mid-October for fall break." She smiled, almost shyly. "Thanks for the car. It'll make it lots easier to get back and forth."

"Good. But Ellen . . . what about the other kids? Your friends. Is it all settled?"

"It's all good now. Mr. Bell apologized to a bunch of people. Said he'd been mixed up, and then he said goofy stuff like if he'd had a daughter, he'd want it to be me and how people had misunderstood him. Ridiculous, but it worked, and everyone's moved on to other topics. You said they would." She sighed. "But after the way they acted, I don't know if I'll ever trust them again, not like I used to."

"I'm sorry, sweetheart."

"Not me. Not really. I'm glad I know the truth. I'm extremely glad Mr. Bell isn't my father." She stared at me, perhaps to gauge my reaction. Whatever she read in my face must've reassured her. "I guess you know by now that everyone thinks you and Liam fooled around all those years ago? No one knows the real story. I'm comfortable with that. You are, too, right?"

I nodded and tried to choke down the lump in my throat.

"I'd better get on the road. See you soon, Mom," she said, but she didn't move. She stood there holding the sandwich bag and the drink. Suddenly, she set them back on the counter and rushed over to me. She flung her arms around me, gave me a quick, strong hug, then reclaimed the bag and bottle and was gone out the door.

I ran after her but stopped myself on the porch. "Wait, Ellen. Please?"

She paused in the yard. "What?"

"I need to know . . . Have you forgiven me? Will you ever be able to trust me again?"

She fixed those dark eyes on me and tilted her head to the side. With a small smile she said, "I'm not saying that what you did was right, but if I ever have a child who needs someone to love and protect them, and it can't be me, then you're my first choice."

With a last nod, she got into the car.

As she drove away, I blew her a kiss and waved. The car horn honked once as she vanished around the curve.

Nearly overwhelmed by the encounter, the embrace, and the promise, I leaned against the posts and ran my fingers lightly over the carvings. No butterflies here, thank goodness.

After a few minutes, I sat in the rocker. I was still there an hour later when Roger's SUV came into view.

He parked and walked over to join me on the porch. "She's gone now?"

I nodded.

"Are you upset?"

"Yes," I said, and smiled. "And no."

"There's no pleasing you, Hannah Cooper," he joked.

I reached out and took his hand.

These days there were two rockers on the porch. "Have a seat," I said.

"How did it go?" he asked as he sat and stretched out his legs.

"She said Spencer admitted he'd had it all wrong, and he apologized to folks about saying all that stuff."

Roger feigned surprise.

"Don't bother," I said. "I know someone spoke to him, and I think it was you."

He shrugged. "He's foolish. Not necessarily a cruel man, but self-centered. I pointed out a few realities to him, and he decided to do the decent thing."

I laughed. "He did wrong when he told the truth, but the decent thing when he agreed to lie?" I touched Roger's arm. "I think I must be a bad influence on you."

"Whatever you're doing, it's working. No complaints here." He stood and pulled me to my feet.

Roger wrapped his arms around me. He spoke into my hair. "I have loved you for many years. You never asked me to hang around waiting. I made that choice on my own. I was wrong to blame you."

I put my hand lightly on his cheek. "I'm glad you did wait. I couldn't ask anyone to love me as I was, with so much to hide and knowing in my heart that one day it was bound to fall apart, and I didn't know I could love anyone else this much. I thought every bit of love I had in me belonged to my daughters. I'm not sure all my problems are resolved even now, but I hope you'll continue hanging around with me to find out."

He stepped back, his expression serious, but his hands were gentle as he caressed my arms. "One more thing we need to deal with, Hannah. Something that's seriously overdue. Wait here. I'll be right back."

One more thing? *Enough already.* But I waited.

Roger walked to his SUV and pulled something large from the backseat.

Whatever was wrong, at least I'd have his help with the problem, and its solution, too, if I needed him.

Roger paused at the foot of the steps and held up a board. It was a painted sign, carved and artistically weathered to look like an antique, but it was new and wonderful. Perfect for the cabin and for a fresh start.

Aloud, I read the words, "Cub Creek Pottery."

"Yeah," Roger said. "The old shop relocated, I hear." He grinned. "I picked this sign up cheap from a local woodworker. He does good work, doesn't he? Think you can find a place to hang it?"

After Roger left, I went to Ellen's room and stood at the window again. There was no shadowy figure on the cemetery wall. The small figure hadn't returned, and I knew she wouldn't. The past was now officially in the past.

Ellen had arranged a few trinkets and personal items, including a hairbrush and a framed photo of Gran and Grand, on top of the dresser.

What about the clothing in those bags she'd carried? Why had she expressed that odd concern about whether I would approve of where she put them?

I opened the top drawer and found something unexpected amid the T-shirts and pajama bottoms. I lifted it out carefully.

The baby book.

I hugged it to me and rested my cheek against the top edge.

Also in the drawer, nestled next to the book, I saw a carefully glued and mended blue butterfly pot. There were a few small gaps where the pieces were chipped or missing, but that was OK. I knew where they were.

They were safely and securely held in my heart.

Forever.

ACKNOWLEDGMENTS

Many thanks to Kelli Martin, my editor at Lake Union, for her support and encouragement, and to Lindsay Guzzardo, my developmental editor, who worked with me to make this the best book possible. This story involved challenging, often difficult, life events and choices, but telling Hannah's, Ellen's, and Gran's story meant a great deal to me, and Lindsay's help was amazing in bringing it together.

Lake Union provided an amazing team to help me with *The Happiness In Between* and *The Memory of Butterflies* and I'm very grateful. In addition to Kelli and Lindsay, I'd like to thank Stacy Abrams for keeping my stories free from timeline or grammatical embarrassment, Toisan Craigg for her excellent and patient proofreading, Laura Klynstra for the outstandingly gorgeous covers, and others whose names I don't know but whose contributions to the team make it all work.

Thanks to my husband, who is my rock and support through the long hours of writing and the emotional toil of creating stories to share with readers, and sincere gratitude to my first readers, Amy, Amy, Jill, and Julie, who help me understand what works and what doesn't.

Most of all, thanks to the readers who take the time to enter my worlds, whether along the North Carolina beaches or in rural Virginia amid the forests and dark, winding roads, and who stay awhile, and who share their own experiences and their reading enjoyment with me and others.

QUESTIONS FOR DISCUSSION

1. How might things have been different if Hannah had gone to college after graduation, as intended? How might this have affected George Bridger's decision and his granddaughter's life?

2. What did you think when Hannah made the decision to keep the child? Did she make a rational choice? Was it the right choice? Later, she says she would've come forward if the child's father had returned earlier. Do you think she would have?

3. Secrets were kept from Hannah by her grandparents, and Hannah, in turn, keeps secrets from her daughter. Ultimately, Hannah confesses the truth to Ellen yet, at the end of the story, she tells one more lie, deliberately and with forethought, to protect her. Would you have done the same?

4. Themes of love, truth, loss, and acceptance recur throughout this story, but the predominant theme is that of birth and rebirth, both literally and figuratively, in the references to metamorphosis, the Cooper cemetery, and Hannah's clay figurines. Which recurring motifs or symbols spoke to you?

ABOUT THE AUTHOR

Grace Greene is an award-winning and *USA Today* bestselling author of women's fiction and contemporary romance set in the bucolic reaches of her native Virginia (*Kincaid's Hope, Cub Creek, The Happiness In Between, The Memory of Butterflies*) and the breezy beaches of Emerald Isle, North Carolina (*Beach Rental, Beach Winds*). Her debut novel, *Beach Rental*, and the sequel, *Beach Winds*, were both Top Picks by *RT Book Reviews* magazine. For more about the author and her books, visit www.gracegreene.com or connect with her on Twitter @Grace_Greene and on Facebook at www.facebook.com/GraceGreeneBooks.